Rocked Under
By
Cora Hawkes

Table of Contents

Title Page..p.1
Contents...p.2
Copyright...p.4
Acknowledgments..p.5
Chapter one.. p.6
Chapter two..p.12
Chapter three..p.21
Chapter four...p.30
Chapter five..p.41
Chapter six...p.49
Chapter seven..p.59
Chapter eight..p.66
Chapter nine...p.73
Chapter ten...p.79
Chapter eleven...p.88
Chapter twelve...p.97
Chapter thirteen...p.107
Chapter fourteen..p.111
Chapter fifteen...p.118
Chapter sixteen..p.123
Chapter seventeen...p.130
Chapter eighteen..p.135
Chapter nineteen..p.141
Chapter twenty...p.148
Chapter twenty-one...p.157
Chapter twenty-two...p.163
Chapter twenty-three...p.170
Chapter twenty-four..p.177
Chapter twenty-five...p.184

Chapter twenty-six..p.191
Chapter twenty-seven..p.196
Chapter twenty-eight..p.206
Chapter twenty-nine..p.217
Chapter thirty...p.223
Chapter thirty-one..p.231
Chapter thirty-two..p.235
Chapter thirty-three..p.244
Chapter thirty-four..p.255
Chapter thirty-five..p.260
Chapter thirty-six..p.271
Chapter thirty-seven...p.281

Copyright © 2013 Cora Hawkes

All rights reserved. No part of this book may be reproduced in any form without written permission from the author, except that brief quotations embodied in critical articles and reviews are permitted.

This is a work of fiction. The names, characters, places and incidents are products of the author's imagination or have been used fictitiously. Any resemblance to actual persons, living or dead, events, or locales is entirely coincidental.

Cover photo © Konstantynov at http://www.shutterstock.com/gallery-116797p1.html

Edited by Christine Dentten www.christinedentten.com

Contact Cora Hawkes:
Email: corahawkes@gmail.com
Website: www.corahawkes.blogspot.co.uk
Facebook: www.facebook.com/cora.hawkes
Twitter: @CoraHawkes
Goodreads: www.goodreads.com/corahawkes

Acknowledgments

To my fiancé, thank you for putting up with the many nights I totally ignored you while I wrote this and for all your support, you're my rock, I love you! For my daughter who is also a bookworm and loves rockers, thanks for supporting me, babe. I love you! To my three little men who have had to share me with this book, I love you all very much. To my sister who has called me everyday and pushed me into finishing this, and to my parents for having faith in me, I'm lucky to have you guys, and I love you all so much.

Chapter One

September 2005.

Ashley pulled up by a large house in a quiet neighbourhood on the outskirts of town and cut the engine.

"Uh, are you sure we got the address right?" Ashley asked with an edge to her voice.

"Why're you asking *me*?" I turned towards her, "You put it in the GPS thingy, not me." I looked up at the house with the white picket fence and the high, pointed roof. "And anyway, it looks like the same house as in the picture mum showed me."

"No effing way!" Ash chuckled, looking pleasantly surprised. "This is going to be so much fun!" she squealed. Her high-pitched voice made me cringe.

I frowned. "What is?"

She ignored me as she looked out the car window again. "The address did seem familiar... ." she said under her breath, her eyes squinting up at the house.

"Familiar? What are you going *on* about, Ash?" I cried.

Ash finally looked at me and must have noticed the worried expression on my face. "Oh, it's nothing to worry about," she swiped a hand through the air, "one of my friends lives in the apartment above ours."

"Oh." For a moment I had thoughts of someone really bad living there. Something occurred to me and I laughed, giving her a *duh!* look. "How could you not recognise the address? We didn't even need the GPS."

She shrugged defensively. "*Bloody hell*, Em," she took the mick out of my accent, "you know my memory is like a sieve. Do *you* know your friends' addresses?"

I sighed. She had a good point — I didn't. "What's she like then? Is she a student too?"

A cheeky grin spread across her face. "Not a she, a he — and he's *very* likeable. I've known him since kindergarten." A faraway look entered her expression briefly.

"Shit, Ash," I moaned, "Is this someone you fancy?" I could just imagine her sneaking up to his apartment in the middle of the night.

She looked at me and frowned. "No, and don't you get any ideas about him either." She opened the car door before I could get her to explain. "Come on."

Ash was the total opposite of me physically. She had fine, straight, light-blonde hair that stopped above her shoulders, and a petite, willowy figure that the guys went crazy over. We both had blue eyes — hers were light, like topaz, while mine were more like dark sapphires.

I eased out of the car and stretched my legs. We'd been driving for hours so I was as stiff as a board. I dug around in my bag for the set of keys that had been posted to me at my mum's house while we made our way up the paved path to the front door. I pulled them out and unlocked the door. Inside were two more doors — ours and Ash's friend's entrance, which led to the upstairs apartment.

I unlocked our door and stepped into the lounge. It was roomy, with cream walls and a mahogany wood floor. The early afternoon sun was shining in through the window, brightening everything. There was an old couch and an equally old TV, but not much else. There were two double bedrooms, mine had an en suite. The whole apartment followed the same colour scheme — cream walls and mahogany flooring. It was very different from the places back home, but I didn't mind that at all. I loved the change, embraced it even.

8

We had the basic things we would need, and I was overjoyed that I had had the foresight to buy my own bedding and towels because the ones that were there looked like they hadn't seen a good wash in a while. Once we had all our boxes in from the car, we set about cleaning the windows and kitchen cupboards before unpacking our things.

It was evening by the time we were finished so we ordered a take away and sat in front of the TV with a bottle of wine to celebrate moving in.
"What's the guy upstairs like?" I asked as I polished off my noodles.
She looked up, a grin touching the corners of her mouth. "Scott?"
"Yeah, Scott."
She frowned, "I'm sure you met him before." She shook her head. "Anyway, he's a nice guy." She put her fork in her mouth. "He'll be a senior and he's the lead singer in a rock band." She chewed.
I could feel my eyes widen. "A rock band?" I had a vision of a spiky-haired, tattooed guy, who had wild orgies that ended when the sun came up. So much for quiet study time.

"Yeah, he's got a reputation around here but it's not as bad as it sounds."
"What reputation?"
"He's hot, Em. I mean, seriously hot. He doesn't take any crap from anyone and he… Uh… Has some commitment issues. He's an asshole when it comes to girls because of it. Shame, really." She continued to load food into her mouth.
Worry creased my forehead. He didn't sound that nice.
Ash giggled. "Don't look so worried. He's a good guy really — a good friend — He's got a bad side to him but I doubt you'll see it."

"Right," *he sounds like a dick*, "and he's your friend?"

"Like I said, we were at kindergarten together and we've been friends since. I told you about him a few times, actually."

I racked my brain. She may have done but I couldn't remember so I shook my head.

"*Jeez*, Em! Were you even *with* me when we talked?" Her lips were a tight line as she waited for my answer.

She was referring to the many overseas phone calls we used to make to each other before I moved over here. We used to spend hours talking but when things got hard it was more like her talking and me half-listening while I had other things on my mind. *Slam!* My brain shut that door and I concentrated on Ash again.

"I'm sorry, Ash." My eyes pleaded with her to understand.

She sighed, "Don't worry about it." She flicked her hair over her shoulder. "Anyway, he's got serious commitment issues and he's *never* had a girlfriend." She paused. "The reason I'm telling you this now, is because I know how you feel about that type of thing and I just wanted to warn you about his reputation before you get all starry-eyed like the rest of the girls do."

"You said he was '*very likeable*'!" I mimicked in an accusing tone.

She laughed. "He is, as long as you don't sleep with him."

My eyes widened. Why would she think that I *would* sleep with him? *What the f—?*

"Look, honestly, he's a good friend and I've known him forever. He's loyal and if you need help or a shoulder to cry on he's there."

Ash obviously thought a lot of him and cared for him a great deal. I wondered if it was more than that, but I didn't want to ask since it would be admitting that I hadn't listened to her on the phone.

Rocked Under ~ Cora Hawkes

"Is he very noisy?" I had to ask since the guy was in a rock band and lived right above us.

"No, and don't worry, the guys don't rehearse here. You'll like him. You should have no problem with him and I promise he won't try anything with you."

Try anything with me? Did this guy think with his little head or something, because that's what it sounded like?

Anyway, she didn't have to worry. I had no intention of getting involved with a tattooed, spiky-haired rock dude who wore his waistband below his arse cheeks, slept around and had commitment issues. That was the type that had me running for the hills. My mum didn't haul me away from England for me to make the same mistake she did — and I wouldn't. In fact, I was pretty much terrified of having any kind of relationship deeper than liking. I had seen my mum suffer and become a shell because of a man — a man that she had clung to no matter what he did.

What I had put her through was awful, and she had already spent so much of her life suffering at the hands of my dad. Her divorce had been very straightforward and the settlement was huge. She would never have to work and neither would I if I didn't want to. When we arrived a little over six months ago, my mum had insisted that I go to college, get an education — be normal. My childhood had been anything but normal. She wanted me to stop worrying about her and make a life for myself. Now that he was out of the picture, I could choose what I wanted to do for the first time in my life. It felt great and I wanted to make her proud more than anything to make amends.

I felt better leaving her knowing that she had bought a house near my aunt — Ashley's mum. I decided to study the music industry. I loved music and it was my only real passion. I didn't want to perform — I wanted to be behind the scenes, in the hustle and bustle, managing.

"So, when do I meet him?" I asked, feeling a whole lot better about meeting my new neighbour.

"He's away visiting his dad in the city, but he'll be back in a few days to rehearse before he goes on stage Sunday night."

Sunday came around quickly. We spent the last few days making the apartment more homey. We filled the kitchen, went shopping for things to make the place our own and by the time we had finished we were both happy with it. Ash and I got ready to go to Macy's, a rock and alternative music bar that was a five-minute walk from our place. I would meet her friends, but I was also hoping to make a few of my own as her friends were mostly juniors and seniors.

It was my first night out since England, and boy had I missed it. I had never stayed in at the weekend before I moved over here. I loved to dance — it had been the one time where I could be myself and let it all go. I was nervous as hell about starting college. I would be a freshman, and Ash a junior, but I was so happy to be going to a place where I would know at least one person. Ash and I had similar interests even though she was a couple of years older. We had always stayed in touch by phone and on Facebook, and we would see each other a few times a year. She had been my rock over the past few months.

Chapter Two

Macy's was a huge place on the edge of the town. As we approached I could hear muffled rock music coming from inside. I had sweaty palms and dragonflies were dancing in my tummy because I was about to meet Ashley's friends for the first time. She said I would be fine, that they would love my accent and that they were already dying to meet me.

"Do I look okay?" Usually I didn't need to ask. I wasn't an unconfident person — I just wanted to make a good first impression.

She looked down and then spent a long time scrutinising my black skinny jeans, which were tucked into flat, black, flat, calf-length boots. She looked slowly up all five foot four of me, past my hip-hugging, red, fine-knit jumper to where it slouched slightly off my shoulders. She then ran her eyes over my face. "You look great, as always." She shook her head, smiling.

I grinned at the way she had checked me out. She knew a quick look at me wouldn't make me believe her if she said I looked good. I managed to sneak a peek at my reflection in a parked car window just to double-check. My almost-black, wavy hair hung down just past my breasts. I looked okay, I guessed. I wished I had straightened it. Unfortunately, I got most of my features from my dad. My olive complexion, dark hair, curvy figure and rather over-large nose were all visible trademarks of my dad's Italian heritage. But my dark-blue, almond-shaped eyes were my mum's, and they were definitely my favourite feature.

Loud music and body heat enveloped us as we walked through black double doors into a huge, square open space that was brimming with people. There was a large raised stage in front of us at the far end with a band playing a heavy rock song that I didn't recognise. A large bar lined the wall to the left of us, already packed with people waiting to be served. The bartenders looked rushed off their feet, just like any nightclub. Tables and couches were dotted around the edges of the dance floor. The floor itself was a big space, which was crammed nearest stage with college students dancing and waving their arms in the air, trying to get the band's attention.

"It's always busy on the nights Scott's here," Ash said as she craned her neck and looked for her friends. "They're over there, come on."

"Is that Scott?" I pointed to the stage. If it was, then I didn't like his music.

Ash wrinkled her nose. "No, he's on later." She looked at me and lifted her shoulders as she smiled excitedly.

She took my hand and hauled me through the moving, sweaty bodies to a table to the left of the stage where a guy and a girl sat talking animatedly.

"Hey, hey!" Ashley sang-shouted. Two heads swivelled towards us.

"Ash!" The girl jumped up and almost ran around the table. She was around my height with a rounded figure and short, fine, light-blonde hair.

"Meg!" Ash was squeezed in a death grip.

I noticed that the guy's eyes were on me curiously. I smiled at him shyly and looked down at my feet until Ash introduced us.

"I want you both to meet Emma, my cousin," Ash said proudly.

The guy with short, light-brown hair stood up. "Hey, dweeb! I'm Newton." I laughed awkwardly. *Dweeb? Really?*

I glanced at Ash with a frown and she leaned close to my ear, "He's playful. Just go with it."

His hand shot out towards mine. I took it and said hello while looking into his friendly eyes.

"Good to meet you. British, huh?" he winked at me, his warm, brown eyes twinkling.

Rocked Under ~ Cora Hawkes

I nodded. I'd have to think of some nerdy, dumb thing to call him in return.

"I'm Megan. It's so good to meet you. Ashley has told us all about her beautiful British cousin." Her voice bubbled out of her and filled my ears.

I forced a laugh, a knot of alarm flaring in the pit of my stomach. "I hope not too much." Because really, they didn't need to know too much.

"Aw, don't worry! It was all good," Megan said as if reading my mind. She grinned at me and looked at Ashley.

Phew! My stomach went back to its normal state.

"You're gonna have to keep an eye on this babe," Megan said to Ashley as they shared a knowing look.

I frowned. Why would they need to keep an eye on me? I wondered for a second what it was that Ash hadn't told me. I made a mental note to grill her about it later.

"I'll keep an eye on her for you, Ash. Don't worry — she'll be safe with me," Newton winked at me.

I felt relieved that the introductions were over. It's always horrible being the newbie, especially in a group of friends who have been hanging out for years already without you. I felt like a bit of an intruder. Ash and I sat opposite the others and we slipped into an easy conversation. They were asking me to say stuff like 'tomato'. My accent was the highlight, which I didn't mind for the moment because I knew they would get tired of it.

A few drinks later and I was feeling relaxed. The alcohol had dulled my initial nervousness and left a feeling of excitement that I had missed. This new start would be good for me — my future was looking bright for once. I watched, envious, as everyone danced, moving their bodies and shaking it all out.

"So, *Dweeb*, you wanna dance?" Newton stood over me.

"Yes, please, *Buttfluff*," I got up as Newton threw back his head and laughed.

"Buttfluff." He tested the word in his mouth like he was tasting wine. "I like it. Let's go!" He caught my hand and dragged me out to the middle of the floor, through the squash, and then turned to me.

Dancing was my favourite thing in the world. I could let go on the dance floor like nowhere else. I began to move but felt like a robot at first after not having danced for so long, but after a while I eased myself into it like I hadn't had a nine-month break from nightclubs.

Newton placed his hands on my waist and leaned close, "You like living here?"

"Yeah," I nodded, "It's not too different from home." I was smiling my head off as the beat caught me and thumped through my body. I closed my eyes, raised my arms, swung my hips and just enjoyed it. Newton removed his hands to do the same.

After a while I felt hands on my waist again and a mouth half-shouted, half-whispered in my ear, "You know you're ugly as hell, right, *Dweeb?*" He pulled back to look at me with a cocky grin on his face.

I laughed while shaking my head but I let him keep his hands on my waist. I liked this guy. He was funny with a warm and relaxing presence that rubbed off on me.

"Just sayin'," he shrugged. "We'll have our work cut out for us keeping Scott away from you."

"Why?"

"Didn't Ash tell you about our famous friend?"

"Yeah, but I think you're both probably exaggerating a bit. He can't be that bad!"

"He's not bad, just loves the ladies and, unfortunately, they like him a lot too." He wiggled his eyebrows. "He's got a different girl every night — puts Casanova to shame."

"Well, don't worry. I can look after myself when it comes to guys." He didn't look so sure, but then he had only just met me so that was okay. He would see soon enough. The guys at home had no chance, and neither would they here unless I wanted them to.

I was making my way to the bar a little while later to get the next round of drinks when the lights went off around the stage. The crowd cheered and whistled and heaved towards the stage in a mad rush to be at the front. My interest snared, I watched and waited to see who was playing next. A single blue light lit the stage, its beam shining down and outwards towards the crowd. A man's silhouetted figure stood in its path. He stood there motionless, like a black phantom, while he looked out at the audience and the pack of screaming girls at his feet. My heart raced as the excitement that hummed through the atmosphere got under my skin, infecting me.

The drummer started a slow beat and Mr Silhouette started to sing deeply. My breath released slowly as his low voice penetrated, vibrating intimately through the floor to my feet and up my body, making me shudder, leaving me feeling as though I had been violated in the most sacred of places.

His voice was deep, hoarse. I couldn't wait to see all of him. I *needed* to see his face, because surely someone with that kind of presence and his kind of voice couldn't also be blessed with a face to match? I didn't have to wait long. The rest of the lights came on when the guitarist came in and the girls at the front of the stage screamed even louder. I froze as I studied his form, greedily committing every detail to memory. Everything else faded into the background — my vision went dark around the edges until he was all I saw. I let my gaze take a leisurely stroll up his body, from his long, jean-clad legs to his lean hips. My eyes roved unashamedly over his chest, taking in the way his black T-shirt hugged his just-right muscles. He raised his tattooed arms and I watched in fascination as his biceps tensed when he gripped the microphone tightly and then flexed his fingers slowly.

My breath was rushing in and out as I bit my lip and continued to stare at what was surely God's gift to women. Lastly, I looked at his face. I was blown away again by the beauty of him. Dark, silky, overgrown hair, which was a sexy mess, hung over his right eye and he swept it casually back. He had high cheekbones, and full lips that were almost making out with the mic. He was outstanding. I had never seen anyone like him, and yet he seemed familiar in a strange way. I wanted to get closer — to see the colour of his eyes, and if he had dimples when he smiled.

I sat there with my elbow on the bar, my chin resting on my fist, holding my mouth closed while I was mesmerised by him, by his presence — it filled and covered the room like a sensual, black, silken sheet. He looked to the left of the audience with a smile that lit his eyes and he waved. I followed his gaze and saw Ash and her friends waving back. My chin fell off my fist. That was Scott Mason?

My wide, surprised eyes looked back at the stage and collided with a dark, intense stare that was studying me intently. My breath hitched, or maybe I just stopped breathing altogether, as his intense, curious gaze trapped mine. I couldn't tear my eyes away. It was as though he was singing to *me*. My bottom lip said goodbye to my upper one as I struggled to get air in. Our eyes held for what seemed like endless minutes. I felt caught. Rabbits and headlights flitted stupidly in and out of my addled brain.

Feeling hot all of a sudden, I knew I was blushing and groaned aloud as I rolled my eyes at myself— and then I openly cringed at actually groaning out loud and rolling my eyes at myself. *God, Girlie! Get a damn grip!* His eyebrows drew together very faintly as he cocked his head to study me while keeping the ballad going beautifully. I looked away. My face felt warm. He must have thought I was crazy, sitting here pulling faces at myself. I told myself that he was probably used to girls making utter idiots of themselves over him.

I couldn't believe that I had just ogled a guy like that. I never did that kind of thing openly. *Ever.* I grabbed the tray of drinks that had been sitting in front of me and returned to our table. He had to be seriously lacking in the personality department, I decided as I set the drinks down more roughly than I normally would have done. *No* guy had *ever* made me feel that way, or act that way either. I mean, I just didn't do the whole 'eye-stripping' thing that other girls seemed to think was okay.

I sat down and Ash leaned in close to my ear. "That's From Under. Scott is the singer," she nodded towards the stage, and pulled back to see my reaction.
I forced a natural smile. "I figured it was."
She whispered in my ear again, "You'll meet him later."
I pursed my lips and nodded. Meeting Scott didn't sound like such a good idea any more — I might as well have just joined the groupies at the front.
I caught Newton's eye. "Dance?" I mouthed, nodding to the dance floor. Alcohol had definitely made me braver — I needed more.
"With you? Do I *have* to?" He flashed a smile as he stood and we were off like we'd known each other for years rather than just a few hours.

Scott's voice filled the bar as we danced on the edge of the floor. I watched him on stage and had to admit grudgingly that they weren't just good, they were amazing to watch and listen to. They were one of the best bands I had seen live, and that was saying something since I had seen so many after years of Glastonbury Festivals and gigs in London. I reluctantly decided that Scott Mason made them — without him the rest of the band would be lost. He was breathtaking on stage.

Their style was a blend of heavy rock and soft ballads. Scott's voice was haunting — deep and raspy all at the same time for the ballads, which made shivers run down my spine, and he could shout his way through the heavier songs very well too, all while strumming wildly on his guitar. I knew, I just *knew,* that From Under was going places. I turned away. The way Ash had described Scott, he sounded like a big-headed idiot, and why wouldn't he be? He had everything going for him.

After an hour or so of pure rocking, I squeezed my way over to where Newton was dancing with a girl. He turned away from her when he saw me approaching.
"You okay, *Dweeb*?" he asked.
I was about to nod when Scott started talking.
"Thanks for a great night. Got one more for you single ladies out there!" He didn't even sound breathless after all the singing he'd done.
I rolled my eyes as I swear I heard almost every girl in the place, single *and* attached, squeal with pleasure.
He caught my eye and my stomach trembled stupidly. He winked and flashed a killer smile that showed straight, white teeth and dimples.
My tummy did a somersault. *Was he flirting with me?* I ignored the stomach trembles, hardened up and gave him my 'so-not-interested' look before turning my back on him. He had no chance

and I couldn't wait to see the look on his face when he found out who his new neighbours were. Ash hadn't told him yet — she had wanted to surprise him.

He had most of the ingredients that made him a recipe for a lady-killer. As a guy, however, he was missing one key ingredient — morals. People like him, people who slept around with no respect for women, were arseholes.

Newton dipped his head close to my ear. "Looks like Scott just claimed you, and *damn*, I liked seeing you turn your back on him."

"Claimed me?" My brows were furrowed in confusion.

"Yeah, *claimed*. It means that he likes you and will try to get in your panties by the end of the night."

My jaw dropped. *Seriously?*

"The females go all mushy for Scott, so this is me warning you."

My chin lifted. "He can bloody well try, but he's not my type and I'm pretty much one-hundred percent sure I'm not his either." *I'm not a slut.*

Newton cocked his head slightly as he gazed at me and then smiled, "I think I believe you."

Chapter Three

Newton left me to dance on my own, claiming exhaustion. I watched him go back to our table and sit close to Ash. I did a double-take — he was sitting *very* close to her. I watched as half her body touched his side and she twiddled with her hair. I smiled to myself. Ash had the hots for him. I wondered if he knew, but then he was cosying up to her too. Meg was nowhere in sight. Scott had left the stage and had been replaced by classic rock that played from speakers. Merrily numb and foggy-headed, I danced with a few guys. I was sorry to see that the night was ending. I wanted to stay and dance all night long. I didn't care that I had college the next day or that I was a bit hammered. This was the first time I had been out in so long that I had forgotten how much I loved it. My cheeks were actually hurting from overuse of my smiling muscles.

A gentle rock ballad slowed the pace of the bodies moving around me in unison and I swayed my hips to the slow, heavy drumbeat. I could feel the bass quivering through the hardwood flooring. The haunting, melodic riff lulled me as a warm tingle spread over my skin. I felt someone — a presence — dancing behind me, almost as if they were dancing with me, moving with me. Time seemed to slow right down as I felt him almost touch my body here and there, like a whisper of air across my skin, teasing me. I waited for his hands to touch me but our secret dance went on and on, neither of us willing to make a move just yet. There was a heat building between us that was rising by the second. My breath went in and out shallowly as my lungs seemed to shrink.

I was coiled so tight that I was ready to turn around and just at that moment warm hands slid onto my hips from behind me and held them with a gentle firmness as they swayed slowly. Shivers shot through me so fast that my body flinched ever so slightly. I couldn't see who it was, but I didn't care. I was losing myself to the music and the sensation of his hands holding me, guiding and taking control of my hips, making them move slower, wider. His warmth invaded my back as he came closer and closer until his body made light contact. I trembled with an unusual feeling that zinged though my veins. Whoever this guy was, his hands were no stranger to feminine skin, that was for sure. My breath held as I felt him lift a hand off my hip to gather my hair away from my shoulder. A faint mix of mint and alcohol teased my nostrils as his warm breath fanned my exposed neck.

Anticipation clenched my stomach when the tip of his nose rubbed softly down my neck. Sparks shot all over me as his lips touched where my shoulder met my neck, grazing gently from side to side, over and over again, in a gentle assault. What felt like a day's stubble scraped my sensitive skin as the hand still gripping my hip pulled me backwards into him. He was moving with me in such a way that I was panting, the rigid part of his jeans pressing into my backside. His hands moved to my shoulders, ran slowly down my arms and gripped my hands intimately, taking them with him to my lower tummy as his mouth made its way up to my ear. I was losing it. I had never felt as sexy as I did right then.

My heart was hammering and all thoughts leaped from my mind. All that was left was him, and what he was doing and making me feel. I wanted him closer so I released a hand and raised my arm to loop it around his neck, holding him there as delicious sensations assaulted me. His free hand slid firmly up and down my side. He released a throaty chuckle close to my ear, and then ground his hips into me, torturously slowly, as we swayed. A dull throb started between my legs. I could feel what I was doing to him and it excited me as nothing had before. I matched his rhythm, straining to get closer. He released my hand to grip my hips with both hands and squeezed slightly.

His breathing became heavier and I heard a hiss pass his teeth before he pressed them firmly to my neck. He gently bit me, then licked the same spot. I groaned aloud again as I grabbed his neck tighter, holding him to me. My breath was coming out short and shaky. Everything seemed so far away — it was just the two of us and the music. It vaguely registered that he was walking us backwards. I didn't care — I was too far gone now, he was driving me crazy. His lips, firmer now, were on my jaw as he sucked and licked. I had never felt this before with anyone. I wanted to rip our clothes off right then. His hands tightened again as the tug of his lips on my jaw and neck deepened to a level that was almost primal.

A growl escaped his lips and pulsated over my skin. I could hear his breath rasping out of him. Without warning, he spun me around. His hands clinched my hips and pushed them back against a wall as he detached himself from me and leaned his forehead against mine as we tried to catch shaky breath after shaky breath. I opened my eyes, wanting to see his face.
I gasped. I was looking into the dark gaze of Scott Mason. "What the hell?" I yelled, pushing him away as hard as I could.

The surprise on his beautiful face might have been funny if this had been a laughing situation, but I had pushed him straight into a massive guy standing behind him.
The big man turned around and fisted Scott's shirt. "Watch where you're fucking going!" Big growled, his lip curling, showing yellow, crooked teeth.
"Take your hands off me," I heard Scott say in a quiet voice. I noticed that his hands were balled into fists at his sides.
"Or what?" Big laughed cruelly, looking behind Scott to me. "Aw! Am I showing you up in front of your girl?"

24

Scott's fist had connected with Big's nose before I even knew what was happening.

Big stumbled back in shock. "You're gonna fuckin' pay for that."

Scott didn't waste any time. He stepped in closer, punched him again and then grabbed his head and brought it down to his knee, hard. Big went to the floor.

I stood there, trying to disappear into the wall. Lingering lust, anger, embarrassment, and now guilt, all swirled within me. Scott whirled around then, his frowning eyes went straight to mine and I could only stand there gazing back at him, wide-eyed and speechless. He came at me. A ripple of fear ran down my spine. Ash had said something about his bad side, but my reaction to realising that it was Scott I had been dancing with had been swift and unstoppable. Would getting him into a fight put me on his bad list? I tried to shrink further into the wall as he gripped my hand and, without looking at me, dragged me away across the packed floor to the opposite side of the crowd where he put me against the wall *again*.

He placed his hands either side of my head and stood over me. His nostrils flared slightly, whether from exertion or anger I didn't know, but I hoped it was the first. His eyes held mine darkly as he calmed himself down.

"What was that for, babe?" he finally rasped.

I groaned inwardly. His voice had an intimate edge to it that had my pulse working overtime again.

I was mortified that I had danced with him like that — and that I had then pushed him away straight into someone and started a fight. In my defence, I had had no idea that it was him behind me, touching me that way, with those hands...*Stop it!* How could I have been so stupid? Now he was watching me questioningly, waiting for a reply.

"What was what for?" I asked, my voice hoarse.

"Why did you push me away? I thought we were having a good time." His hand came up to stroke my cheek gently. His intense eyes seemed to darken visibly and his brows drew together. "God, you're a beauty."

I gazed at him and the world slipped away as he looked at me like no one had ever looked at me before — as though I was his special something and I fascinated him like nothing else did or ever could again.

I took a shaky breath and snapped myself out of it. He was so much more dangerous close up than when he was on stage. He was a real pro at this stuff — I had to remember that.

I knocked his hand away and shoved his hard chest lightly.

He looked sullen and his perfect lips parted as if he was about to protest.

"I'm not interested," I said as loudly as I could so I wouldn't have to repeat myself and made a move to walk away.

His hand hit the wall blocking my exit.

I gritted my teeth. He obviously didn't like being told 'no'. The egotistical arse has probably never heard the word slip from between a girl's lips. Tough.

"You're British?" He seemed surprised. Had he really only just noticed?

"Wow, you're quick aren't you? Yes, I am."

"What's your name?" His breath held.

"Emma." I felt triumphant as his breath whooshed out of him and he turned his back on me. He dragged his hand through his hair agitatedly. I was so glad at that moment that Ash had my back and had obviously warned him away from me.

He turned and watched me hesitantly for a moment. His eyes took a slow journey from my face down to my feet and back up again.

Rocked Under ~ Cora Hawkes

26

"Fuck," he muttered as he swiped his hand over his mouth and chin.

He clutched my hand again, more gently this time.

I instantly felt hot and uncomfortable.

"Come on, I'll get you back to Ash." He started tugging me along behind him across the sweaty dance floor. He glanced at me over his shoulder, "I'm Scott, by the way."

"I know. Your reputation precedes you." I pulled my tingling hand out of his grasp, "I can make my own way, thanks."

He stopped abruptly and I collided with his back. My hands went to his sides of their own accord for support, while he whipped his behind him lightning fast and grasped my hips to steady me. My legs almost buckled as I felt the hardness of his backside on my abdomen. *Jee-SUS!*

He squeezed slightly before dropping his hands and turning around to face me. I took a much-needed step back. My body was misbehaving in response to his closeness, like an allergic reaction.

"My reputation?" He began to cross his arms and I saw blood on his knuckles.

I grabbed his hand. "You're bleeding," I said, holding his hand up to show him.

He shrugged, "It'll happen if you hit someone a few times. It's no big deal."

I noticed that his knuckles were covered in silvery soft lines from previous fights. I looked up. "I'm sorry for causing *that* fight." I dropped his hand.

"He deserved it," he said dismissively. "Look," he stepped closer, "You shouldn't dance with guys like that if you're not gonna follow through. You could get into a lot of trouble."

What a load of bull. I had been taking care of myself for a long time now. "What kind of trouble?" I looked up at him wide-eyed and blinked, playing innocent.

His eyebrows rose a touch.

Anyway, it wasn't as if I had meant to act like that. I didn't know what had got into me. He had made me feel something that I hadn't before, that was for sure, and I didn't like it — not with him anyway.

"Fuck, babe," he groaned, "You know what I mean."

I found his voice the sexiest sound in the world. I needed to get away from him — *now*.

"Sorry, but I don't." Should I let him squirm some more? He really looked uncomfortable. I loved it, but decided against it. "Can we get back to Ash now?"

Without saying a word he grasped my hand again and dragged me behind him towards our table where Ash, Meg and Newton were sitting.

They clocked us and I noticed Newton's surprised expression as he saw our joined hands. Scott adjusted the seat next to Ash and sat me in it like a child. My temper flared.

Ash grinned at Scott, "I see you've met your new neighbour."

Scott froze, his brows inverting as he looked from Ash to me and then back again. "What?"

"Emma and I moved into your building." I could tell Ash was enjoying this a lot.

Scott flashed a frown at me before turning back to Ash, "I gotta go. Later."

I watched him walk away, shaking his head. His gait was smooth and sure. When he was almost lost in the crowd he turned his head and looked back at me darkly before disappearing into the bodies on the dance floor. I turned to look at the rest of the gang. They were looking at me like I had grown another head.

"What?" My brows rose. "Do I have horns on my head or something?"

"Or something," Newton said.

"Shit, Emma, what did you *do* to him?" Meg asked.

Rocked Under ~ Cora Hawkes

Ash was studying me quietly.

"I didn't do *anything*."

"Oh shit!" Newton started laughing, "Did you just blow Scott off?"

"I told you *Buttfluff*, he's not my type." That just made him laugh even harder.

"No shit!"

I rolled my eyes. "Right," I slapped my palms on the table, "Whose round is it?"

I needed a drink. I may have blown Scott off but he had affected me like nobody else ever had. I didn't like that and it wasn't something I could let on to anyone — it would just be too embarrassing after telling Newton that Scott wasn't my type. And then there was Ash. What would she think after everything my family had been through? My mind started doing a replay. I jumped up from my seat, "The next round's on me."

Macy's was emptying slowly and I watched Ash and Newton dancing. She hadn't told me she had a boyfriend or a thing for Newton, but it was pretty obvious that she liked him a bit more than a friend. I could tell by her little give-away looks and the way that she lowered her lashes to hide her eyes if he made eye contact for too long. They would make a cute couple. Did Newton even know she had a crush on him?

I didn't dance again after Scott brought me back. Suddenly, I felt a prickling sensation, as if someone was watching me. My brows pulled together and I looked around. Scott's hooded, dark stare connected with mine. Awareness slammed me full pelt. A hotness overwhelmed me and took my breath away. My heart stalled and then restarted painfully. *Is it possible to have a heart attack at my age?*

He was leaning against the wall next to the stage in almost darkness, with his hands shoved into his front jean pockets, shoulders slumped and head down. But his eyes were on me and they wouldn't release me. I didn't know how I had sensed him, given the distance between us, but I had. I let my breath go slowly as I looked away when he didn't. I felt so awkward and uncomfortable under his scrutiny that the urge to get up and hide was immense. I bent my head, letting my hair act as a curtain, and fiddled with my charm bracelet as I squirmed, fully conscious of his eyes on me — like he resented or even disliked me.

I didn't look up again until we left, and then I kept my gaze forwards, on my goal — the exit.

Chapter Four

"Over here!" I heard Newton shout across the humungous cafeteria at lunch a few days later. It had been a busy morning. I was starving and ready to eat a horse *and* its rider. He was sitting at a big, round table with Ash and Meg. Ash had asked Newton yesterday why Scott hadn't joined them for lunch like he usually did. Newton had looked briefly in my direction before looking at Ash with a shrug of his shoulders. "He's been busy."

I pushed all thoughts of Scott to the back of my mind, annoyed that I was thinking about him again. After that first night I had only seen him once, and that had been in our communal entrance. I had been coming in while he had been going out. I remembered it like it had been ten minutes — and not two days — ago.

I had been opening the door in a rush to get in out of the pouring rain, which already had me looking like a drowned rat, when the door had been pulled out of my grasp. I had looked up and seen Scott standing there, looking down at me with a wry grin on his face. My breath had held and my heart had started stuttering as I noticed his eyes — they were an intense shade of dark green that stood out from his tanned skin. I had had that same feeling that he seemed familiar, but I had shaken it off.

"Hey," he had said, the grin still playing at the corners of his lips and his eyes twinkling at me gawking up at him.

My cheeks had grown warm at being caught. "Hello," I had replied, my British accent more pronounced.

"Are you coming in?" An eyebrow lifted.

I had jumped when I realised I was blocking his way, standing there staring at his gorgeous face. "Oh! Sorry. Yep, I'm coming in." *You are an idiot!*

He had moved aside. "You're soaked to the fuckin' skin." He had been looking at my sodden and now transparent blouse.

I had hastily crossed my arms and pretended to shiver. I had felt my cheeks go warm with the humiliation of being caught in the rain with just a thin blouse on over my bra. "I don't know where this rain came from, it was nice half an hour ago." *Why did everything I say to him sound so lame?*

He had chuckled quietly in the most melodic way imaginable. "The weather tends to be unpredictable."

"I'll remember that," I had smiled up at him.

He had been still for a moment as he watched me, a very slight frown marring his perfect face. After a moment of him having my heart in my throat again he had very abruptly said "Later." And with a strange smile he had gone. I had stood there for a while just shaking my head at myself for having stared at him like a hungry dog.

That guy was truly too damned perfect for his own good.

The smell of food and the rumble in my tummy tugged me from my reminiscence and brought me back to the cafeteria.

"Hey!" I plonked myself down on a hard plastic chair next to Ash.

"Good morning, *Dweeb*?" Newton asked.

"Yeah, but now I'm bloody starving." I put my hand on my stomach, hoping it wouldn't growl.

"See, I told you you'd be fine here," Ash chimed.

I smiled and looked around while the others talked about their lessons.

Giggles coming from the table next to us caught my interest. Two girls were whispering and practically drooling over someone who had just walked in. My back stiffened as I felt those green eyes on my back. It could only be Scott — I never reacted to anyone the way I did to him.

I found my head turning in his direction automatically — I couldn't help myself. My eyes found his hooded ones instantly and my lungs squeezed as I looked at him. He was wearing faded blue jeans and a tight-ish black T-shirt with a faded motif across the front that hugged his muscles in all the right places. His dark hair shone in the light. He looked hot — too hot for a cafeteria full to the brim with hormonal girls — and I was one of them. He smiled as a hello before diverting his attention to the giggling girls.

"Scott!" I heard Newton shout across to him, calling him to sit with us. I needed a minute to get my breath under control, so I jumped up, ignored Ash's questioning look and went to get my lunch.

In the ten minutes it took me to get my food I didn't look at our table once, but I had a tingling sensation every time his gaze touched me, making me feel uncomfortable. I wished he would stop. I wasn't a strange, exotic creature — I was British for Christ's sake, and not even the only one on campus. Maybe this weirdness would fade, or something, once we knew each other better. I kicked myself for the hundredth time for getting carried away the other night with someone I hadn't even bothered to look at first. I should have turned around. Not for the first time in my short life, I cursed alcohol.

I sat back down with my lunch.
"...Awesome last night, man." Newton was talking to Scott.
"Thanks. We got three nights a week there this semester." He shrugged as if it was nothing great.
I looked up into green eyes. My heart lurched but I hid it well and smiled at him coolly, but I was sure it didn't reach my eyes. This was ridiculous. I fumed silently. No wonder he got away with what he did — he was gorgeous with a capital 'g'.

I knew that someday he would be big. I *knew* it. He had the right sound, the right image, the overwhelming presence. Oh yes, the bad-boy image together with his looks would take him places.

Someone cleared their throat behind me. I turned around to see Adam, a junior I had met on my first day who had been flirting with me ever since. He had asked me out that morning and I had said I would think about it and let him know.

"You made up your mind yet?" he grinned.

I laughed at his impatience. "I have," I said and looked away, teasing him.

I hadn't thought about it really. Adam was a few inches taller than me, with blonde hair, warm, chestnut eyes and a great body. I could tell he played sport.

"Well, yes or no, woman?" he put on a disgruntled air.

"It's a yes," I smiled and then noticed everyone at our table watching our exchange.

"Guys, this is Adam." I then went on to introduce Adam to everyone. They gave him a cool welcome, not like the warm one they gave me when I was introduced the other night.

Adam nodded around the table. "So, do you want to meet or am I picking you up?"

"When?"

"Tonight," he grinned.

We decided to meet at seven outside Macy's and then he was gone. I liked Adam. *He's safe!* I blinked at the thought and looked away.

"Hey, British!" A guy I had met in class walked by our table. "I hope they have *to-MAH-toes* in the salad today." He winked at me and walked on.

I laughed aloud as I remembered him trying to copy my accent during class. The others were looking at me and I explained about his British lesson and how he said he would help me with some of the different spellings over here.

"Em, we don't know Adam very well," said Ash, voicing her concern.

"Yeah, you shouldn't just hook up with anyone." Newton looked stern and I was surprised that was even possible for him.

"He's not just anyone, he's in one of my classes," I defended.

"Still...." said Ash.

"Oh, he's nice, you'll like him." I waved her worries away. I needed to get out and make friends on my own. I couldn't hang around Ash's friends all the time.

"I'm going to be calling you every hour," Ash said seriously.

I laughed. "Okay, *jeez!* But it's only a date. It's not like I'm hooking up with a total stranger either." *Like I did the other night.* I sneaked a look at Scott from under my lashes. His lips tightened as he looked away from me.

"Leave the girl alone, guys," Meg butted in.

I looked at her gratefully and changed the subject. "What are the rest of you doing tonight?" I asked.

"We're at Scott's for a movie," Meg replied and looked at Scott with a cheeky grin. "Wasn't it my turn to choose the movie?"

Groans erupted around me.

"Fuck, no!" Newton grabbed his head. "No more Jane Austen adaptations, Meg."

Meg looked offended. "Actually, I was thinking of a horror."

"What's wrong with Jane Austen?" I loved Jane Austen.

"Nothing, if you haven't seen Pride and Prejudice a hundred times already," Newton replied.

Scott's eyes met mine across the table. It was like I had an invisible string attached to him, pulling me in, making me aware of every move he made. His dark expression cleared after a second, and he smiled, showing me his white teeth and those dimples again.

After my last class I was starting to make my way home when my hand was taken from behind. I turned and came face-to-face with Scott.

"What're you doing?" I said breathlessly, trying to sound cross. I hated being grabbed, touched or watched by strangers.

He was so beautiful. My hand in his tingled and I stilled as I saw the way he was looking at me — the same way he had done the other night. *God, you're a beauty.* His words echoed in my head and then his expression cleared again.

"I need to talk to you," he growled and my stupid heart tripped over itself.

I didn't want to talk about Macy's. "O–kay."

"About the other night..." he hesitated.

I wriggled my hand out of his. He took a step back and put his hands up as if in surrender. "Sorry." He shook his head slightly. "You know I didn't know you were Ashley's cousin, right?"

"Yeah, I know." I looked away and closed my eyes briefly against the embarrassed heat that was turning my skin red as I again had unwanted flashbacks.

"It wouldn't have happened if I did," he sighed and looked away. "I'm sorry for treating you that way."

He's sorry? Could this be any more mortifying?

"Look, it's no big deal. Don't worry about it. Let's just forget it happened, okay?" I wanted to forget so badly. "I was drunk," I shrugged as if it had meant nothing and that his gaze was not making my insides quiver. How could I feel like this over *him*?

"So," he drew the word out slowly, "Friends?" He held his hand out to me.

"Friends." I forced a smile up at him and put my hand in his for a second to shake it, again hoping that this awkwardness would go away once we had known each other longer. At the moment I couldn't stop thinking about him, but I had to try, seeing as the guy was one of Ash's best friends, not to mention that we shared a building.

I wanted to forget about the whole thing and so did he, so I was willing to give it a good go. He had already taken up way too much of my brain space as it was, and maybe I wasn't his type after all. Or maybe he wasn't as bad as everyone was making him out to be?
"You going home?"
I nodded.
"Same. I'll walk with you." He pocketed both his hands and we started the walk home.

I could see every girl we passed watching him, admiring him. I peeked at him out of the corner of my eye to see if he noticed it too, but he didn't seem to — he wasn't taking one bit of notice of all the attention he was getting.
He smirked sideways at me. "What?" he asked.
"Nothing." *Shit!* I averted my eyes.
I heard him sigh. "What brings you over here anyway?" he asked.
"I…Uh…My mum and dad just got divorced and it seemed like a good idea." I didn't want to think about that just then. My past was where it should be — in the past and filed in my head under 'no entry'.
"I don't want to pry if you don't want to talk about it." He must have sensed that I didn't want to talk. And why did he care anyway?
"My mum's family lives over here and as we don't have any family left over there, we moved here," I offered, trying to make it sound simple.

He studied me quizzically. "So your mom was born here?"

"Yeah, she moved to the UK after she married my dad and had me." I couldn't help the way my lips turned down at his name and gave myself a mental kick when Scott's eyebrows raised a fraction.

"Your dad doesn't care about you being over here?"

Hell no! "No, he doesn't." What was this anyway, twenty questions? I didn't want to talk about my dad at all.

"What about you? Do you like being in a band?" I really didn't want to know anything about him — I really didn't — I just didn't want to talk about the past anymore.

"I wouldn't be doing it if I didn't like it." His eyes were twinkling at me and somehow I think he knew that I had deliberately changed the subject . "We're doing a tour next summer when I graduate."

"Really?" I had a real interest in music. "Where?" I wanted to know more instantly.

"National. We want to cram as many dates in as we can."

"That's so interesting." I knew my face was lighting up but I couldn't help it. I didn't want to find anything about him interesting, but he was making that very difficult for me.

He laughed and my eyes widened as I was hit by a wave of desire all over again. His laugh was warm and deep and made him seem even more eye-poppingly beautiful than he already was. I released my breath slowly while looking away from him so I could catch my breath. I looked at the cracks in the pavement.

"Do you play anything?" He seemed totally tuned into me now.

"Piano, but I don't want to be a musician like you. I want to be involved in the business side of things."

"Piano, huh? How long have you played?"

"Since I can remember. Apparently my dad insisted I be taught as early as possible." *Oh, yes! His perfect daughter.*

"You must be good then?"

Rocked Under ~ Cora Hawkes

I wasn't just good, I was a pro. But I didn't want to boast so I just smiled by way of an answer.

"Hmm..." he cocked his head slightly and looked at me thoughtfully. *What is he thinking?* Our gazes locked for a moment and I looked away before he could read me.

We were halfway home now and I had to grudgingly admit that he was a nice guy. He reached into his pocket and pulled out a packet of cigarettes.

He lifted the packet to offer me one. "Smoke?"

"Non-smoker." I squeezed a smile out. "I suppose I should tell you how bad those things are and that they'll kill you one day, but I'm guessing you already know that."

He put the cigarette between his lips and lit up. "I'll give up the day I graduate."

"Just like that?" I teased.

He nodded, "Just like that." His mouth curved in a smug grin.

We had grown silent again. I racked my brain for something to get the conversation flowing. Silence between us wasn't a good thing — it made my mind wander to memories that were better left alone.

"What do your parents think about you wanting to be a rock star?" *How lame do I sound?* Very.

"It's just me and my dad, actually, and he's always had my back in everything I do. My mom fucked off when I was a baby and only seen her a couple of times since."

Trust me to put my foot in it. "I'm sorry. Now *I'm* prying."

"It's nothing," he shrugged, "It was a long time ago and I've never known any different so…" I felt bad for him. Growing up without a mum must have been hard. I imagined him as a little boy with nobody to wipe his tears away, nobody to kiss away hurts. I stopped myself from thinking that way about him. In no way did I want to think of him as being vulnerable.

I swallowed as I thought about my own mum. She had had such a sad life — but no more.

"You and your dad are close, then?"

"Yeah, he's away a lot so we don't see much of each other, although we talk on the phone." His face softened and I could tell that he loved his dad very much.

"Hi, Scott." We both looked towards the blonde who sat on the wall twirling a lock of hair between her manicured fingers.

Scott winked and smiled sexily at her. I wondered if she was the one for tonight and then give myself a mental thump. Why did I care anyway?

We were almost home now and I wanted nothing more than to have a shower.

"You still meeting Adam at seven?" I thought I had seen his jaw tense but I couldn't be sure.

"Yeah."

"Do you want me to walk you there?"

I frowned. Why would he want to walk me to meet my date? "Um, no thanks, I'm good."

"Okay. Everyone'll be at mine when you get back. You and Adam can join if you want."

This felt weird. Here I was talking to the guy who I had almost had sex with about the guy I was dating tonight.

"Thanks, we might." I went to get my key but he beat me to it and held the door open for me. I mumbled my thanks as I walked in.

"Maybe see you later, then," he said.

"Yeah." I turned to unlock mine and Ash's door.

"Emma?" His quiet rasp was almost breathless and right behind me. Shivers ran up my neck as I realised that that was the first time he had said my name — and it sounded so good.

Rocked Under ~ Cora Hawkes

I turned to face him with a frown. His intense gaze held mine as he came closer. He reached out a hand and my breath held as I wondered what he was going to do. He took my phone out of my hand, punched in a number and pressed 'call'. A few seconds later I heard his phone ring and he hung up, tapped the keys and handed me back my phone.

"I've got your cell and you've got mine. If Adam gives you any shit, call me." His gaze bored into mine.
"Why? You barely know me." It just slipped out. I cringed at how rude I sounded. I only wanted to know why he was trying to protect me like I was his little sister or something.
He paused before answering. "You're Ashley's cousin."
"You don't need to look out for me out of duty just because I'm related to Ash, you know." It annoyed me that he would pretend to care just because of Ash.
A half-smile appeared. "Friends look out for each other, don't they?"
Yes. We were friends.
I closed my door and leaned against it. Maybe Scott Mason wasn't such a bad guy after all.

Chapter Five

Adam was already waiting when I arrived at our meeting place. He took my hand immediately and walked to the nearest diner. The whole time I was thinking about how his hand was nothing like Scott's big, strong, calloused hands. Adam's hands were soft and gracefully thin. I sighed to myself. The sooner I stopped thinking about Scott that way the better. I turned all my attention to Adam and tried to stop comparing him to Scott.

The diner was busy. We wound through the tables to the only one left. Adam pulled my chair out for me and then handed me a menu. I ordered a burger and chips. Adam laughed as he corrected me — fries, not chips. It was annoying to be corrected but I didn't say anything. He'd get used to me.
Ash had called me twice already and I had had to explain to Adam that she was worried about me. We talked and got to know each other — actually, he talked and I got to know him. He watched horrors while I hated them, he listened to mostly hip-hop while I thought it was terrible, he didn't have the time to read while I made time to read. We had a lot of differences, but don't opposites attract anyway? He knew what he wanted in life — a good job, a wife, a family and maybe a dog, in that order. He was a bit young to be thinking about all that already and I hoped he wasn't spouting all that just to impress me. He was handsome in a warm, wholesome kind of way and I knew my mum would love him. What mum wouldn't like him? By the end of our meal we were comfortable with each other and he held my hand over the table.
He sounded grounded and safe. I cringed. There was that word again — safe. Twice in one day now. He was safe and Scott was dangerous. Okay, he was a bit up his own arse, but this was only the first date and maybe he was desperately trying to make me like him?

"What're you thinking?" he asked, breaking the comfortable silence as we walked back to my place.

"Just stuff." I looked at him and smiled.

"Share?" Adam asked.

"I was just thinking about what a great guy you are. I've had a nice time tonight. Thanks." He stopped and I looked up at him.

He was watching me intently. "You're so cute," he whispered as he touched my cheek gently.

I knew he was going to kiss me, and I didn't feel panicked by it at all.

He came towards me slowly, all the while looking at me as if asking permission. When I didn't stop him he put his lips on mine tentatively at first. When I didn't pull away he brought his other hand to my cheek and deepened the kiss. His tongue was stroking mine softly and I brought my arms up and wrapped them around his neck. He was so gentle with me and I liked it.

He pulled away to look at me and grinned.

We walked on, our hands meshed together, until we reached my place.

He walked me right to my door. "I really had a lovely time tonight, Adam. Thanks," I smiled, my hand still in his.

"So," he drew it out, "do you want to go out again?"

"Yeah, I'd like that," I nodded.

He stood there and reached for my other hand to pull me in close for another kiss. He kissed me the same way he had before, but my body wouldn't relax into it. I kept thinking that Scott could walk out the front door or look out the window any minute and see me kissing Adam, and I had no idea why I should be thinking that while I was meant to be enjoying Adam's attention. Why should I care if Scott saw anything? I'd just met him and I can count on one hand the number of times I'd spoken to him. Adam didn't notice my discomfort and continued to kiss me.

After saying goodnight I went inside and remembered that everyone would be upstairs at Scott's for a movie. I debated for a minute whether or not I should knock on his door and join them. Would it send the wrong message to Scott? I didn't want him to think that I wanted to see him, but everyone was there and it was way too early for bed. Argh! *What am I doing?* I was obsessing over him and I barely knew the guy. What the hell was wrong with me?

Without thinking about it anymore, I tapped on his door. A few moments later, Scott appeared. He didn't say anything but just looked at me darkly as he came forward to take my hand. He had light, denim jeans and a faded green shirt on that looked fantastic on him. His gaze never leaving mine, he came close and as he did a faint twang of alcohol hit my nostrils. I squinted at him through the dim light and confirmed that he looked slightly drunk.

He looked over my shoulder. "Where's your date, what's his name, Adrian?" He stepped towards me.

"Adam?" I corrected. "He left."

"Come up then." He pulled me through the door and up the stairs to his apartment.

The door was open when we got there and we walked straight in. Scott's apartment surprised me. It wasn't dingy, as I expected it would be. I thought it'd be dark, with empty beer bottles littering the floor, maybe a few week-old takeaway boxes on the coffee table, but I was wrong.

Inside the door was an open-plan lounge and diner. It was a big room with clean, white walls and splashes of deep red here and there. There was a large, white, leather couch shaped like a 'u' that would have been big enough to seat about ten people. Ash, Newton and Meg were splayed out on it, stuffing themselves with popcorn, all eyes riveted on the gore that was flashing across the massive flat-screen TV. There were big double balcony doors that overlooked the town below. Then my eyes came to rest on his piano. Sleek and black and shiny. My fingers spasmed just looking at it. It had been so long since I had played and I missed it, although a part of me didn't want to play again.

I felt Scott watching me and I couldn't resist looking at him with a smile. "You have a nice place."
He raised an eyebrow. "Why are you surprised?"
I shook my head. "Guys aren't known for their cleaning, you know."
He was so good-looking. His eyes, half-closed, instantly held mine. A tingle of awareness zinged over my skin. I took a breath, releasing my hand and breaking the contact at the same time.
"Hi!" I raised my hand to the guys.
Grunts and half-hearted smiles of welcome came my way as their eyes stayed glued to the screen.

My hand was taken in a soft grip. I looked down to see that Scott had abducted my hand again. I hated the way he took my hand all the time. My lips parted to protest.
"I'll get you a drink," he said, cutting me off, and dragged me through a door near the dining table and into the equally clean, tidy kitchen. His hand was doing things to my equilibrium. I thought this was odd, because when Adam had held my hand it was just that — a hand. Scott's hand was warm and strong and forceful. I felt aware of every bit of skin that his hand was touching, and I didn't like it. He didn't let my hand go as he went over to the fridge and opened the door.

His thumb started stroking slow circles on the sensitive part between my thumb and forefinger, sending fire shooting down to my belly, I hated it — I didn't want to feel this at all.

"What do you want?" He opened the fridge door wide so I could peek inside.

What I wanted was my hand back. Honestly, I could walk on my own without his helping hand. After all, I was nineteen years old — a big girl. Why did he think he had the right to get inside my personal bubble? I barely knew him.

"I'll have a beer, please." I tried pulling my hand away gently, but when he didn't get the subtle hint I asked, "Can I have my hand back?"

"Does my touch bother you, babe?" His gaze pierced mine.

Hell yes! "No," I said too fast. My face heated and my stomach flipped.

He frowned and looked at me with his head tilted to one side. I wanted to look away so much but I refused to back down. My face got hotter as his eyes burned into me and then, after what seemed like minutes, he released my hand.

"I'm holding your hand cos I like it. I'm not flirting." His lips twisted. "You're not my type," he shrugged and turned back to the fridge.

Not his type? Why did that infuriate me? By the sound of what I had heard, he went for girls that laid down for him on the first night. Damn right I wasn't his bloody type. I was far from a slag.

"You're right, I'm not your type. I'm not a slut." I raised my chin defiantly.

He turned abruptly, his brows pulling together as he studied me. "What the fuck is with you?"

"Nothing, I just don't want you to take my hand all the time. I'm not a doll," I huffed and crossed my arms as I looked away from his intent stare.

"I'm a touchy person," he shrugged. "Stop overanalysing."

Rocked Under ~ Cora Hawkes

"I'm not overanalysing anything. I don't see you ever holding Ashley's hand, or Meg's," I pointed out.

"Why you being sensitive?"

"I'm not. I barely know you and you keep invading my bloody bubble."

"Bubble?" he chuckled. "Do all Brits have brooms shoved up their asses, or is it just you?"

I gasped and my jaw went slack. How dare he? "Wow, your ego is really something, but no, we don't have brooms shoved up our anything." I gave him the best glare I could manage. "I just don't want you to get the wrong idea about me because of the other night. I don't want you to think that I'm interested in you or anything, because I'm not."

His expression sobered as I spoke.

"Really? Not interested?" He moved towards me slowly, like a panther tracking its prey, its eye on its goal. I edged back with every step he took until my lower back came up against a counter in the centre of the kitchen. His hands went either side of me as he lowered his head towards mine. I could smell the boozy haze he was giving off, but there was a scent that I remembered from the other night mingled in with the alcohol — and it was far from unpleasant.

My heart sped up and wanted to burst out of my chest as his head came even closer. He stroked his cheek against mine and I froze as his stubble scraped my skin, sending unwanted tingles all over me. One of his hands came up and fingered the dip at the bottom of my neck where my collarbones met. I could feel my pulse kicking rapidly against the gentle pressure of his stroking finger.

"Hmm...." he mumbled.

My eyes closed in embarrassment as I knew he had all the proof he needed that he affected me.

He moved away slightly to look at me. "This might not be interested," his fingers touched my temple in a feather-light caress, "but your body's telling me a different story."

My heart doubled its speed. "My body isn't telling you a thing." What else could I say to make him back off?

He stepped away from me until he was leaning against the counter opposite me. He shoved his hands in his pockets, his eyes never leaving mine. Something had shifted in the atmosphere, a tension between us that was heavy and suffocating. I held his stare with my head held high, daring him to say I was lying. He watched me squirm longer, his head cocked. After a minute, a faint smile transformed his features. He grabbed two beers from the fridge and came close again, placing mine on the counter behind me.

"You're right." He shook his head in apology. "Wishful thinking, I guess."

Feeling way out of my comfort zone, I grabbed my drink and headed back to where there were other people. Wishful thinking? What did that mean? He bothered me. He bothered me big time and I didn't need it. I needed to just see him as a friend, nothing more. I wondered if I would feel this way about him if we had been introduced in the normal way — but I knew that I probably would. From the moment I saw him on the stage, I was a goner. I may as well join the fan club and wear the bloody T-shirt. Okay, so maybe he was like this tonight because he was a bit drunk, but he got to me like nobody else ever had. I wondered if that was what was referred to as a chemical reaction — lust at first sight. There was no way I would even entertain the idea of love at first sight — I really didn't know how someone could love a person when they had just met them.

I remembered Ash saying that he didn't do the 'boyfriend' thing but that he made a great friend. I could believe it, because although I was angry, it was only at myself for reacting to him so strongly when I was usually so cool. Our talk on the way home earlier had shown me a side to him that was different from the side I saw when he'd been drinking, and I liked him that way. I had felt sorry for him earlier when he told me about his mum — every child should have a mother.

I got comfy on the couch and gazed into the TV. I had missed too much of the movie to get into it but at least it was something to pretend to watch while my mind went into overdrive. Scott came in after me and sat beside me, but he didn't touch me again, and he didn't say much either. I finished my beer and made an excuse about getting an early night.

Chapter Six

Everyone was already sat at our table when I arrived in the cafeteria for lunch the next day. Even Adam was there waiting for me, watching me as I walked towards them — and then my step faltered as another pair of eyes, this time hooded and intense, tracked my every move. Would I ever get used to that stare? Adam stood and put his arms around me before kissing me thoroughly in front of everyone. I heard cheering and wolf whistles in the background and knew that this was a show of possessiveness on Adams part. I didn't like it but I let it go while Scott was watching us.

"Hey, babe," he smiled as he pulled away from me.

"Hi," I replied with a strained smile as he kissed my forehead.

I sat and chanced a peek at Scott, who was looking away at something else. He seemed in a bad mood and I could see the muscles in his jaw clenching. Hangover, maybe?

"So I take it you guys had a good time last night?" Meg wiggled her eyebrows up and down. She had been too engrossed in the film to bother asking.

"Yeah," I glanced at Adam.

"Aw! You two make a cute couple," she said in her *Tweetie-Pie* voice.

Halfway through lunch a girl sashayed in and caught my attention, mainly because of what she was wearing — or wasn't wearing. She had on a mini skirt, or was it a belt? I looked closer. Yep, a mini skirt trying to be a belt, with a skimpy top that showed off her tanned tummy and ample cleavage. Her eyes zeroed in on Scott and she went out of her way to walk past him. I smothered a chuckle. She was being so obvious and looked bloody ridiculous too. I shook my head — the lengths that girls would go to was hilarious, and cringeworthy for other girls to watch.

"Hi, Scott," she purred as she got near him. As she was about to walk past, Scott whipped his hand out and grabbed her into his lap.

She squealed with laughter and I couldn't help but grimace. What was *wrong* with me? Why did I care what he did?

"Hey," he said right before kissing her. I watched in shock as his hand crept slowly up the outside of her bare thigh stopping just at the top, where his thumb stroked slow circles on her exposed skin.

I swallowed past the lump that had formed in my throat and turned my head away.

"Here he goes again," Meg said rolling her eyes. Everyone else just carried on as if this was normal behaviour for him.

"Same old Scott," Newton mumbled as he eyed the girls thigh.

"Are you two going out again?" Ash asked me expectantly.

"Tomorrow," Adam answered for me without asking me first.

I wanted to yell that he hadn't even asked me yet, but again I let it go. I felt grouchy.

"We're all going to Macy's tonight. Wanna come?" Meg was looking at me and I noticed that Scott had stopped eating the girl's face, although his attention was still on her.

"Might as well. Who's playing?"

"Scott."

"Great." I tried to sound pleased but Scott's eyes darted to mine with a faint frown, catching my fake enthusiasm, so I gave him my best smile to let him know that I didn't mean it. I was rewarded with a smile and a wink that made my pulse quicken.

Macy's wasn't as crowded as it had been the first night. There were spaces between people and seats to spare.

"Does anybody want to dance?" I shouted over the music at nobody in particular.

Ash laughed, "I think you guys have probably guessed by now that the girl *loves* to dance." She smiled at me, "I'll dance with you, cous. Come on."

As we got on the dance floor the music stopped and the stage lit up. Scott and his band were in place. Excitement welled up in me as he started with an upbeat song. Just like before, the girls made a mad dash to get to the front. He saw Ash and me instantly and winked as he thrashed his guitar and sang with a smile. My heart fluttered as I smiled and waved shyly at him. The song had me moving fast, but I kept up.

About halfway through, Ash pulled me off for another drink. "God, Em! You really can dance the night away!"

Dancing was all about letting go for me. At home it had been the only way I could let it all out and maybe lose control a bit. Ash would never understand the demands that were put on me from an early age.

It had led to me getting a fake ID at sixteen, just so I could get into the nightclubs. I was so happy when I turned eighteen, the legal age for drinking in England. Now I had to have another fake ID — I had been horrified when I found out that the drinking age here was twenty-one.

I quickly downed my vodka, along with a glass of water to hydrate, and made it back out onto the dance floor.

Later that night, I spotted Scott dancing suggestively with a girl with long, dark hair and a slender body. They were dancing close, face-to-face. He had a hand on her waist and I watched in envy — no, not envy, *disgust* — I watched in *disgust* as his other hand went up to her cheek and then threaded itself into her hair, where he balled his hand into a fist and pulled, making her look up at him. His lids were heavy and his attention was all hers. His head went down to her but as he did his eyes found mine. I flinched at the blatant hunger burning through him into me. I turned and looked away quickly, not wanting him to notice how my smile had slipped and that my eyes had squeezed closed. Why should it bother me to see him like that with someone else? I pushed the thought to the back of my mind with a shake of my head. No points for guessing who the lucky girl would be tonight — *unlucky girl* — I meant, *unlucky!* She wouldn't be lucky with him — no girl would be.

I danced away from them and straight into an attractive blonde man. "Whoops! *Sorry!*" I shouted at him over the music.

He grinned, showing blinding-white, over-bright teeth, and started to move with me. I stayed with him through a couple of songs until he got cocky. He put his hands on my waist and tried to pull me closer. I pulled myself out of his grasp and away from him but he reached for me again and clamped his hands onto my hips, squeezing me to keep me there. I wriggled and pushed against his chest but he wouldn't let go. The first threads of fear licked at my spine, my heart tripped and then took off at speed.

"Get off me!" I shouted.

He let go abruptly. He was being dragged backwards fast. Scott was pulling him away and said some words to him that looked heated but that I couldn't hear. I hoped he wouldn't hit him, although it would be no less than he deserved — 'no' means 'no'. Scott pushed him back with force. Blonde guy went flying backwards into the arms of the waiting doorman and was hauled outside by the back of his shirt. Relief washed over me in warm waves and I took a deep breath, not realising that I had been holding it.

Scott turned and came back to me. His shadowy face made his anger look menacing.

"Thanks, but I could've handled him," I lied.

He shook his head and looked at me hard. "This isn't fuckin' England, Emma! That dick wasn't going to fuckin' stop!"

His fury blasted me and I took a step back. I didn't want his anger directed at me.

He frowned like he was in pain and his gaze softened as he stepped forwards. He gently gripped my upper arms as he leaned down to my ear, "You need to be more careful, okay?"

His closeness was disturbing me. I managed a stupefied nod of understanding. I was super-aware of his warm hands touching my bare skin. How could it be that every time he touched me I felt like this? It was annoying — I didn't want to feel this way. My body was reacting all on its own, without me telling it that it was okay first.

"Come on, I'll dance with you," he smiled.

I hesitated and didn't know how to say 'no' in a kind way. "No, it's okay, I was going to sit out for a while anyway."

"It's only a dance, Emma. No funny business, I promise," he said with a mischievous smile.

I realised I couldn't say no. He had just helped me out when he didn't need to, and what was one dance, anyway? It would be over before I knew it.

I nodded and he gripped my hand, then twirled me away from him so fast that a surprised giggle escaped my lips. Seconds later I was laughing loudly as he spun me around and around until I was squealing with dizziness and falling all over him. We were getting odd looks from everyone as we danced ballroom to rock. Adrenaline was pumping through my veins, and it had nothing to do with the exercise.

The music changed tempo and he pulled me into him. Awareness came back tenfold and I stiffened in his arms.

He looked down at me, the corner of his mouth lifted in a half-grin. "Relax, Emma. It's only a dance between friends, right?"

I caught a tender look a second before he replaced it with a cocky grin. "I've not known you a week and I already know that dancing with you is never just a dance."

Rocked Under ~ Cora Hawkes

I regretted saying the loaded words instantly. I didn't want to remember the way we met. I averted my gaze, hoping Scott hadn't heard me. I thought I felt Scott stiffen but realised I must have been imagining it when he next spoke.

"Really?" he teased, but it appeared forced. "What else is it then, babe?"

I had walked into that one. I shook my head. "Never mind."

The brunette he had been dancing with earlier came up behind him and put her arms around his waist, her hands pushing me away.

She eyed me viciously and then changed her expression a split second before Scott turned to look at her. "I missed you, lover." Her sultry voice grated on me.

I pulled away from Scott but his grip tightened on my arms.

He turned to look at me, a frown on his face. "Stay." He turned his head back to the brunette. "Take your hands off me. I'll find you later."

She opened her mouth to argue but then huffed and stalked off, throwing a dirty look in my direction.

He pulled me close again but I pushed myself away. "That wasn't very nice. I saw you with her earlier." How could he treat girls that way and get away with it?

His eyes became hot. "I know you did."

I flushed and looked away as I disentangled myself from his arms. "You should go talk to her. You were a dick."

"You're going nowhere. She can fuckin' wait."

I was in his arms again. "You shouldn't treat girls like that."

He frowned, "She shouldn't have treated you like you were invisible."

There was no more talking. We moved together and I'm sure that to Scott it seemed like a normal dance, but to me it felt like more, and as his legs brushed mine, tingles shot out from the area to heat the rest of my body.

Did he know the effect that he had on me? Did he know what he was doing? Already I knew his scent, the smell that was only him. There was that familiarity again but I couldn't put my finger on it.
"You okay, babe?"
I jumped at the sound of his whispering voice near my ear, his breath skittering across the sensitive skin. I shuddered as I looked up. He was closer than I'd thought. His eyes snared mine, burned through them. My lips parted in surprise. His eyes were like lasers looking right through me. His gaze dropped to my mouth as his grip tightened. Suddenly, he looked away, grinding his jaw. Was he angry with me? I couldn't tell.
The music changed again, a faster beat, a guitar thrashing out a frenetic riff. I sighed with relief when Scott moved away and asked if I wanted a drink. I nodded and left the floor with him.

We all left Macy's together. I looked at Ash and did a double take — she was holding Newton's hand and looked very happy about it. I would interrogate her later. Meg was pressed up against some guy I had seen in the cafeteria at school and Scott had his arm around the brunette that he had sent away earlier like a child. I could not believe that she was with him again after the way he had talked to her — she obviously had no self-respect. The looks she kept throwing my way were of pure hate, but I ignored them. My heart squeezed as I realised I was alone. I wished Adam was there. I was the odd one out, and while they all walked on ahead, I lagged behind.

Scott turned a moment later and frowned. He released his girl and came back to walk with me.
"Want some company?"

Rocked Under ~ Cora Hawkes

"I don't need a babysitter, Scott. I'm a big girl, you know." I didn't want him to feel sorry for me.

"Take it easy. I'm only walking with you. It's no big deal," he chuckled as I carried on walking with my arms crossed.

I heard him chuckle again under his breath, "There's no need to get your panties in a twist."

"My knickers are just fine! Just go away. You can't leave her again — do you *want* to see me murdered?" I joked, although I wasn't entirely sure it was one.

He frowned. "Girls like her don't give a shit. You think she gives a fuck about me?" He crossed his arms. "None of them do and I like it that way. She'll wait for me anyway." His cocky grin reappeared.

Of course she would, who wouldn't wait for him? He was gorgeous, a total stunner.

He was so sure of himself and confident. The thought of him going back to her was doing something strange to me, creating a heaviness deep in my belly.

"Why do you do that?" My mouth seemed to be working on its own tonight. Too many vodkas.

"Do what, babe?" he asked lightly, his attention all mine.

"Why do you sleep around so much?" I whispered, knowing full well that I had no right to ask.

His eyes widened and he looked up at the sky for a moment. "Why do you ask?" His voice was quiet.

"Ash told me that you've never had a girlfriend." Why was I talking about this with him?

He sighed before looking back down at me. "She told you that, but what she was really doing was warning you off me." He was looking at me seriously now.

"No," I lied, "she just told me." I looked away.

"I don't believe you, but I can understand her wanting to protect you, especially from me." He shook his head. His tone had been serious but then he smiled softly at me.

I was momentarily stunned by him.
"You still haven't answered my question," I reminded him gently.
"I...I'm not into relationships," he shrugged as if it was nothing, but I knew he was lying.
"So, basically, you sleep around because you can get away with it and you think that having a girlfriend would hold you back and you'd get bored."
Very briefly, I saw his face crease with pain, but it happened so fast that I could have imagined it.
"Why? Were you thinking of applying for the position?" His grin was cheeky as he steered our conversation back onto safer ground.
I blushed. If only he knew how much I thought about him.
"Wow, is that a blush?" He looked surprised and then laughed loudly.
"Shut up!" I cringed as I punched his shoulder, my face burning hotter. "And no, I wasn't applying for anything, I'm seeing Adam, remember? I'm sort of taken," I said proudly, holding my head high.

He sobered then and looked up again at the sky.
"He's lucky," I thought I heard him say under his breath.
"Huh?"
"I said, 'he's lucky'. But if he treats you bad, he's going to turn unlucky real quick." He looked serious.
I frowned. I didn't understand what he was saying.
He sighed and put his arm around me, holding me close. "If he hurts you, babe, my fists will hurt his face."

"Scott, I told you. I can look after myself." I tried to push his arm away but he tightened his hold.

"It's not up for discussion, Emma."

I let it drop for now. I kind of liked his protectiveness, but it was a bit much as we had only known each other a week or so.

Chapter Seven

The next few weeks went by quickly and it was the beginning of October before I knew it. Adam had quickly become a fixture in my life. That first date had turned into a regular thing, with us hanging out a few nights a week. The guy liked to kiss but he never pushed me for more, which I found a bit bizarre since most of the guys I had dated had tried to get into my knickers almost straight away.

Ash and Newton had grown closer in the last few weeks, too. They spent a lot of their time with their lips locked together. I had probed Ash about it and she had told me that she had liked him for a while but he had never seen her as anything more than a friend. She seemed to float on a pink-tinged cloud wherever she went, and I envied her for her carefree nature. Newton was at our place most of the time, but I didn't mind if Ash didn't.

Scott had become a good friend without me even realising. When we were all together, I noticed that we sought out each other's company. We mostly talked music, but he looked out for me too. A week before, he had started rehearsing with the band more and Newton had said that they were writing new music. I found myself excited about it. I enjoyed watching him play a bit too much, I knew that — and I think he kind of knew it too.

That first night at Macy's seemed distant in my mind, but there would be the odd time when I would feel his intense stare on me and I knew, I just *knew*, that he was remembering it too. I would catch him looking at me when he thought nobody was taking any notice of him. It was at times like these that I felt like he was looking straight into me — that he could see *me*. Most of the time though he was just like any other guy-friend, although I admit that I didn't feel as comfortable with him as I did with Ad or Newton.

There was this awkwardness between us that, no matter how hard I tried, just wouldn't go away, and I wanted it to. The more time I spent around him, the more of a mystery he became. He was such a dick when it came to girls, but with his friends and with me he was totally different. It was as though he was two people sometimes. To the outside world he was Scott Mason, bad boy and womaniser. In private he was Scott Mason, caring and loyal friend. He had taken a place in my thoughts and I was used to him being there. I wondered about him all the time, and felt ashamed that I thought about him more than I did Adam. Other times, I thought about the night we met. The memory would creep up on me at the most inconvenient moments, like when Adam was kissing me.

"Hey, hey! Are you ready for tonight?" Meg did her signature eyebrow wiggle as she danced her way to our table to music that was only in her head.
"Hell, fuckin' yeah!" Newton raised his hand and high-fived her as she passed him.
I giggled at them, "Oh my God, guys!"
Tonight was the opening of the new nightclub, Soundz, and we were all going together. I hadn't been in a nightclub for a long time. Memories began to filter through my head like flashbacks — I stared ahead, not seeing anything, and felt a frown appear. I stopped myself from going there. This was my new life and there was no way I was going to let my past ruin my fun tonight. I had always loved going clubbing at home — I used to count down the hours until the weekend. I pulled myself back to the present, hoping nobody had noticed me space out.

I looked up and straight into dark-green eyes that were studying me intently. I felt a jolt of surprise go through me and my heart stopped for a moment. Feeling flustered, I bit my lip to stop it trembling and smiled at him.

He frowned. "You okay?" he mouthed silently.

I nodded and looked down quickly, fiddling with the lid of my drink. Sometimes Scott was too much for me and I needed to kind of reel myself back in. His attention seemed to cross the line between friendship and, something more. I don't know, maybe I was imagining it — I could have been.

"…And I know Em is looking forward to it," I caught Ash saying just in time to reply.

I could feel Scott's inquisitive stare on me, trying to suss me out. "You know me so well, cous." I replied as naturally as I could.

To keep my hands busy I reached out, stroked my fingers through Adam's hair and heard him groan with pleasure. I gasped as he snatched me off my chair and into his lap. I flailed, trying to pull my short, knitted dress down further. He planted one of his hands between my knees and kissed me heatedly while moving his hand further up. He had never been this forward in front of everyone before. His hand between my thighs reminded me of the time I had watched Scott do it to that girl — the way he had slowly slid his big, strong hands up her thigh and then stroked her with his thumb. Adam was still kissing me but I was getting turned on thinking about someone else.

Shit! Fuck! I was breathless and getting a wetness between my legs that shouldn't be there while I was thinking about Scott. I realised I had both hands clenched in Adams hair, clutching him to me. *Oh God!* I felt disgusted with myself. I couldn't believe I was imagining Scott kissing me while Adam was oblivious. I took the heat out of the kiss slowly and then buried my head in his shoulder and closed my eyes, too ashamed to look up. I hated myself. Not for the first time, I felt like I had cheated on Adam.

I snuggled closer to him. I wanted Adam, *not* Scott. *Adam, Adam, Adam, Ad*…When I opened my eyes, Scott was in my line of sight. His head was bent as though he was looking at the table.

He had a faraway look in his eyes and his mouth was a tight line that made his usually full lips look flat.

An hour before we were due to meet, Adam called me and told me that he couldn't make it. He had forgotten about an assignment that he had to finish by Monday and it would take him all weekend to get it done. He said to go ahead without him and to have a good time. I thought about cancelling too, but to hell with it, I thought. I really wanted to go. I did feel sorry for Adam, though — he had sounded grouchy as hell about it.

After blow-drying and straightening my hair, I applied my make-up, nightclub-style. I lined my eyes in black, smudged it in for the smoky effect, then added mascara. I loved the way the black brought out the blue in my eyes — they were exactly the same deep blue as my mum's kind eyes. Then came the blush and the lip gloss. I put on black, low-waisted skinny jeans and a pair of black, strappy heels, and added an emerald, backless top. I was ready to go.

Soundz was pretty much like most other nightclubs I had been to back home — a large dance floor with a DJ, a bar and tables and chairs. The bar was at the very back below a huge balcony. I looked up and saw another dance floor, along with another bar. The club was already jammed full, mainly of students. It was dark, except for the lights flashing and moving in time with the beat.
"Shots!" Meg shouted, and headed for the bar.
We followed her for shots before moving out onto the dance floor, where we stayed. I let myself go and felt the beat take me and lift me away.

A few guys came to move with me every now and then, but I didn't take any notice and they soon took the hint. I felt tingles down my spine and knew Scott had arrived and spotted me. I didn't bother looking for him though. I would see him later. I was still cringing, an after-effect of the scene in the cafeteria. I hated kissing Adam in front of him, although earlier it had been more than kissing. I was embarrassed. I felt like Scott could see me for the faker that I was for being with Adam. Don't get me wrong, I liked Adam a lot, but there were no deep feelings there — and that was the whole point. I didn't want undying love. I didn't want to be vulnerable in that way. I didn't want someone to have that kind of power over me. I knew I was being stubborn but I had made a decision a long time ago and I was sticking to it. Scott scared the crap out of me sometimes. Nothing made sense to me when Scott was around me. Everything seemed to be in limbo, like there was no certainty to my feelings or his. He always brought girls back, he drank a lot and he had got into a fight four times since I had known him. Scott was trouble with a capital 't'. There was a vulnerability to him sometimes though that I didn't understand, because he was one of the toughest guys I knew. I didn't get it. I didn't get *him.*

The next time I went back to our table, Scott was the only one there and he had not one, but two skimpily clad, vaguely familiar blonde girls all over him. My stomach felt heavy and I just wanted to hide my face. I smiled at him but it felt stiff and I knew it didn't reach my eyes. I totally ignored the girls, who were looking me up and down. It was like Scott had said — they didn't give a shit about him so I never gave them the time of day. I learned quickly that it was all about who was beautiful enough to have him — girls *actually* boasted about it. I wanted to rip him from their roving hands and tell him that he was worth more than that. But Scott had also told me that he liked it that way. *Ugh! Stop it, Emma!* He could stop it, but he liked it, so it was his own damn fault.

I sat down and Scott pushed a drink towards me. "Vodka. The last round was mine."

"Thanks. Sounds like you've already had quite a few," I teased. I hesitated before taking a sip.

He shook his head with a grin, "Nobody's messed with it, babe. I've had it in front of me the whole time."

I trusted him completely so I knocked it back and slammed it down hard.

"Have you met Holly and Paige?" he asked with a smug smile on his face.

What was the smugness about? I said hello anyway and flashed a fake smile before sweeping my gaze back over the dance floor.

What was the point of him introducing them? I knew I would never talk to any of them again — tomorrow it would be someone else. Where were the others anyway? I felt like a third wheel sitting there — or should I say *fourth?* I wished Adam had been there. I scanned the room for someone I knew but it was too crowded.

"Wanna dance?" My head shot back when nobody else answered and I saw that Scott was asking me.

I was about to say yes but then I glanced at his decorations — if looks could kill I would have been six feet under.

"Um, no, it's okay," I turned and watched the floor again for our friends. It was probably for the best anyway.

A warm hand lifted mine off my lap. I closed my eyes briefly as his warmth soaked into me. I looked up into Scott's smiling face.

"Come the fuck on, babe." He led me onto the dance-floor.

"Thanks," I shouted near his ear, "but you didn't have to, you know."

He leaned in closer. "Dancing with you is not a hardship, trust me." He pulled away with a big smile.

We danced until our feet ached. He was a good dancer. He started mimicking the bad dancers around us and I laughed so hard that my stomach muscles protested. Later on, the others found us and joined in. He didn't touch me and he kept my personal bubble free. He was just Scott — and I loved it.

Rocked Under ~ Cora Hawkes

Chapter Eight

We exited the club in a fit of giggles.
"Are we going to yours?" Meg asked Scott.
Scott shrugged, "If you want."
"Um, I think I'm gonna go back to mine," I said and hurried on, "I'm pretty tired."
"Come on, Emma!" Newton came over and hung his arm over my shoulder.
I looked to Scott for help but he was watching me with hooded eyes.
"Okay, I suppose I could sacrifice a few hours of beauty sleep for my friends," I giggled and everyone whooped at once.

When we got to Scott's my eyes were drawn again to his piano, standing by the balcony doors, and I couldn't resist the pull of it. I strolled over to it and let my fingers run lightly over the keys without pressing down so as not to make a noise.
"Do you want to play?" Scott said quietly, just behind me.
Yes! "Are you joking? I won't play well now. I would never embarrass myself on purpose," I joked, although I had played tipsy so many times at home.
"Maybe some other t…"
"She's lying!" Ash butted in, "I've seen her play wasted before!" Ash had obviously had the most to drink tonight.
"Thanks, Ash." I didn't want to play in front of them.
"Won't you play for us, Em? *Please!*" *Oh, God!* She was turning into a five-year-old before our eyes.
"Okay, okay!" I rolled my eyes as I looked at Scott. He was smiling at me in such a cute way that my pulse stuttered.

"Woo-hoo! Emma's gonna play on Scott's piano so settle down. This is a rare public performance!"

That sounded all kinds of wrong. I looked up to see if anyone else had a dirty mind. I blushed when I saw Scott place his hand on the back of his neck, shake his head and look at the floor, trying to smother his smile.

"Come on then, Em. I'm dying to see you play with Scott's piano." Newton burst out laughing and then Meg started too.

I huffed, not very happy with Ash *at all,* and sat down. Right, no pressure or anything, I thought as everyone sat on the large couch except for Scott, who leaned against the balcony doors with his arms crossed, just waiting, watching. My blush deepened, probably to beetroot, as I let my fingers say hello and flex over the keys.

"What do you want me to play?"

"Play that one that you played a few years ago when we visited." I tried to remember,."You know, the slow one you played after Christmas dinner."

Great! That was my dad's favourite. I nodded and turned my attention back to the piano. I let my fingers roam, my shoulders relax and then the song played out its hauntingly tragic melody. I closed my eyes as I played, the song carrying me away. The sound filled the room, echoed off the walls and bounced back to me as I fed it more. A sadness crept in and shivers went down my spine. On and on I played until I lost track of time and surrendered to the moment.

Silence. I had finished but nobody was talking. I opened my eyes and everyone was sitting there with their mouths gaping. Ash was grinning her little ass off. I looked at Scott, he was studying me intently. Pure desire shook me. I took a quick breath and looked away.

"*Goddamn, Dweeb!*" Newton shouted, breaking the ice, "You can *play!*" He sang his words. "I almost leaked man-tears."

"What did I tell you?" I heard Ash say with pride.

"Wow, Em. You are amazing," Meg shook her head as if clearing it.

"I guess I'm okay."

Scott's quizzical gaze held mine. The rest of the world fell away and my brain went fuzzy. Too much booze, maybe? What was he thinking when he looked at me like that? The familiar heat spread over me and up to my face. I felt hot and I was blushing a—bloody—*gain!*

I stood. "*Phew!*" I sighed, "It's hot in here, isn't it?" I fanned my face with my hand.

Scott pushed himself away from the door, where he had been leaning with his arms crossed. Then, without taking his eyes off me, he took my hand and led me to the balcony doors. He broke eye contact as he opened them and the cool night air hit me instantly as he pulled me outside onto a large balcony with two chairs and a table.

His hand was sending tingles up my arm. Little flames danced along my skin. I pulled my hand out of his and he frowned.

"That's much better." I hated the silence between us. I wanted him to say something.

"You're fuckin' talented, babe," he said hoarsely.

"Hmm…Thousands of pounds worth of lessons, so I hope I *am* talented by now." I smiled brightly to dull the charged atmosphere a bit. "I haven't played for a while," I looked out over the town, "and I hate playing for people." I bit my lip.

I heard him inhale quickly, then a hand came under my chin and turned my face back to his. "Teach me," he said simply.

Awareness coiled in my stomach when he touched me. It was quiet out here and dark and, worst of all, we were alone. I wanted to go back inside.

"Teach you?" I looked confused. "Teach you to play the piano?" I was surprised that he would ask me. "Are you serious? I've never taught anyone anything."

"Yeah, I'll pay you for your time."

Could I teach someone? I'd never tried to teach anyone to play before. I had always been the student.

"If you're willing to pay then why don't you pay a professional to teach you?"

"You *are* a professional, babe." He cocked his head and looked confused. "Don't you know that?"

"Maybe, but I've never taught anyone before." I didn't know if it was a good idea. Actually, it was a terrible idea.

"Just think about it."

So, he wanted me to teach him to play the piano. Money held no appeal as I already had much more than I needed. We all crammed onto the couches in front of the television with bowls of popcorn. Ash and Newton had a couch to themselves, but after the popcorn had gone they disappeared downstairs. Scott, Meg and I settled on the other. Halfway through the movie Meg fell asleep, only to stand up twenty minutes later, sleepwalk to the window, where she paused for a few seconds, and then sleepwalk back to the couch. We watched in a silent fit of giggles as she threw a load of cushions onto the rug and laid down on them. The smallest cushion served as a teddy, which she bundled in her arms. Two minutes later, as our giggles were starting to subside, she got up again and stomped down the hallway into a bedroom.

"I wish we'd caught that on camera," I giggled.

"She does it all the fuckin' time," he said, passing me a beer. We had moved to the kitchen after the movie. He leaned against the counter opposite me with his hands buried in his front pockets watching me with a faint smile.

"Where's your dad, anyway?" I took a swig from the bottle.

"He lives in the city to be closer to the office."

"Did he remarry after your mum left?"

"He wasn't married to my mom. He was already married but they were separated." He smiled. "My dad was forty when he met my mom. She was half his fuckin' age." He shook his head, "Big fuckin' mistake. When he found out she was pregnant, apparently he was over the moon but my mom wasn't. Anyway, a few months after I was born she left. My dad bought me up. He never remarried. There have been women, but he's never settled. He just put all his spare time into me." He smiled softly as he spoke.

"He sounds great."

"Yeah, he is. He's in his early sixties now but he refuses to retire," he rolled his eyes and looked at me.

"How long have you lived on your own for?" I was curious about him. He never really talked about himself and I found that I wanted to know more.

"Since I was seventeen." He came to lean on the kitchen counter beside me.

"And you're twenty-two now?"

"Uh-huh," he bent his head in a nod.

"You've been alone a while then. Don't you get lonely?" I frowned, feeling sorry for him, and then my eyes widened. "Oh *wait!* Here I was feeling sorry for you but I totally forgot that you're hardly ever alone," I laughed but it didn't sound right, "You have a girl here every night."

He actually cringed and looked at the floor in what I thought was shame.

I carried on. "I bet you could get any girl you wanted," I said playfully to hide my very real and annoying curiosity. "Have you ever been turned down?"

I was feeling brave but I just didn't understand it. How could anyone live like that?

He looked up with a sheepish smile and shook his head at me, "I'm not talking about that shit with you, Emma," he laughed and looked away.

"Why not? Do you even *know* how many girls you've slept with?"

"What about you, babe?" His attention turned to me and his eyes narrowed. "How many guys have you been with?"

My face grew warm and I knew I had turned bright red. "That's none of your bloody business," I snapped and looked away.

I heard him suck in his breath and I looked up.

His expression had sobered and he cocked his head slightly, "You're a virgin." His voice had turned soft. It wasn't a question, it was a statement.

I was so embarrassed my face was flaming hot. "I..." I crossed my arms. "...That's a really personal question, Scott."

"How the fuck did you do that?" I didn't like the way he was looking at me, like I was subject matter in a test tube.

"What?" I snapped.

"*How* have you not been with anybody, Emma? I mean, fuckin' look at you."

I sighed. "Look, I just never felt that strongly for someone, okay?" I shrugged like it was no big deal, but it was.

"Does Adam know?" he asked, serious now, his voice lowered.

"Yeah," I murmured, "He doesn't mind waiting. He doesn't think it's that big a deal."

Scott was looking at his feet and he nodded before looking up. His eyes found mine and held them. There was something lurking there but I couldn't put my finger on it.

"It *is* a big deal, babe. You don't know how fuckin' rare virginity is at your age." He swept his hair back. "Don't waste your first time, it's something you'll never forget."

I didn't want to talk about this anymore, so I looked at my watch and shook my head to make a show of being shocked at the time. "It's really late. I'd better go."

"You don't have to go. You can crash in my room if you want — with me." His cocky grin appeared.

I froze and frowned at him.

He raised his hands. "Don't hit me, I'm kidding," he laughed. "But seriously, I'll sleep on the couch if you want to stay."

I thought about it. What would Adam think about me sleeping in Scott's bed? If it was him sleeping in another girl's bed I'd be angry as hell.

I forced a laugh, "I've only got to walk down the stairs, but thanks anyway."

Once I had got into bed I couldn't get my thoughts away from Scott and what my first time would be like if it was with him. I tossed and turned for a few hours with unwelcome, steamy images playing behind my eyeslids. When would I get over it? Scott was a friend for Christ's sake and I was starring alongside him in a bloody porno almost every night as I fell asleep. Did he do the same? *Of course he doesn't.* He has a girl there most nights. Why the hell would he think of me?

Chapter Nine

Scott's door was ajar so I went through slowly, tapping on the door as I passed it.
"Hello?" I called to the empty lounge.

Ash and I had been shopping when my phone beeped, alerting me to a new message. It was Scott and he wanted me to come and see him when I got back. I had known what he wanted straight away, it was obvious after last night, but the question was, should I do it? I had hastily tapped out a text saying that I was shopping with Ash and that I'd be a couple of hours. I had debated for a few seconds whether or not to add a kiss on the end. I usually did with everyone else, so I did.

"Come in, babe," I heard from the kitchen, "Be there in a minute."
I made my way to the couch and flopped down. I looked around for any mess but I couldn't see any. How the hell did this guy have a tidier place than me? I shook my head. He really was almost perfect. Scott came in with two mugs of coffee. His dark, glossy hair was damp from a shower and he wore a pair of torn, old jeans low on his hips. His chest was bare. How could any body look so sexy without even trying? His muscles moved fluidly with him — he didn't have an ounce of spare skin anywhere.

"Coffee?" He set the mug and the sofa dipped as he sat next to me.
He relaxed and threw an arm over the back of the sofa where I sat. Heat emanated from his bare arm to my nape, sending warm tingles through me.
"Thanks." I reached forwards for the mug and took a hesitant sip, careful not to burn my mouth. "I know what you want to ask

me." I leaned back again, back towards his heat, and tried to forget that he was shirtless, which was virtually impossible.

A lopsided grin appeared. "Yeah, I think you got a pretty good idea too."

"You want me to teach you to play the piano, don't you?" I raised a brow and turned my body towards him. Big mistake — he did the same.

His chest was right in front of me in all its rippled glory. His smell enticed and overwhelmed me. I put the coffee to my lips just so I could smell something different. Colourful tattoos decorated his skin from his shoulders to his wrists — sleeves, I think they call them. His chest and back were also painted in black with bright colours here and there. I averted my gaze and squeezed my eyes closed as my fingers twitched, itching to trace the lines of ink.

He nodded. "If you can teach me for an hour on a Saturday, then I'll help you with your assignments."

It would look odd if I refused and I could spare an hour once a week for him. I liked his company most of the time, but when he was half undressed, like he was now, all I could think about was reaching out and touching his skin.

"Chuck in a cocoa with marshmallows and cream while I'm here and you've got a deal." I put my hand out for him to shake.

He chuckled. "Fuckin' deal, babe." He took my hand in a firm but gentle grip. His eyes bored into mine and his smile slipped slowly away.

I heard a sigh as his hand held mine. My lungs squeezed. All I wanted to do was to pull him to me, but Scott was the one person I couldn't get involved with, he'd take my heart and give it the best time of its existence before obliterating it, and like my mum, I wouldn't survive that kind hurt. I mustn't ever forget that. I couldn't.

I pulled my hand out of his. "Um...First lesson next week?" My voice was gruff.

"Works for me," he shrugged and reached for his coffee. "What're you doing for the rest of the day?" He took a sip.

"I was going to read for a couple of hours. Why?"

"You read?" His eyes widened and then turned wicked. "What kind of books do you read?"

"None that you'd be interested in," I blushed.

His eyes darkened along with his smile. "Why you blushing, babe? I think I'd be *very* interested to read what you do." His voice turned throaty.

I bent my head and my hands came up and pressed against my hot cheeks as I groaned, "I doubt it."

The corner of what looked like a photo sticking out from underneath his coffee table grabbed my attention. I bent down and retrieved it. It was a picture of a young woman with long, blonde hair and blue eyes the colour of the sky in summer. She was pouting into the camera cheekily but her eyes looked cold, almost sly.

Scott went still beside me.

I looked at him questioning eyes. His lips turned down and his eyes looked sad as he stared at the old picture.

"Is this your mum?" I asked, taking a wild guess.

"Yeah." He swiped a hand through his hair and took the picture from me, shoving it down the side of the sofa like it was an empty wrapper.

"She's pretty, but I'm guessing you get your looks from your dad."

"Yeah, thank fuck." He stood abruptly and walked over to the window.

Shit. He didn't know his mum and I had put my foot right in it.

I went over to him and placed a hand on his warm shoulder. "Scott, I'm sorry. It was stupid of me to say that. Sometimes I don't think."

He turned and my hand slipped down to his forearm.

He placed his hand on mine and entwined our fingers. "Don't be sorry, Emma. I'm good. Just gets me sometimes, you know?"

"Yeah, I do." I thought about my dad and poked the thought away. "You can't choose your parents."

"The only reason she ever turns up is for money. The last time was when I was fifteen and my dad told her he wouldn't be giving her any more. We haven't seen her since." His attention was on our joined hands.

I didn't like seeing him like this and it was my doing. I wanted to cheer him up, make him smile again.

"Hey, you want to hear me play the guitar?"

He looked up, surprise in his eyes. "Please don't tell me you're a pro at that too."

"Show me where it is and you'll find out," I smiled.

I had never picked up a guitar in my life — and it showed. Scott handed me a beautiful, black acoustic guitar. I didn't even know how to hold it but I tried my best, and at least Scott was smiling again, which is what I had aimed for.

He chuckled and moved his hand down over his face to try to hide his amusement. "You don't hold it like that…Here…"

I was sitting on the edge of a big footstool and he came to sit behind me. He shifted forwards until I was sitting between his hard, warm thighs. I was so aware of him that I froze. I didn't dare move. He came closer and put his arms around me to reach the guitar. His naked chest came into contact with my back, making my core temperature rise to dangerous levels. His scent was enveloping me, taunting me, and this time there was no escape.

His head peered over my shoulder causing the hairs on the back of my neck to stand on end.

"Hold it like this," he whispered close to my ear as he moved my hand into the right position.

His breath tickled me, making a shudder run down my back.

He paused for a second and I thought he had noticed. "And if you," he slid his hot hand under my thigh gently and lifted it for me until only my toes were touching the floor, "raise your knee, you can rest it here."

"Okay," I whispered. It was all I was capable of saying with his hands all over me. Maybe this wasn't such a good idea.

He took his hands away and rested them on my thighs. "Now try." His voice was gruff.

I started playing but my mind was focused on the parts of my body that he was touching. I was dreadful. He was just so *there* that I couldn't have concentrated if my life had depended on it.

He turned his face towards my neck and I heard him inhale through his nose gently. His grip on my thighs tightened as he shifted closer to my backside and his forehead hit my shoulder heavily.

Shit! I'm going to spontaneously combust any goddamn bloody minute now if he doesn't stop.

I stopped playing abruptly and took a shaky breath. "I give up. I think I'll stick to the piano." My voice was stilted and I hoped he hadn't noticed. I needed to get out of there.

He sighed and lifted his head. "Good idea."

He moved away and took the guitar out of my hands without looking at me. Cool air hit me where his warmth had been, making another shiver run down my spine but for a different reason.

He placed the guitar against the wall. "You want to watch a movie or something?"

I stood up. "I'd better go. I have dishes and laundry to do so…"

He nodded, put his hands in his pockets and looked at his bare feet. "I'll see you later?" He raised his green eyes to mine.
"Yeah. What time are you on?"
"Nine."
I smiled. "Right, we'll see you there." I turned and walked to the door. I needed to be away from him right then before I got lost in those eyes of his and forgot myself.
"Babe?"
I loved it when he called me *babe*. I opened the door and looked over my shoulder with questioning eyes.
"Thanks."
"For what?" I asked.
"For giving a shit."

Chapter Ten

"You're teaching Scott to play the piano?" Ad asked. "I didn't even know you *played* the piano." He smiled, but I could tell he wasn't happy that Scott knew something about me that he didn't.

We were sitting at our usual table at Macy's. Ash, Newton and Meg were thrashing it out to the music by the stage.

"Well, nobody except Ash knew and when we were at Scott's last night she made me play," I cringed. "I don't really like playing in front of an audience," I added.

Ad seemed to feel better about the fact that I had been forced which annoyed me — he shouldn't feel pleased about me being forced to do anything.

"So you'll be spending more time with him." He made it sound like I was doing something wrong. "When will *I* get to see you?" he moaned.

"I can still see you in the evenings."

Ad sighed and looked at me, his eyes warm again. "I know, babe. I don't really mind. Guess I'm just jealous that you'll be spending time with another guy."

"Hey," I said, nudging his shoulder with mine, "You're still my man."

He smiled and pulled me to him. "Yeah, babe. I am."

He kissed me softly just the way I liked it. I slipped my hands under his jacket and grabbed his shirt with my fists to deepen the kiss.

Scott came on stage and started with one of the band's ballads. Ad stood, pulling me up with him, and lead me onto the floor. He pulled me into his arms and we started to move to the slow song. He was stroking my back in a soft up-and-down motion with the backs of his fingers and I closed my eyes as I relaxed into him.

Scott's sad voice was filling the bar with a heartbreaking song that I hadn't heard before, about wanting something that was out of reach — something that was too good to ruin. I opened my eyes and found Scott watching me while he was singing. He had such a bleak look in his eyes that I unintentionally squeezed Ad, the force of his gaze almost hurting me. Ad's arms tightened and he looked down at me. I was still frowning and looking at Ad but I was thinking about Scott. That look...Was he still upset about his mum? I felt guilty at once.

Too late, I caught myself staring up at Ad with my lips parted slightly.

His head descended to mine in a deep kiss. His arms came around me, holding me in place while he kissed me. Then his lips travelled down my neck. I closed my eyes as I tried to enjoy it but it wasn't doing anything for me. I opened my eyes again and Scott was still staring at me. He looked away almost immediately, but not before I caught that same look clouding his brilliant, green eyes.

I watched him sing the rest of the ballad as he gazed, unseeing out over the audience, his expression strained. I wanted to reach out to him and erase whatever pain he was feeling. I wanted to fold him in my arms and hold him, be there for him. I blinked. *What the...? Why the hell am I thinking like this?*

I yanked Ad's arm. "I need a drink," I shouted near his ear.

He nodded and pulled me off the floor.

Later, when Scott came off stage, groupies pounced on him, slinking their bodies around him and touching him like snakes. He extracted himself, obviously not in the mood tonight, and went backstage. Twenty minutes later he joined us for drinks — his drink for the evening was Jack Daniel's. He sat quietly for an hour, talking only when spoken to and smiling in all the right places. He downed shot after shot. Something was up with him but I chose to keep quiet. The others didn't seem to have noticed anything and it would have looked odd if I was the only one to comment on his off mood.

He caught me staring at him and I forced a smile. He didn't return it but held my concerned gaze with his half-lidded one. A frown pulled at my face and I looked away, peeking back seconds later to find his stare still pinned on me. I turned my attention to the couples on the floor, who were making the most of love hour. Was he angry with me? He couldn't be angry with me. Maybe he was just in a mood. He had been fine earlier.

A strong hand came in front of my face, startling me. I looked up to see Scott standing over me.
"Dance with me." His eyes were pleading as he watched me for an answer.
I looked to Ad for help but he was deep in conversation with Newton. Should I? I looked around the table but only Ash had her attention on me, and she was frowning. I looked back up at Scott. Excitement buzzed through me as anticipation took over. If I refused, he would think that I wasn't comfortable with him.

The best I could do was to dance with him and maybe find out what was up, make him smile again. It felt like his mood was balancing on a fine line and I didn't want to tip him either way — I knew that he was a loose cannon when he had been drinking.
I nodded and put my hand in his. Scott led me to the other side of the floor, by the side of the stage, so we were shielded from our table. My heart was hammering in my chest and I knew he had had a lot to drink.

Scott pulled me close just as another power ballad started to flow through the speakers. I tried to keep our bodies apart but Scott was having none of it. He pulled me closer into him and wrapped his arms around me. There was no choice but to snake my arms around him too.

I leaned back to look at him. "Are you okay? You've been quiet tonight."

The corner of his mouth lifted. "I am now."

He pulled me close again and I laid my head on his chest.

I am now? What did that mean?

His hands slid around to my back and slipped under my top. His thumbs were stroking slow circles on the bare skin of my lower back. Tingles shot through me.

"Scott, what are you doing?" I looked at him with questioning eyes.

His head came down to my ear, "Shh." He nuzzled my neck, at the same time pushing his hand into the small of my back, forcing me into him. My arms flew around his neck so I wouldn't fall backwards.

We moved together, swaying, clinging. His hands tightened on me as his lips touched my shoulder gently. I shuddered violently and gasped. My mind went blank, my last thought being that I should stop him, but it was near impossible and my willpower withered with my mind.

He had so much power over my body — it was his. It was like he knew exactly what it wanted, and how to make it his. His hands slid slowly up my bare back and gripped my shoulders, the tips of his fingers digging into the skin above my collarbones. My head fell back as his lips traced my chest and then moved to the dip at the bottom of my neck, kissing up to my ear. I was trembling with want. The intensity of him, together with the music spelled danger.

I never wanted this moment to end. Our bodies were melting together.

"Scott," I heard myself moan as he played me with expertise and precision, the same way he handled his guitar. I sunk into an oblivion where there was just me and Scott, the music cocooning us in our own heaven.

Suddenly, he moved his hands and brought them up to cup my face quickly, desperately. His eyes searched mine and the naked need in them jolted me. I couldn't do this. I couldn't. He was too much. He would destroy me, swallow me whole and spit me out in the morning. My eyes widened as the noise around us came crashing back to my ears. *Shit!* I looked around for any sign that someone had seen us, but thankfully no one had.

I stepped away from him and a look of pain shot across his face.

"I need the bathroom," I said, slipping away before he could say anything.

I slammed into a stall and leaned back against the door. What was I thinking? Ad was out there somewhere. What if he had seen us? *Fuck it!* Scott was dangerous. I realised in that moment that I cared about him. I cared that he was sad. I wanted to take his sadness away and make him smile, but at what cost? I brought my hands up and covered my hot face, shaking my head. I should have said no to him.

He was drunk and we were meant to be friends, nothing more. I let my hands drop. I would go back out there and stay away from him for the rest of the night. With any luck he would have been distracted by another girl by now. A pang of jealousy streaked through me. Why did he have to be so…So…*Him?*

Before going back I ran my hands under the cold tap until I had cooled down. I opened the door and walked straight out but my arm was seized and I was hauled sideways. Before I knew it Scott was standing in front of me.

Rocked Under ~ Cora Hawkes

"Why'd you run off like that?" Anger radiated from him.

"I didn't run anywhere, I walked. I needed the bathroom." I held his gaze.

"Don't..." he started.

"Scott!" a girl shouted.

"Fuck," he muttered under his breath.

I looked at the redhead stomping towards us with determination, her beady eyes on Scott. I wanted to punch her in the face. Whatever was up with him, he sure as hell didn't need someone who didn't give a crap about him.

I was about to tell her to back off when Scott hauled me to him.

"Come here." He put his arm over my shoulder and hugged me to him. My heart kicked at his closeness. He put his hands either side of my waist and turned me towards him.

He was pulling me close to him. "Scott, no…"

"Just help me out here, okay? I can't deal with her shit right now," he whispered close to my ear and then slowly dropped his mouth down to my neck. He didn't move his lips, he kept very still, but I could feel his breath on my skin, coming in and out in shorts puffs. His hands were gripping me tightly but our bodies weren't touching. He was rigid. Like stone.

"Scott! I'm ready to go!" I heard her whiny voice cry.

His grip altered. He was about to move. He came in closer to me and put a leg between mine. I knew that he wanted to get rid of her so I played along. I snaked my arms around his waist slowly so she could see them. I felt him jump so slightly that I barely felt it.

"Fine, Scott! Don't think you'll have another chance with me!" the bratty girl said in anger.

I didn't know if she was still there watching us so I stayed still until he decided to move. After a moment I felt his forehead hit the part of me where his lips had been and heard him sigh.

I turned my face to him at the same time that he turned his to mine. Our noses touched. Our eyes met and my heart skipped a beat. A shiver of pure desire ran through me.

He turned around, grabbing my hand at the same time, and led me through a door near the stage. We emerged into an empty, dimly lit hallway.

Scott pulled me close, cupped my face and looked at me for a minute. A frown tainted his handsome face — he looked like he was at war with himself.

Another shiver ran through me and I literally froze. I was lost in his expression and I wanted him. I needed him to kiss me.

He must have seen the desire in my expression. He lowered his head with intent in his eyes.

I bit my lip. *I shouldn't be doing this.* He was watching my mouth. His thumb moved from my cheek and rubbed along my bottom lip, pulling it free from my teeth. I felt heat start to lick along my skin again and I trembled slightly — I was sure he felt it.

He inhaled quickly and held his breath as he moved his hand to the back of my head and held me there.

My heart was hammering inside my chest and my lips parted in a gasp as I tried to get more oxygen into my starved lungs.

His head came closer and he rested his forehead against mine. His eyes slipped closed and he inhaled deeply. "Emma," my name was a whisper of need from his lips, which were so close to mine, "your beauty goes so much deeper than your skin." He shook his head. "I don't want to taint that goodness in you but I…." he swallowed.

Goodness? If only he knew. I wasn't good. I could be very bad when I was pushed far enough. "Scott, you're seeing something that isn't really there. You barely know me. What makes you think I'm so good?"

"What makes you think you're not?" he growled.

Rocked Under ~ Cora Hawkes

I closed my eyes. I was trembling. I wanted him to kiss me so much and I knew that I needed my head checked for wanting it. My lips felt dry and I had the urge to poke my tongue out to moisten them. As my tongue flicked out of my mouth it made contact with his lips.

He groaned. His grip on me tightened and he slid his tongue along my upper lip before his lips met mine.

His kiss was gentle, barely there, testing. Our breath mingled in short bursts, and as our kiss went deeper so did my need for him. His tongue slipped into my mouth and slowly, firmly, stroked me. I moaned low in my throat. Scott increased his pressure and his hands went down to my butt. Heat licked through me as an ache began, the dull throb of desire telling me to surrender all, right there and then.

Scott ripped himself away from my lips and buried his head in my neck again. His chest was moving up and down rapidly.

He groaned and squeezed my ass harder, pushing me further into him. "Shit!" he groaned into my neck, sending little vibrations through me, "I want you so bad."

He was all over me. His hands were undoing me in ways that would stay with me forever. I knew why girls went crazy for him, why they couldn't resist him — he was sex on legs. I felt as though he needed me now, that his life depended on him having me.

Our kiss was exquisite, the best I had ever had, and I wanted it again and again. *Oh, God! What the hell am I doing?* I had to stop this now. I needed to get away from him otherwise I would be in his bed within the hour. I had taken too much of him today and — I hardened up — he was so good at getting girls into his bed that he'd tell them anything they wanted to hear. I bet he'd used that line loads of times before. He couldn't think much of our friendship if he was willing to ruin it for one night in the sack with me. The thought pissed me off.

"Scott, stop. You've had way too much to drink and you're so going to regret saying all this in the morning." I put my hands up to his chest to gently ease him away.

He lifted his head, a frown marring his beautiful features. "Is that what you think?"

A door slammed somewhere in the distance and he dropped his hands, tucking them into his front pockets. I ignored the loneliness that swept though me and turned my head in the direction of the door. I could feel Scott's gaze glued to me, studying me.

Chapter Eleven

The guys of From Under were walking towards us, laughing and joking.

"*Goddamn!* She's hot!" I heard one of them say.

"Oh, *baby!*" another said with a whistle, while the other two just stared.

I forced a smile and looked away.

"Hey, man, what's up?" one of the quiet guys, with messy blonde hair, said in a deep voice.

"Not a lot," Scott replied and then looked at me. "This is Emma, Ashley's cousin."

He nodded to the first guy, "Emma, that's Alan. He's our bass guitarist."

Alan had a dark crew cut and dark-brown eyes that had a wicked gleam in them.

"Hey, baby," he said with a grin and a wink.

"Hello, Alan," I said with a smile.

Cries of "*Whoa!* British?" and "You never said anything about her being British?" came from the group.

I forced my smile and turned to Scott, who was doing the same. His eyes told me that it wasn't over.

Scott nodded to the next one, "That's Bone, our drummer." Bone had thick, dirty-blonde, wavy hair down to his shoulders, twinkling, hazel eyes and an easy smile.

Bone lifted a hand in salute and nodded, "Hey, good-looking."

"This is Jason, he's on guitar." Jason was a beach blonde with messy hair and coffee-coloured eyes.

"Yo!" he said in greeting.

"And Mike, our technician." Mike had short, light-brown hair with the brightest aquamarine eyes I had ever seen on a guy.

"Hi there," was his welcome.

Bone came forwards and took my arm, "Come and have a drink with us, darlin'."

We all went into a room that was a lot like a living room, with sofas, a TV, a table and chairs and a kitchenette.

I chose to sit on the sofa and Scott made sure he sat next to me, while Bone sat on my other side.

"Aw, you coulda sat on my lap, baby." Alan feigned hurt and I smiled.

"Shut up, Al," Scott scowled.

"*Jeez*, Scott. Lighten the fuck up, dude." Alan winked at me again.

I tried to hide my smirk. I'd have to watch myself around Alan.

I glanced at Scott from under my lashes and my coy gaze clashed with his. He had his eyes on me and his gaze held mine. I wasn't looking forward to us being alone again. I didn't want to face what had just happened. I couldn't blame Scott because I had wanted it too, but the idea of how little he thought of our friendship niggled at me. Maybe we weren't such good friends after all. Maybe all this time he had been building up to get me into bed. *Shut up!* I doubted he would go that far to get someone in bed when he had a different girl every night.

"Who wants beer?" Bone asked, and everyone apart from Scott and I answered.

"Scott, beer?"

Scott glanced sideways briefly at Bone, then brought his gaze right back to mine. "Yeah. Emma'll have one too."

I was going to need it if he was planning on keeping his gaze locked together with mine like that. I couldn't take this anymore. I wished he would just stop — stop the tension between us. I needed a breather but I had to stay and have at least one drink with them.

"She had the best ass I ever seen, man," Alan was boasting.

"Man, I saw that ho," Bone started as he put an opened beer in front of me, "She was all ass, tits and teeth, man. What the fuck do you see in girls like that?"

"He likes dumb girls. That way they don't give a fuck if he's got a small wiener!" Jason said quietly and then burst out laughing with Bone.

"Fuck you!" Alan said chuckling. "At least I can get a nice piece of ass."

I took a swig of my beer and tried to see the funny side of their banter, although I really couldn't have done if I'd tried.

"Whatever, pretty boy," Jason sniggered, flipping him off, "You're a slut."

"And I love being one," Alan's eye twinkled as he spoke. "Speaking of sluts," he looked at Scott, "where's your ride for the night — or is that rides?"

My stomach tightened as Alan and Bone chuckled. I didn't want to hear about Scott's rides. I didn't want to think about him with a girl at all just then. I hated admitting it to myself but it made me feel things that I had no right to feel. My niggling annoyance with him escalated.

He looked at me and I looked away. I couldn't even fake a smile for him.

I lifted the bottle to my lips and swigged until it was empty.

I couldn't look at Scott. I didn't want my anger with him to show. He might have thought it was funny to play with someone's feelings like that, but I didn't. All my life I had been centred on a man just like Scott. Maybe I should flirt with one of these guys, just to show him that I didn't just do that for him.

I leaned slightly closer to Bone. "Why do they call you Bone?" I asked, smiling up at him.

His eyebrows raised and he smiled. "I've had the name since I was eleven and fell from a tree."

I frowned, trying to get why falling out of a tree would give him that nickname.

"I broke my elbow and some of my bone was sticking out."

I cringed as he rolled his sleeve up.

"See? I had to have surgery to put it right, a ton of stitches and a lot of physical therapy." He showed me a large scar that ran from just above his elbow to halfway down his forearm.

"Ouch," I winced and held my hand up to touch it. The scar tissue was bumpy and soft at the same time. "Does it still hurt?"

"Nah, aches sometimes when it's cold but I'm a big boy, I can handle it," he beamed at me as I rolled his sleeve back down for him.

"I've never broken anything, but I have a big scar on my hand where I had stitches. Look."

He took my hand and examined my palm.

"I got it when I was seven."

Bone ran his finger up and down the scar gently.

"I was trying to climb over a metal mesh fence and fell, catching my hand on a sharp bit on the way down."

He bent his head and kissed my palm. His stubble tickled me and a giggle escaped my lips.

He looked up. "You even laugh attractively," he grinned wickedly and then frowned as he looked over my shoulder.

I turned around to see what it was and Scott was looking daggers at me. I couldn't have cared less.

Scott stood up. "I have to get home early."

Everyone believed him but me — I knew he was lying.

He grabbed my hand and started yanking me roughly away.

"See you guys!" I waved as I was literally dragged through the door.

Rocked Under ~ Cora Hawkes

He pulled me along the corridor and out the back entrance of Macy's into an alley, without saying a word or looking back at me.

I wrenched my hand out of his. This had gone too far. Who did he think he was, dragging me around like that?
"What is your problem, Scott?" I asked heatedly, crossing my arms.
He crossed his arms too and looked at me, his jaw tensing, his eyes narrowed. "You are, Emma!" He uncrossed his arms and strode towards me, stopping abruptly a foot away.
"What have I done?" I hadn't done anything wrong that I could think of — well maybe apart from flirting with Bone on purpose. "Please tell me because I really don't know what's wrong with you tonight." I was getting more and more angry.

"You were flirting with Bone!" He pointed an accusing, threatening finger at me. "You don't need to be giving guys like him encouragement."
"No, Scott. Don't make this about Bone when we both know it isn't." My voice was rising. I stepped forwards and jabbed my finger into his chest, hard. "You have been acting weird all night so don't say this is about Bone! And don't fucking talk to me like you own me because you don't and you never will!" I finished, panting with anger and frustration.

His stance changed as I said the last words and his face fell slightly. I remembered the anguished look he'd had on stage and some of my anger started to drain away.
I sighed. "Scott." I made my voice softer. "Why are you being like this? I don't want to fight with you."
He studied me for a moment. "You wanna know what's wrong with me?" His voice was tight and both his hands came up to grip my upper arms.
"*Yes.*"

He seemed to be warring with himself as he walked me backwards until my back slammed against a wall. He was looking down at me darkly, his jaw set, and I couldn't tear my eyes away from his as I saw different emotions flicker through them — anger, pain, want, need, something else that was an alien look for him, then back to anger.

The only sounds I could hear were the dull thump of the music in the bar and our breathing. His was heavy and laboured. He smacked one hand on the wall above my head while the other gripped my waist tightly.

I frowned as I realised what was happening. "Stop it, Scott." My hands came up to his chest to push him away but my feeble attempt only made him angrier.

He grabbed my hands and pinned them above my head.

I looked up at him and saw his dark-green eyes blazing down at me. "You know what I want." He hissed the words at me.

He crushed his body against mine.

My eyes widened in shock as electricity shot through me. My hands went to his hips in surprise.

He quickly released my hands and drove his hands into my hair, pulling my face up to his. He held my gaze and I closed my eyes to hide myself from him.

He placed his forehead against mine. "I can't stop this," he whispered roughly, "I can't stop wanting you and seeing you with Ad is…It's driving me fuckin' crazy." As he said those last words he drove his hips into me with a low groan. "I want to take you right now, in a goddamn back alley and against this fuckin' wall. It's so fuckin' wrong and I'm a scumbag piece of shit that doesn't deserve to even look at you."

My eyes flew open. His gaze was desperate, needy, lustful.

"Scott," I whispered, broken. I had nothing else to say. I couldn't tell him I wanted him. I couldn't tell him not to stop. I was Adam's. "Stop." I said finally, just above a breathy whisper. I dropped my hands to my sides and balled them into fists to keep them there.

Scott stiffened and stepped away from me.

I didn't know what to say to as I stared at him. He was panting as I was. "I'm not one of your groupies, you know that."

"Yeah, you're my *friend.*" I didn't miss his sarcasm and I frowned.

"What's that supposed to mean? You don't want me as a friend? Fine, fuck you! I don't want a friend that doesn't respect me as such and molests me any chance he gets!"

He raised his brows, hurt, and then turned away. He was quiet for so long that I almost turned around and went back inside, but I waited for him. His great shoulders rose, he held in a breath and then let it go slowly as his hand went through his hair.

"Sorry, Emma." He turned his bleak gaze on me. "Jesus, I'm fucked up thinking that…." he shook his head and looked at me.

He came towards me and took my hand. "Come on." His voice was quiet and calm.

"Where are we going?" I wasn't sure I wanted to go anywhere with him now.

"Back inside."

He led me back into Macy's, back through the corridor and back into the noise and crush of bodies.

"I'm going home. I'll see you tomorrow." He squeezed my hand before letting go — before leaving me standing there, wondering what the hell was going through his head.

I went to find the guys after watching him leave. I sat down next to Ad and he asked where I had disappeared to for an hour. I told him part of the truth — I went to meet the band. He didn't like it but I really couldn't have cared less if I'd tried. Ash eyeballed me from across the table and I knew that we'd be having a talk when we got home.

All I could think about was what Scott was about to say when he had trailed off. *"Jesus, I'm fucked up thinking that…"* Thinking that *what?*

"What's going on between you and Scott?" Ash didn't beat around the bush. We had been home two minutes when she just came right out and asked.

"Nothing's going on." I fiddled with my charm bracelet as we sat on the sofa.

She looked at my bracelet and frowned. "Are you sure, Em?" She didn't look so sure that I was telling the truth.

I didn't want to lie but nothing had really happened and I didn't want the questions that would follow if I was honest with her. I couldn't tell her after she had warned me about him, and she would kill Scott if she found out he had come on to me. I didn't want that. I wanted to forget and move on. Telling another person would make it harder to forget, more real. She would always be watching, so I had to make sure she believed me.

"Yeah, you know he's not my type. That whole bad-boy thing is definitely not me."

"Why did you disappear with him for so long? And I know you danced with him." Her look was stern.

"We danced. He asked if I wanted to meet the band and I said yes. I had a drink with them and we talked and then I came back," I shrugged.

"Right," she said slowly, studying my face.

I threw my hands in the air. "Oh, Ash! Stop with the Sherlock impersonation."

"Scott's different with you — he treats you different to the rest of his friends."

"Probably because you have all been friends for years and he's not known me long?" I looked at her like, *duh!*

"Hmm…Maybe."

After that she let it drop, but I could tell she wasn't convinced.

I woke up in the morning to a text message on my phone that was sent at 3.48 a.m.

Scott: *Im sorry 4 bein a dick. 2 many shots. Ur friendship is important an I dont wanna lose it. Pls 4give me.*

Chapter Twelve

It was freezing. The trees had been stripped bare, their branches like gnarly fingers reaching for the watery winter sun. I wrapped my jacket closer around me against the wind as I crossed the street. I almost ran home from meeting Ad at the diner for lunch. The last few Saturdays I had been teaching Scott the piano. Well, I say teaching, but he really only needed practice. He picked it up naturally, as I thought he would. His first lesson had been the day after he had kissed me at Macy's — awkward was an understatement. He had apologised again and again until I had asked him to let it drop because I didn't want to remember it.

I knocked on Scott's door and waited for him to answer. The door opened and my stomach fluttered at the sight of him.
"Hey, babe. Come in. I'll be a sec."
He was wearing nothing but a pair of jeans again and the effort it took each time to avert my eyes from his solid body was increasing.
"Okay, take your time," I smiled.

He turned and walked away. His jeans hung low on his hips and I felt a flutter as I watched the muscles in his back move as he walked.
I sighed and walked through to the living room, where the piano stood by the balcony doors.
As I arranged the music sheets I had brought with me, I heard him coming back. "Are you ready for…"
A girl with dark, shoulder-length hair walked out, wearing nothing but one of Scott's shirts.

She was beautiful, in a sickly kind of way. I felt an ache in my gut as I thought about both their states of undress. Had I interrupted something? Jealousy reared its unwelcome head but I had no right to feel that way so I pushed it away and smiled.

She perched on the edge of the couch, crossed her legs and smiled tightly. "So, you're the piano teacher?" she looked me up and down.

I didn't like her. "Yes, I'm Emma," I smiled. It was forced, but I gave myself points for trying.

She reached up to play with her hair. "Scott's just getting some clothes on. He must've forgotten that you were coming over. We woke up late and spent the morning in bed," she said with a sly smile.

She *wanted* me to know what they had been doing. I didn't want to know. I didn't want to picture Scott with anyone. I kept telling myself I didn't care, but I did.

Fucking slut! "How nice for you," I said sweetly in my posh voice.

"Yeah, it's always the same with us," she smiled dreamily.

I started to laugh but covered it well with a cough. I didn't say anything, I didn't call her a liar. I knew that she had only met Scott last night. Let her have her fantasy — I've had enough of him.

I had a vision of them in his bed, him lying on top of her, rocking into her gently…

I shook myself. I needed to stop it. I had told Scott weeks ago to stop so I had no right to think that way about him and I wouldn't — soon. Things would just slip into place and he would be more like a big brother than…

Scott walked in and the room shrank before my eyes. He put his arm around the girl but his attention was on me. "Hot cocoa?"

"No thanks, I just had one at lunch with Ad," I smiled.

His smile or gaze didn't falter. "Okay." He looked at the girl and kissed her.

I turned around and pretended to rearrange the music sheets. I didn't like seeing him kiss her at all. I didn't know why I had to feel that way. After all, I had blown him off, not the other way around. I could do this. I just had to ignore it and pretend it didn't bother me. I was a good actress, I had been acting most of my life. I liked to think I could handle myself by now. My back stiffened slightly as I became more hopeful. I mean, I would be here two hours tops, and once our lesson started it would be fine.

"Get dressed and go now," I heard Scott say.
"Okay, I'll come back later," she replied.
"Sorry, babe, I'm playing later."
"Well, I'll meet you there when you get off then."
Oh dear, this is where it got ugly.
"Just leave me your fuckin' number and I'll call you when it's a good time."
"I'm not a slut, Scott. I thought we connected," she said quietly.
Yeah, they had connected alright. Maybe if she had wanted him to respect her she shouldn't have opened her legs after only hours of knowing him.
"We did, baby," he crooned. "I'll call you. Just leave your number."
I felt sorry for her a tiny bit. Perhaps she really liked him. But then I thought about it. — nah, she'd only just met him.

Five minutes later, Scott kissed her goodbye at the door with her number on a piece of paper in his hand.
As soon as he closed the door he balled it up and threw it in the bin. He was amazing. How did he get away with treating girls that way?
He stalked towards me with an easy grin on his face. "Now, I'm ready."

We spent an hour and a half practising, going over the songs that I had assigned him to learn. I picked out his mistakes, which were very few, and corrected them.

"You want a drink now?" he asked after we were done, and I nodded.

While he was gone I let my fingers roam over the keys, playing of their own accord. Scott sat back down beside and put down our drinks.

He stalked my fingers on the piano with his eyes. I groaned inwardly. How could he make such a normal thing seem sexy? The way he was looking at my fingers, like he wanted them on him, made my toes curl.

I watched him as I played, his mouth parted slightly. The atmosphere in the room thickened, we were being wrapped in a tension of our own making. My fingers slowed as my heart sped up. God, I should stop this now. There was definitely something there between us, I could feel it, touch it, smell it — it was as real as it was uninvited.

I slammed my fingers down on the keys and he jumped. He gazed at me with slumberous, drowsy eyes. "Right, I'm off. Got a load of work to catch up on before tonight."

Scott stood and gazed down at me in a way that told me he wanted me. His jaw tightened as he fought it right along with me.

"You at Macy's tonight?" His voice was a low rasp.

"Yeah, I'm meeting Ad there." I picked up my music and sifted through it to find his assignment for the week. I would have picked something more complicated but I had no doubt that he'd be perfect at it anyway — he was perfect at everything he did. "Here's what I want you to learn this week," I said, handing it to him.

"Thanks." He scanned the sheet.

He really was the most gorgeous guy I knew. Even his hands were sexy. I looked around his apartment to take my eyes away from him while he studied the paper. My eyes came to rest on a picture on the wall that I must've missed. I walked over to it to get a closer look. It was a picture of an older Scott and a younger Scott. They were in a boat with sun hats on. They were holding a large fish between them. Scott looked to be about ten, his father in his forties.

"That's Dad and me," Scott said right behind me.
I flicked a glance at Scott and found him watching me with a wry grin.
"You look a lot like your dad, you know." I smiled at the image of the cute boy with the bright, happy eyes.
"I don't know if that's good or bad," he laughed.

I took another look at the photo. His dad had the same dark-green eyes, the same nose, the same hair. I noted that they had different mouths — while Scott had full lips, his dad's were thin. His dad was almost as handsome as his son — he was good-looking for an older man.
"You don't need me to tell you that that's a good thing."
"So, you think my dad's hot?" he teased, wiggling his eyebrows.
I laughed. "He's a total babe!" I teased, rolling my eyes, the tension between us easing.
"So, that also means you think I'm a 'total babe'?" He was still smiling but somehow I felt that something had shifted.

I tried to keep it light. "I think your dad's way hotter," I giggled when he pretended to look offended.
My phone started buzzing. The caller ID was unknown. I frowned as I answered it.
"Hello?"

Rocked Under ~ Cora Hawkes

"Emma?"

"Dad? How did you get this number?" I hissed down the phone as I turned my back on Scott.

"Does it matter? We need to talk." His voice seemed strained.

"No, I have nothing to say. Don't call me again."

"Emma, wait!"

"I can't talk now." I hung up on him.

My heart was in my throat. It had been so long since I had heard his voice. There was nothing that he could say that would take away the misery he had inflicted on us. I wanted to forget what he had done, to leave the past behind — ignore what he once was, the good memories of what my dad used to be to me, my hero. It had all been a lie. I felt my eyes sting as I thought about it. I sucked in a breath and looked down, willing the tears not to come now. Please, not while I have company.

"Are you okay, babe?" Scott put a comforting hand on my shoulder from behind me.

The softly spoken question just made me want to release the tears even more and my body shook with the effort to keep them in.

"Yeah," I whispered. My throat was hurting so much. "I'll see you later." Without looking back, I almost ran to the door.

Before I could get there, my wrist was seized and I was swung around to face a concerned Scott. He held my hand in his and put his other up to my cheek while he searched my face.

My lips were trembling and my eyes were going to start streaming at any moment. I closed my eyes. I didn't want Scott to see me cry.

"Baby, what's wrong? Was that your dad?" he frowned, his thumb sweeping back and forth across my cheek.

The tenderness in his eyes was my undoing and my tears came. I yanked my hand out of Scott's and threw my hands up to cover my face before it crumpled with pain.

"No, baby, don't hide." He took my hands away and gathered me to him.

I buried my head in his chest and it all came out. The hurt of years came pouring out of me in great shuddering sobs that racked my frame, hurt my throat and stung my eyes.

He stroked my hair while holding me tightly to him. "It's okay, baby." Hurt and raw disappointment burst out of me in thick tears that wouldn't stop. I was scarred by the unfairness of everything that happened. Shattered by everything our family used to be and what it had become, because of him. I wanted to beat something, stamp my feet and scream. Memories kept flashing through my mind — Dad smiling indulgently down at me. Dad chasing me around our big garden and letting me get away on purpose. Dad tucking me into bed every night. My dad... — I stopped and gave myself a mental shake.

How *could* he? How could he call *now?* I hated him. I never wanted to hear his voice or see him again. My father — my hero. What a total fuck up my hero had turned out to be. I wanted to reject the good memories I had of him, they were worthless now.

After a while, Scott lifted me in his arms and carried me over to the couch where he sat down with me in his lap.

I began to settle down and Scott was still rocking me and holding me, his hand softly stroking my arm.

"Do you wanna talk about it?" he whispered.

I shook my head into his wet chest. "No. I'm sorry for crying over you." I didn't want to look up at him yet. I was too embarrassed. I couldn't believe I had just cried like that in front of him. I had never really let anyone see me cry. I was so used to putting on a brave face, but now that I didn't have to any more I supposed I was out of practise.

"You can cry on me any time you want, Emma." His chest expanded and fell heavily. "I don't fuckin' like seeing you like this, babe."

I took a deep, shaky breath and relaxed into him. I was tired and my eyes felt thick and heavy.

Scott was quiet. I took another breath and inhaled his scent. He smelled faintly of his aftershave — I loved that smell. He also smelled damp. I put my hand up and felt his chest, solid and damp with my tears. His breathing became deeper and I put my ear to his chest. His heart was beating fast and strong.

Something had changed in the last minute, making the energy around us heavy, weighted. I felt him underneath me as I wriggled slightly. My breathing stopped and my skin became hot as I felt him grow beneath me. I pulled away from his chest slowly and gazed at him as he continued to harden. I froze and stayed absolutely still, not wanting to encourage him. My eyes must have been like saucers as I looked at him, my face was flushing and I bit my lip nervously.

He inhaled and squeezed my arm as he took me off his lap and placed me on the couch before standing up.

"Do you want a drink?" He went to the kitchen without waiting for an answer or looking at me.

I let my breath go quickly and adjusted myself after he had dumped me like a sack of potatoes. I was relieved that he had got up when he did, because I didn't think I would have been able to move away from him at that moment.

He had looked so concerned about me. I had witnessed a tender side to him that I knew few girls had. I closed my eyes as I recalled him hushing and whispering comforting words to me. What am I doing thinking like that? That path led to heartbreak, and madness, to losing the ability to act rationally.

I wanted to leave. I needed to be alone with my thoughts for a while. My dad had shocked me. I wondered how he had got my number — my mum wouldn't have given it to him.

While Scott was still in the kitchen I went to the bathroom. I looked in the mirror and blanched at how awful I looked. My eyes were puffy and red, my lips were full and I was pale. I splashed cold water over my face and finger-combed my hair as best as I could.

Scott was waiting for me when I came out. He was leaning against the wall with his arms crossed, watching me as I walked back to the couch.
"You okay?"
I nodded. "Yeah, I'm going to go." My voice was scratchy.
"I'm here if you need to talk about anything."
I nodded again. "Thanks, but I really don't want to talk about things that are best forgotten." I couldn't talk to anybody about it. It was a part of my past that I planned on leaving firmly behind in England. "You won't tell anyone about that, will you?" I twisted my hands together nervously as I bit my lip.

He cocked his head to the side, watching me in that adorable way that made my heart jump. "Of course not." His brows were drawn together, his mouth a tight line.
"I can't believe I cried all over you like that. I'm not usually a girl that cries, you know?"
"Babe, you sure you don't want to talk?" He was studying me.
I fidgeted under his gaze. I bet he hated girls that cried. I couldn't talk to him about this.

Rocked Under ~ Cora Hawkes

I shook my head and cringed as I felt the beginning of a headache. "I'm fine, really, I just…" How could I explain it all to him? He and my dad were alike in the way that they loved their women. My new friends here had no idea what I was, what I had been — And I didn't want them to know either.

"Emma?" He was standing in front of me now. "You went away again."

"Sorry, I'm just gonna go. See you later?" I asked.

"Yeah." He walked me to the door. "Emma?" he said, just as I was about to walk out.

"Yeah?" I looked over my shoulder.

"We're going to Soundz after Macy's tonight. You in?"

"Probably." I wanted nothing more right then than to get pissed and dance all the horrible feelings out of me.

Chapter Thirteen

Once I was back in my apartment I called my mum.
"Hello, darling. How are you?" she asked in her light voice.
"I'm fine. Are you okay?" I asked. I didn't know if my dad had contacted her for my number.
She sighed. "He phoned you," she said knowingly and I knew then that she gave him my number.
"How could you, Mum?" I said gently. I didn't want to upset her more than she had already been upset. The last few months she had actually started to come out of herself, like a hedgehog coming out of hibernation after a long, harsh winter.

"He's your father, darling. I couldn't say no to him even if I…" She sighed again.
"I'm sorry. He caught me by surprise and I suppose I was just shocked." I had always known that there would be a time when he would try to contact me, but I hadn't thought it would be so soon.
"I know, darling, but he sounds…" she paused, "…Different."
"Oh no, Mum! Please, don't."
"It's all right, Emmy. I know more than anyone how he gets."

"Mum, you're a beautiful woman," I began, getting ready for the spiel. "*No*, you are a beautiful, *rich* woman who has a kind heart and always helps others, and you deserve to have a *life!*" I was getting angry and it was at times like this that I didn't regret what I had done so much. "We moved here to be with family and it was the right thing to do. You will meet someone who loves you like you deserve to be loved, and I know you have a lot of love to give to someone who deserves it." I took a breath. "You have everything going for you, Mum. Did I forget to say that you also have a very beautiful daughter who adores you?" I added, because she deserved, *needed* to hear it more often than I actually told her.
I heard her chuckle. "I love you too, my heart."

After hanging up my headache got worse, so I lay on my bed for a while to try and get rid of it. My mind drifted to Scott and the way he had held me. He cared about me, I knew that much, and I felt the same way about him but I felt guilty because of Adam. What would he think if he knew Scott had been there when I needed a shoulder to cry on? He would be hurt and I didn't want that on my conscience.

I awoke later to banging on my bedroom door.
"Emma?" Ash called.
"Come in," I croaked, half asleep. I pulled myself up to test my head. My headache was gone.
"Are you okay?" She stood with her hands on her hips, worry written all over her face.
"I had a headache." I looked at my phone to check the time. It was half six. I had been asleep for hours.
Ash's face softened as she came in and shut the door. "Are you feeling better now?"

"Yeah." I thought about telling her about Dad's call but I didn't want to talk about it with her yet.
"Are you coming out tonight?"
I thought about staying in to finish some work, but I wanted to get out — I didn't want to sit here on my own with my thoughts. "Yes, give me half hour and I'll meet you all there." I got up to turn the shower on.

"How did Scott's lesson go?" Ash searched my face.
"Good. He's a lot better than he lets on."
"So he hasn't tried anything with you yet?"
I turned and frowned at her, "Why do you ask?"
She lifted her shoulders, "I was only asking."

"No, he hasn't." I looked away from her and my hand went to my bracelet. Had Scott ever tried it on with Ash? "Has he ever hit on *you*?"

She fidgeted and crossed her arms.

"Ash," I pressed, "have you ever slept with Scott?" I held my breath, waiting for the answer, and I knew what it would be.

"Yes," she whispered, letting her breath out in a whoosh. "It was years ago. Well, about three actually."

She looked embarrassed and I wished I hadn't asked. "Oh."

"We'd been friends since I can remember. In his senior year of high school he…He changed. He was suddenly hot and I…*Oh God*," she covered her face with her hands, "I went after him."

I came to sit beside her on the bed. I was shocked. Why hadn't she ever told me? Why hadn't Scott ever said anything?

"You remember me telling you that I was in love and I was sure he was the one?"

I nodded and groaned inwardly as I remembered her gushing about someone about three or four years ago.

"Well, that was Scott," she sighed.

"Shit, Ash, I had no idea." A thought occurred to me. "So he was your boyfriend for a while?" I frowned, "I thought you said that he'd never had a girlfriend."

"He wasn't my boyfriend, although I wanted him to be. I was popular in school and when my friends started crushing on him, I wanted to be the one to be able to call him my boyfriend first." She looked at me, wanting me to understand, but I didn't.

How could she have been so shallow? Why hadn't I listened more?

"What happened?" I needed to know.

"We were drinking and I came on to him." She curled her lip, disgusted with herself. "Afterward he didn't talk to me for a week and I was embarrassed and hurt that he had treated me that way — like I was any other girl. We had an argument and didn't talk for months. Everyone at school knew about it." She shook her head. "I knew it was my own fault for pushing him when he didn't want me that way, so in the end I valued his friendship more. We made up and have never looked back," she sighed.

"Do you still like him that way?" I asked.

She was quiet for a moment. "The thing is, I know he would make someone a great boyfriend — I'm jealous of that, but I don't think he'll ever settle. I do look at him sometimes and think '*wow*', but that's the effect he has on all girls."

I looked away. I knew all too well that he did.

"So, has he made a move on you?"

"No," I lied. How could I say yes after what she had just told me?

"Good. He better not, either."

After our argument a few weeks ago he seemed to have got the message. We had to keep it that way. If Ash found out about us, she wouldn't be happy, and Ash was my family. I couldn't upset her like that because I had a suspicion that she still had feelings for him.

Ash left me to get ready. What a day, I thought. First Scott's lesson and then the phone call from my dad and then Ash telling me she and Scott had…I couldn't think about it.

Chapter Fourteen

I showed up at Macy's a bit later than I said I would and Scott was already on stage. As I made my way through the crowd I felt his eyes on me and I looked at him and waved as normally as I could. He winked with a wicked grin while he sang.

"Hey, babe," Ad pulled me onto his lap and pushed two drinks towards me, "You missed the first two rounds but I kept them for you."

"Thanks." I knocked the first one back and picked up the other one to sip it.

"You okay?" he asked, his eyes twinkling.

"Yeah." I was lucky to have him, I reminded myself. He was kind, loyal, and safe. I hadn't put a lot of time into him lately and I wanted to show him that I appreciated him.

I leaned forward to whisper in his ear, "Want to dance with me?"

"Thought you'd never ask," he beamed, and we got up to dance to one of Scott's slower, ballad-like songs.

I went into Ad's arms and we moved to the slow beat. I closed my eyes as I rested my head against his warm chest, feeling drained. Today had been one of those days that should've been skipped — or maybe I just shouldn't have got out of bed this morning. I lost myself in thought, inhaling deeply through my nose and releasing slowly. My thoughts turned to Ash and Scott. Why hadn't she told me sooner about them?

I opened my eyes at that moment and looked into Scott's gaze. He stood gripping the mic tightly with both hands, watching me, always watching me. I held his stare as I moved, with Adam holding me tightly, slowly. Was there anyone who hadn't been with him? Scott broke eye contact first and looked down, putting his head on the mic through Bone's solo.

Ad didn't deserve this. He was a cool guy and it was as though I was cheating on him, even though I wasn't really. My feelings towards Scott were more than friendly and I hated myself because Ad didn't know. I felt like I was making a fool of him. Scott was far from stupid, he knew when a girl liked him or wanted him and no matter how hard I tried to hide it from him, he *knew* — I knew he did. The number of awkward moments we'd had — I was losing count. It should have been Ad holding me while I cried, not Scott.

He had seen me break and had not asked any questions. He had just held me. I had seen a part of him that had endeared him to me further and I didn't want that. I didn't want to think of him that way at all.

Scott glanced at me again and I saw his eyebrows crease faintly in barely hidden confusion, as if he could sense my mood. My stupid heart kicked in excitement, not knowing what was good for it.

"Are you okay, babe?" Ad asked in my ear.

I nodded up at him with a smile and reached my arms up, putting my hands on the back of his neck. I gently brought his head down to mine and kissed him.

His kiss was soft, gentle, at first, but after a moment he deepened it, his tongue entering my mouth forcefully. He jerked me to him as if he couldn't get close enough.

He broke the kiss and placed his mouth on my neck. I moved my hair to give him access and let my head loll to the side as he kissed all the way up my neck to my ear.

"Damn, Em, I want you now," he rasped in my ear.

He kissed back down my neck. I looked to the stage but Scott had his back to the audience. As I was about to close my eyes, Scott turned and his eyes collided with mine.

There was a storm raging at me, an anger emanating from him that made me flinch. *I can't stop wanting you and seeing you with Ad is...It's driving me fuckin' crazy.* His words haunted me, but I pushed them away and stopped them from ruining things with Ad. Scott's black look wouldn't let me go, so I broke away from Ad with the excuse that I needed to use the toilet.

I disappeared from both of their sights as soon as I could. I went to the ladies and locked myself in a stall — again — because of Scott.
I hated seeing Scott like that. I was torn. Frustration burned within me that I couldn't be with Ad without feeling bad about Scott's feelings. But why did I feel like that anyway? Scott and I...Well. I didn't know what we were, but I did what we were not. He had said all that to me weeks ago, but he had never stopped bringing girls back and he never hid it from me.

Why should I care? I had had enough crap for twenty-four hours. I just wanted to feel free for a while. I was conscious that I was becoming increasingly aware of trying to please Scott when I should have been concentrating on Ad.
I sighed as I emerged from the stall and walked out. I went straight to the bar and ordered two drinks for myself, which I downed straight away.

My brain was fried and I didn't want to think anymore tonight. I knew that drinking wasn't the best thing I could do, but I didn't care. I had spent most of my life hiding behind a ridiculous façade, but that was in the past. This was the new me. *Screw it!* The rest of our time at Macy's was spent drinking and jumping around the dance floor while trying to hide from Scott's view.

Soundz was as crowded as I knew it would be on a Saturday night. We hung around the bar until a table became free and then we pounced on it. I had been clamped to Ad's side for most of the night so far and I intended to keep it that way. I avoided Scott's dark gaze when I could.

A while later I was dancing with Ash and Meg when I spotted Scott in a corner making out heavily with a girl in a tiny skirt and knee-high boots. I felt my face crease as I watched his hands roam over her, down past her ass to her thighs. From there his hand slid up her skirt and he stroked her right there in front of everyone.

I ground my jaw and my blood boiled, the booze I had consumed fuelling the anger. I hated him at that moment. I hadn't admitted anything to Scott but he kind of had to me. I wanted to get back at him so much.
I seized Ad as he came up to me and planted my mouth straight onto his. Ad pulled away in surprise. I smiled up at him and grabbed his hands, putting them on my butt. He squeezed and angry desire started to heat my skin. I turned my back to him and reached my hands up, gathering my hair over one shoulder as I moved myself against his hips.

The *thump, thump* of the music was deep and I ground myself against him with the rhythm. Ad put his hands on my belly and slipped them under my top, moving them up to just below my breasts. I leaned my head back and put my hands over his. His head came down to my exposed neck and he kissed all the way along it. I raised my arms and looped them around him to keep him there.

I opened my eyes and saw Scott watching me. A jolt went through me at the violence blazing in his eyes. His eyes travelled down me and then back up to my face. I bit my lip, sharp desire penetrating my fuzzy head. I closed my eyes, shutting him out. I turned in Ad's arms, drove my hands through his hair and pulled him fully into me to sate what was happening in my body.

Ad rubbed his hips against mine and deepened our kiss.
"Come with me," Ad whispered near my ear and led me away from the dance floor.
Feeling slightly dazed, I almost tripped on the way. Ad led me past the restrooms down to the end of the corridor and leaned against the wall with me in his arms.
"This is better," he said before he came to me again, and I put my all into it. I kissed him deeply, desperately even — but it wasn't Ad's eyes looking into mine, stoking the fire in me when I closed them.

I seethed. I didn't want to see Scott. I. Wanted. Ad. Scott was out there with someone else and he would never change. A leopard doesn't change its spots and Scott would never be with one woman. I was furious at myself for wanting him so much. I was weak, my body was weak, but I knew my mind would never give in to it.
Ad put his hands underneath my ass and pressed me into him. His erection rubbed against me.

"Ad, I want…"
"I know, babe, me too," he rasped. He turned us around so my back was against the wall.
I ran my fingers through his hair as he kissed my neck. He brought his mouth back to mine.
"Get away from her," came an angry voice.
I opened my dazed eyes and looked straight into Scott's furious ones.

"What the fuck, man?" Ad slurred as he turned.

Scott crossed his arms and stood tall, not sparing me a glance. "You're wasted, Ad. Go and cool down."

"I don't need to cool down." Ad crossed his arms too and the pair eyed each other up.

Ad sounded very drunk now that the haze had cleared a bit and he was swaying from side to side.

Scott stepped closer to Ad, menace in his stare. "You better. You're not laying another fuckin' hand on her tonight, Adam."

What the hell did he think he was doing? I had seen him with a girl not ten minutes ago and now he was behaving like a jealous boyfriend.

Before Ad could say anything I spoke. "Scott, what're you doing?"

He didn't take his eyes off Adam. "Stay out of this, Emma."

"You're not her family and you sure as shit ain't her man, so…"

Scott grabbed Ad's shirt and pulled him in to his chest.

"Scott, stop!" I shouted before he floored Ad.

"Go! Now!" he growled through clenched teeth.

Ad's brows rose and then knitted again angrily. Scott let him go and Ad stalked away without even looking at me.

Great!

Scott was looking at me like he hated me. Well, I didn't care — it was okay for him and not for me?

"What're you doing?" I demanded.

"Stopping you from doing something you'll regret," he growled.

"I wouldn't have regretted it," I said, wanting to taunt him.

He moved forward so fast that I shrank back. He grabbed my wrist. "You wanna be fucked up against a wall in a nightclub your first time?" he snarled.

I felt ashamed then and tears sprang to my eyes. I pushed them back and stood my ground. "Let me go." I tried to yank my arm free but he wouldn't budge. He was right in my face, eyes blazing at me, breathing heavily.

I laughed cruelly. "You're just angry because you can't have me." My drunken tongue was working without my brain's influence.

"Don't flatter yourself," he spat, squeezing my wrist harder.

I gritted my teeth, "Really? You can't stand to see me with Ad! It eats away at you that I prefer Ad to you and the fact that…" I looked him up and down with a sneer, "…You're not good enough for me."

He dropped my hand, like I had burned him and took a step back.

I felt pain tear through me as his face became like granite. *Shit!* I went towards him, "Scott, I didn't mean…"

"Yes, babe, you did," he cut me off and cupped my face. "All that's true, but it doesn't stop you from wanting to fuck me." His eyes drifted down to my lips and back up to my eyes as he came closer. He stopped when his lips were millimetres from mine.

I closed my eyes and revelled in his closeness, his smell.

"Does it?" he whispered. He rubbed his lips against mine ever so lightly in a barely-there caress.

I knocked him back as hard as I could but my body wasn't working properly. "Fuck you, Scott. Go back to your tart because she can give you what you *really* want."

"And what's that?"

"A hard, cold fuck with no ties."

I heard his quick inhale. Then he turned his head and planted a soft kiss on my cheek before leaving me completely and walking away.

Rocked Under ~ Cora Hawkes

Chapter Fifteen

I woke up the next morning feeling groggy and sick. Then I remembered the previous night and groaned into my pillow. Adam had left the club without telling me and it was all Scott's fault. After Scott had walked away I had gone to find the others and got plastered. I didn't see Scott again and Meg had said he'd grabbed himself a skank and taken her back to his place. Oh yes, I got very drunk indeed.

I turned on my side and picked my phone up off the bedside cabinet. There was a message.

Adam: *Hey beautiful, Im sorry. Call me when u read this. X*

I rolled my eyes and turned onto my back. I would call Ad later. He had showed a different side last night, but then he had been very drunk, too. I thought back with a sober mind. I knew why Scott had walked away from me. I had said something that I didn't mean and he had got me back for it. He had proven his point. I needed to make it better. Put it right. I felt awful about what I had said. *Not good enough for me?* Why had I said that? I didn't think that at all. He just wasn't what I needed in a man — he would be so bad for me.

I remembered the look on his face when I said it, the hurt in his eyes, like he believed it. He had done me a favour by stopping Ad and me when he had. I had had way too much to drink and I probably would've let Ad take me against the bloody wall like one of Scott's groupies. I debated calling him to apologise, but he had hurt me too. I needed some time to think without seeing or talking to him. I needed a breather from the roller-coaster ride that we — well, *I* — was on. He wanted one night, but one night would never be enough for me. Not to mention that our friendship would be ruined. How could it not be ruined?

The next week slipped by with Scott and I not really talking. Okay, we said hello to each other and acknowledged each other, but we didn't *talk* talk. I stayed away from Macy's and spent a lot of time with Ad after he had apologised a hundred times first. When I saw Scott, I cringed inwardly and his stare was knowing. I wanted him. There was no denying it or making excuses for myself.

I walked into the cafeteria late at lunch on Friday. As soon as they spotted me walking towards them, they all went quiet. I stopped before sitting down and stared at them, wondering what they had been talking about. I knew they had been yapping about me, that was for sure — Ash and Meg were smiling at me innocently, but Ash had a slight flush on her cheeks which was a giveaway that she was hiding something from me. Newton was studying his phone rather intently and Ad was talking.
"Hey, babe. You okay?" he grinned as he pulled me onto his lap.
I stole a glance at Scott. He was staring straight at me for the first time for a week. My heart started hammering as he held my gaze. Something was up. He hadn't looked at me like that all week, he had mostly ignored me.

He was angry about something — angry, but there was something else there too, something less noticeable lurking behind the anger.
His jaw tensed for a moment before he stood up and stalked away.
I watched him go and wondered what I had done wrong, or maybe if something had upset him. The urge to go after him was so strong but I kept still.

"What's up with him?" I asked anyone.

"Who knows, who cares? Probably a girl or something." Ad nuzzled my neck and rubbed my thigh.

I knew that Ad and Scott didn't like each other, but I didn't want to listen to Ad talking about him that way. It annoyed me. "I'll be back in a second," I said, standing up.

"You're going after *him*?"

"I won't be long." Ad was about to argue but I turned and walked out of the cafeteria. I rounded the corner. Scott was gone. I looked out the window and spotted him. I ran out the door and after him. He was headed round the back of the building, looking for all the world as if he did not want company.

"Scott!" I jogged after him, "Wait!"

He turned to look at me. "Go back inside," he growled as I reached him.

I reeled slightly, not used to him talking to me like that. "I...I wanted to see if you're okay," I said looking away, feeling like a total idiot for caring.

"I'm just fuckin' great," he replied, crossing his arms. Then he sighed and shook his head. "Just go back inside, Emma." He turned and walked away from me.

I frowned. I didn't want him to be like this with me — it hurt. The last week had been hard and I just wanted to take back what I had said.

I jogged after him again and grabbed his arm. "I'm sorry," I took a breath as he turned with a frown, "I'm sorry for what I said at Soundz. I didn't mean any of it. I was drunk and my mouth ran away with me. I know it probably doesn't matter to you that I'm sorry but I wanted to say it anyway. I'm not usually like that. I guess I was just angry and you were right anyway." I took another deep breath. "So I'm sorry for what I said. Just...Please don't be upset with me anymore."

He didn't say anything. He was still angry but a hunted look had come into his eyes.
I frowned, "What's wrong?"
He stepped forward and gently took my face in his hands. "Do you love him, Emma?" he whispered, his voice soft as he searched my face.
My heart was hammering. How did he do that — be harsh and gentle at the same time? My body rejoiced in his hands touching me, my face warmed and flushed.
How did I answer that question? Did I love Ad? I knew the answer was a definite 'no' but I didn't want him to know that. "I...I don't know," I whispered back, looking away from him. "What has that got to do with anything?"

"Because he...Ah, *fuck!*" He turned his back to me and drove his hands through his hair.
"Scott..."
He spun around to face me and came towards me, intent in his eyes. "Kiss me." He cupped my face again and brought his face very close, his lips almost touching mine.
"We can't." I closed my blue eyes against his green ones. I could almost feel his lips, I could feel their warmth close to mine, his every breath touching me in a caress that was tipping me over the edge and sending anticipation shooting through my veins.

He groaned low in his throat and brought his body close to mine. "Kiss me, Emma," he rasped.
His mouth came to my lips gently. He brushed his lips upwards, making my top lip lift and pucker. A jolt, so sharp, went straight to my belly and I could do nothing but sigh as I opened my mouth for him. His mouth then collided with mine in frenzied

desperation as he sucked and then stroked hard with his tongue, in and out, back and forth, in an assault of passion against my lips.

My body wanted this — hell, *I* wanted this. He stopped moving suddenly but his lips stayed on mine and he took a deep shuddering breath. One of his hands went to the back of my head and the other snaked around my waist as he kissed me in the most tender way I had ever been kissed. His lips were slow and gentle now. I could feel tremors coming from him, his breathing was stilted, shaky. I wasn't thinking — my whole being was there and then and in what was happening. He felt, tasted and smelled *so good.* I wanted him this way forever, I didn't want it to end.

He had my body wanting him, singing to him. Our breath was ragged as it mingled and crashed. I could fall so heavily for him. I stiffened. A coldness flowed up my spine to my skull as panic held me in its grip. Falling for Scott would be me falling on my face and spending my life trying to get back up. Once again, my mum's face at her lowest, in her deepest depression, wheedled its way into my mind. Guilt clenched my stomach when I thought about Adam. I had just kissed another guy. He didn't deserve that. Maybe my dad's habits had rubbed off on me too.

Scott must have felt it as reality crashed down around me and I realised what I had done.

He pulled back to look at me, a question in his expression, as if to say, *what's wrong?* But I looked away. "This isn't right, Scott."

He released me and stepped back.

I peeked at him from under my lashes. He was angry at me and I could understand why. I had followed him to make amends, but I had only made it worse.

"Fuck this shit," he said and walked off.

Chapter Sixteen

I decided to skip afternoon class and sent Ash and Ad a text message telling them that I had forgotten something and I would see them later. I trudged home slowly in the cold air, trying to let my mind clear, but it didn't work. As I approached the flat I could hear angry rock music blaring from Scott's open window. That was probably good — he wouldn't hear me going in.

I spent the afternoon going over everything. Why did Scott want to kiss me? Why was he upset? I had a feeling that it wasn't just about last week, it was something else. Questions flitted around my head but I had no answers and it was driving me insane trying find them. I knew I was doing the right thing by being with Ad. I didn't love him, but then I didn't want the mad love every other girl seemed so desperate for.

Scott would get over it. He wasn't the type to hanker after a girl for long. I was only a challenge for him because I said 'no' and I was Ash's cousin. Suddenly the music from upstairs went off and I heard footsteps thumping hurriedly down the stairs. I held my breath, hoping that he wouldn't knock. Did I lock the door? I couldn't remember, but my shoulders relaxed as I heard the front door slam. I went over to the window to watch him. He got in his car, both his hands gripped the wheel and his head flopped forwards.

I was witnessing an emotion that was usually kept hidden and suddenly I felt as though I was breaching his privacy. My heart wanted to go out to him but I needed it to stay whole and safe with me. I didn't dare give a piece to Scott — he would make it crack until it shattered into a million pieces that would take a lifetime to put back together.

I turned away from the window, not wanting to see any more. I was just a challenge, that's all. If I had said yes to him then he would have got me out of his system. But where would we be now if I had been with him that first night? I would hate him for using me and as he lived upstairs it would be awkward for us both. No I had made the right choice, done the right thing as far as our relationship was concerned, and if he was having problems accepting that, then that was his problem not mine. My back stiffened with my resolve. I was probably the first girl to say no to him.

Adam: *B ready at 7. Im taking u out 2 dinner. X*

Me: *Ok. C u in a bit. xx*

"Wow," I breathed later when we walked into the restaurant where Ad had made a reservation, "This place is really posh." I had been in much more upmarket places but Ad had made an effort for me tonight so I made the effort to be impressed.
"I knew you'd like it." Ad took me over to a candlelit table in the corner at the back and a waiter came to pull the chair out for me.
"I love it. What's the occasion?"
"Can't a guy take his girl to a nice place without there being an occasion?" he teased.
"Yes, but you didn't have to, you know."
"I wanted to, so sit back and enjoy, woman."

We ordered our food and talked easily. Ad made me laugh by telling me stories of the pranks he used to play on his older brother. I sat and listened while he did most of the talking, which was usual for him. More and more my mind drifted back to what had happened with Scott earlier. I wanted us to be okay again instead of there being all this bad feeling between us. I didn't want to admit it, but I missed him.

"Emma?"

I blinked and found Ad staring at me. "Sorry, what?"

"I said, 'I have a surprise for you.'"

"Sorry," I shook my head, "My mind was elsewhere. What surprise?"

"I've booked us into a hotel for the night." He grinned cheekily and wiggled his brows.

"Oh." What could I say to that? Was I ready for it? I wasn't sure.

"Look, don't worry. I'm not going to force you to do anything that you don't want to do. Let's check in and see where it takes us."

"Okay. I'll have to let Ash know that I might not be back." I went to reach for my phone.

"I've already sorted that," he waved his hand in the air.

"You have?" I didn't like the sound of that and frowned. "When?"

"At lunch today."

Suddenly, I realised why Scott had been that way with me — he had known about tonight. I thought back to the way he had stomped off as I came into the cafeteria and our argument afterwards. He thought that I was going to sleep with Ad tonight. He'd asked me if I loved Ad. The answer to that was 'no, I didn't', but I cared about him and I thought he felt the same way about me.

"Okay. That sounds good." I smiled but inside I was secretly angry with Scott. I mean, how dare he be like that with me for maybe sleeping with someone when he slept with numerous girls a week?

"Great! I'm ready to go when you are."

When we eventually entered the hotel room, after having spent an hour in the bar, we were giggling at a story Ad had told about something he had done that summer.

"It's nice in here," I said as I looked around the room and slipped my heels off. The decor was golds and browns, very rich and decadent. This must have cost him a bomb.

"Only the best for you, babe."

I giggled at his cheesy words. He was really laying it on thick.

"Have I told you how beautiful you look tonight?" he said as he came closer to me.

I was wearing a black, baby-doll dress with blue heels and jewellery.

"Only several times," I rolled my eyes.

He slipped his hands onto my waist and I put mine on his shoulders.

I knew what he wanted. We had almost done it the other night but…I groaned inwardly as Scott invaded my head again.

"Are you okay?" Ad was looking at me.

"I'm fine." I reached up and kissed him.

Our kiss was gentle. His mouth moved against mine in his usual way. After a while he deepened the kiss, his tongue invading my mouth. It reminded me of another kiss I had had recently. *Ugh!* I didn't want to think about him now — not now, not when I was with someone else.

I slipped my hands under his shirt and pushed him back towards the bed. I was going to do this, and then maybe I would feel closer to Ad and forget about Scott. As Ad's legs hit the bed he spun me around and before I knew it I was on my back with him on top of me.

"Oh God, Em!" he moaned into my mouth as he rocked his hips into mine.

I put my hands down and tried to undo his belt but failed.
"Here, let me." He had it undone in seconds.

Then his hands moved to the hem of my dress and he tugged. I lifted my butt, then sat up so he could remove it. He looked at me for a second with a wry grin on his face. It was his turn. He stood above me as he slid off his shirt and showed his tanned and muscled chest — not a tattoo in sight. Then came his pants. As he pulled them down his cock sprang free and I couldn't take my eyes off it. I gulped. I could do this, everybody did.

He came down on me again and undid the catch on my bra. I put my hands up over my breast in a last attempt to keep my virginity, but he placed his hands over mine.
"It's only me," he laughed.
I closed my eyes as I let my hands fall away, I was exposed to him.
"You're amazing." He kissed me.
I wasn't as nervous as I had always thought I would be. He kissed down my neck and the top of my breast. I gasped. It felt good. I clutched him to me as he rubbed himself against me. I was becoming damp.
"Oh God, you feel so good!" he groaned into my neck as his hands roved over my body with sure movements.

He kissed his way down my tummy and hooked his fingers into my knickers. This was it. This was the part where he removed the last bit of clothing and made his entrance. *Oh, shut up, Emma!* I scolded myself.
He slid them down slowly and then removed them completely. He stood above me, looking at me. I cringed and tried to cover myself.
"Don't be shy, you're beautiful." He fumbled with his jeans and pulled out a condom.

Rocked Under ~ Cora Hawkes

He rolled it on and then he was on me again. "You ready?"

Was I ready? I didn't know but it was too late now so I just nodded.

He kissed me and rubbed himself against me until I was groaning for him to do something before I lost the will to actually do it. Pain tore through me as he thrust himself all the way inside. Tears came to my eyes with the pain.

"Are you okay?" he grunted.

I wasn't, but I nodded anyway, wondering how long it would last for.

He started moving again and it didn't hurt so I relaxed into it. He moved fast and before I knew it, it was over. Was that it? Was that what everyone thought was so good?

"I'm sorry, it's not supposed to be that quick, but you…" he kissed me, "…you turned me on a lot. Next time I promise I'll wait for you."

That's right, I remembered reading that it was harder for a woman to orgasm and that a good lover always made sure the woman came before he did. I didn't want to try it again. I wanted to get dressed and go home, but I was here for the night.

"It's okay," I forced a smile, "I'm just going to have a shower."

I shot up and dashed into the shower, snagging my bag on the way in. I already regretted having done it. I should've waited. I wondered how it would have been had Scott been my first. I quickly chased the thought away and stepped into the shower.

By the time I had finished showering Ad was already asleep. He hadn't even waited for me, not that I had wanted him to, but still. It made me feel used and cheap. I debated whether I should sneak out now or just stay. If I left, I would have to explain everything to Ash and I didn't need that just then.

I couldn't believe Ad had basically made what we were doing public knowledge — okay, they were my friends, but he still should've kept quiet.

I decided to stay. I crawled in next to Ad but made sure to stay on my own side of the bed. I pulled my phone off the bedside table and checked for messages. None.

Sleep was a long time coming, but I eventually drifted off into a light doze.

Chapter Seventeen

I woke up to find Ad draped around me, his legs were wrapped with mine and his arm had me pinned against the mattress. He was still asleep and looking at him now I had mixed feelings about him, and I regretted last night. I wished it had never happened. I had a dirty, used cheap feeling that seemed to cling to my skin, making me want to shower again and again until there was no part of him left on my skin. I flung an arm over my eyes, shielding Ad from my view.

I had done it for the wrong reasons. I hadn't wanted to, but when Ad had told me about him telling Ash and I had realised that was why Scott was off with me, I was kind of angry. I had wanted to show him that I could do it and that Ad meant something to me, but now I saw that it really hadn't been worth it. I had had too much to drink, and it had clouded my decisions. *Damn it!*

I untangled myself from his limbs carefully and slid out of bed. I dressed as fast as I could and got out of there before he woke up. I didn't want to explain why I was leaving, but I knew that we were over. Something about the way he had fallen asleep after I had gone to shower bugged me. Would it have been different with Scott? Somehow, I knew he would've made it special, made me feel precious, if only for one night. I had to see him today for his lesson and his next assignment and I knew it was going to be tough. I considered cancelling but decided against it.

After having spent a long time in my own shower scrubbing my skin, I knocked on his door with a shaking hand. I didn't know what mood to expect him to be in. I was nervous about seeing him after yesterday. Would he know what I had done? Would he be angry?

A blonde girl opened the door. "Hi," she greeted cheerfully, waving a hand in welcome.

I walked in, returning her cheerful hello.

Scott was looking out the window with his arms crossed and turned as he heard me approach. He shot me a loaded look that told me he knew. How the hell did he know — did I have it written all over my face or something?

"Hi, you ready?" I asked, hoping he would forget about yesterday and let me forget about last night. He was gorgeous. Why would any girl in their right mind say no to him? Why had I? Oh yes, I remembered, as Blondie walked up to him.

"I'm off, sugar. See you tonight." She kissed him thoroughly but Scott had his eyes on me the whole time. I looked away. I couldn't watch this. Why did he do it? I had decided that I hated sex, but I was standing in front of someone who loved it.

"Bye," she drawled at me as she walked out.

"How are you?" As we last saw each other only yesterday, I didn't know how he would be around me.

"I'm just great, Emma. How about you — sore?"

I gasped, shocked that he would say that to me.

"I guess you *do* love him," he said and looked away.

"How do you know about that?" I had to ask.

"Ad called me this morning," he said, his voice indifferent now.

"He actually called you just to tell you?" I was shocked. *That total bastard!* I seethed. How could he have done that?

"I need to cancel our lesson today, so I'll show you the piece I learned and you can assign me a new one." Scott changed the subject, his jaw was tense.

I knew he was lying — he didn't want me here. "Are you still angry with me?" I got in his face.

He shook his head. "I'm not. I don't fuckin' care what you do."

If he didn't care then he was doing a poor job of showing it. "You're off with me and I want to know why. I already said sorry about what happened in Soundz. You're confusing the hell out of me so I want some answers."

"I don't wanna talk. I think you've made a mistake, but you know that already, don't you?" He studied me for an answer.

I didn't say anything and stared at the carpet, unable to look him in the face.

He was right.

"Ad wanted you and he got you," he shrugged like it was nothing.

I didn't know what to say and I was angry at Ad for telling Scott. If he had told Scott, then who else knew? I cringed, remembering last night again. I probably wouldn't do it again for a long time.

"So do you want to see me play or what?" Scott asked, his mouth a tight line.

I nodded slowly.

He played beautifully. He was a natural pianist — all he needed was practise because once he had learned a piece, he was fine.

"You're very good for a beginner, you know."

"What have you got for me this week?" He wasn't making small talk and he wasn't smiling — it was as though he wanted me gone as quickly as possible, and who could blame him? But we were meant to be friends, I wanted that at least. Maybe I should just come out and ask him if we were okay.

"Um," I frowned as I rooted in my bag and found what I was looking for, "I brought you two pieces and as you've done so well, I'll give you the harder one." I grinned at him but he didn't return it.

He took it from my hands and turned away.

I knew that he was upset with me, but surely that didn't mean the end of our friendship?

He had his back to me, his hands fiddling absently with the sheets on the piano. I narrowed my eyes as I noticed that he was rearranging them again and again. He wasn't just angry with me, he was upset, too. I just didn't understand it. It wasn't like he had any deep feelings for me. Maybe something else had happened. I found myself wanting to go to him, put my arms around him and hold him there.

"Scott?"

He turned to look at me over his shoulder.

"Are you okay?"

He looked away and put his fiddling hands in his pockets. "Yeah," he came around to face me, "I've gotta go, so…"

So he wanted me to go. This was getting on my nerves. I hadn't done anything wrong and I had already apologised for saying that he wasn't good enough for me. What else was there to be sorry for? I got that he was pissed that I had slept with Ad, but he didn't have the right to be angry with me for that — just like I didn't when he brought girls back.

"Okay, yeah. I've got to get going anyway." A lie but it was necessary. "Same time next week?"

He nodded without saying a word.

I grabbed my bag and walked out without saying goodbye. If he wanted to act like a spoiled child, then fine.

The next week, I avoided Ad like he had leprosy. I ignored his calls and I gave my regular haunts a wide berth.

"What're you doing?" Ash asked me.

It was Friday and we were walking home after class. I hadn't seen Ad in a week and I had barely seen or spoken to Scott either, which was just fine with me.

"What do you mean?"

"I mean with Adam. You need to tell him what a dick he is," she clarified.

"He'll find out for himself tonight." I had spent a week seething about him blabbing about our not-so-great night together and now it was payback time. Everybody knew I had been a virgin and it was humiliating. Nobody had said anything to me, but I knew they knew, and to say I was angry with Ad was an understatement. I was fucking furious. Anger heated me from the inside, making the cold walk home comfortable. I wasn't going to let him get away with it, and maybe next time he would be man enough to keep something like that private.

"Oh no, Em," Ash moaned, "What're you up to?"

"Nothing much, I promise. I'm just going to show him up a bit. Let him know how it feels," I shrugged.

And Scott could bugger off too. He had avoided me for two weeks now, even though I had apologised for what I said, and I couldn't be bothered with any of this anymore. He had no room to say anything. He was a hypocrite through and through.

I'd had enough. From now on I was going to have fun. And as for Ad, nobody made a fool out of this girl and got away with it.

Chapter Eighteen

Soundz was buzzing by the time Ash, Meg and I got there. I walked straight up to the bar and got the first round in. Tonight I was going to enjoy myself and I didn't care what anyone thought or said about me. My skills as an actress would get me through this. Ad would be smiling on the other side of his fake face by the end of the night, and I couldn't wait to see it.

On the dance floor a while later I was dancing with anybody I could and having a fantastic time when I clocked Ad making his way towards me. I turned my back on him and carried on like I hadn't seen him.
I felt a hand tug my elbow hard.
"Em," he came close to my ear, "We need to talk." He sounded pissed off. Good.
"I have nothing to say to you, Adam," I shouted as I tugged my arm out of his grasp and kept my back to him.
"Look, I know you're pissed but it wasn't me who blabbed about it," he shouted.

"Who did then, Adam, because as far as I know it was only you and me in that room? Or did you have one of your friends stashed under the bed?" I was furious all over again.
The stares I had got all week and the whispers... *Ugh!*
"I only told Scott, I swear!"
I spun around. "You're so full of shit. And why *did* you tell Scott, Adam? You did it to gloat!"
Would Scott have told anyone? It didn't fit — he wasn't that kind of person, was he? Why would he have done that? What possible cause could he have had? I remembered the last time we had spoken — he hadn't been too happy to see me. No. Even though I was seeing through a red haze at the moment, I knew Scott wouldn't do that.

Rocked Under ~ Cora Hawkes

"Okay, I did. But he's been after you even while you were with me and it fucked me off." His face was full of remorse but I didn't care. He'd shown himself for who he really was, and I didn't like it.

"Well, you and your little," I looked down suggestively, "prick can fuck off as far as I'm concerned. You shouldn't have said anything to anyone!"

Although my friends knew that Ad had got us a room, it could've been completely innocent for all they knew. I fumed. The actual deed had been embarrassing enough without everyone knowing about it.

I supposed I was angry with myself for having lost my virginity to someone I didn't really want. To be completely honest with myself, I had known that *before* we did it, but Scott had spooked me. I felt like he had crawled into my skin with me and wouldn't leave, wouldn't let me go. I couldn't be upset with Scott because he had done nothing wrong — except for blanking me for two weeks, there was that.

Ad flushed, his mouth a tight line. "You bitch!" He stepped forward and clenched my forearm hard.

"Take your hands off me now!" I tugged, but he wouldn't release me and he was squeezing hard.

"Make me," he laughed.

My hand shot up and I heard the slap over the music. My palm smarted, but at least he had let go.

His hand went up to his face in shock. Then he seemed to grow a few inches in front of me and his biceps bunched as he made fists and stepped closer to me but then stopped, looking around.

"Just get the hell away from me, Ad, we're through." I turned my back on him and continued to dance as though I wasn't bothered in the slightest by him. I hated him.

I felt eyes on me so I looked up. Scott, in all his glorious male beauty, was up on the balcony gazing down at me. As soon as our eyes met he looked away and put his arm around the bimbo by his side. I swore I could see pride in his eyes, but that was probably for the slut by his side. Who would be proud to have that by their side?

And fuck you too! I thought. I didn't deserve him being like this with me. It hurt. I should be upset, not him.

He had barely talked to me in *two* weeks. Well, he could watch away. I swore to myself that I wouldn't spare him another glance all night. I would totally ignore both of them. If there was one thing I was good at, it was putting on a show. Nobody back home could say that I couldn't.

Bone from Scott's band was at the bar and I pushed my way through the crowd of dancers until I reached him.

"Hey, Bone!" I half-shouted as I slipped in beside him.

"Emma, babe!" he yelled with a white-toothed grin.

"Aw! No date tonight?" I asked, flirting.

He shook his head with a mock sad face.

I slid closer to him and grabbed his hand, "Wanna dance with me?"

He looked unsure. "Ain't you already gotta man?"

I came in close to his ear, "Not anymore." I pulled away to look at him. "So, dance?"

He grinned wickedly, "Sure, baby." He put his arm around me.

We moved out onto the dance floor. Bone put his hands on my hips to pull me closer to him. The beat was fast and strong, a steady throb was vibrating through the club.

My hands went to his shoulders and we danced closely together, rubbing and smiling suggestively.

I brought his head down to me. I was well ready to make the message crystal-clear to Adam and everyone else that I was moving on.

He brought his mouth slowly onto mine. His hands roved up and down my back while his lips played with me.
I deepened the kiss, loving the feel of him against me. It was a good kiss, but it was fun more than anything else. He was a good kisser so I enjoyed it while it lasted. I liked this. I felt empowered that I was getting back at Adam this way. Fuck him, I thought naughtily. He hadn't given a damn about my feelings when he told everyone about what had happened between us and that I was a virgin.

I kissed him harder as anger and humiliation fizzed along my veins. I hoped this embarrassed him, I hoped what I was doing in front of half of the students made him feel the way I had felt. Only a few people had known I was a virgin and he had gone and made it common knowledge.
Bone broke our kiss slowly and looked at me, "*Damn*, baby! You can kiss me anytime."
I laughed and noticed that everyone was looking at us. I smiled inwardly and my gaze went to Adam.

His stare was lethal and cold. A bubble of nervousness settled in my tummy but I still felt better — well, I felt a bit better. It still didn't erase the fact that he had gobbed off so everyone knew my private business.
I nudged Bone's shoulder. "C'mon, I'll buy you a drink."

An hour or so later I made my way to the ladies. Ad's eyes were on me all the time and his glare was icy, but I didn't care. He was an idiot and he'd made me believe that he was something he wasn't. He didn't really care that we were over, he just cared about saving face. It wouldn't have surprised me if he had cheated on me. I thought about the times he had cancelled on me. He probably had.

Scott had been watching me with an equal amount of iciness as I danced with anybody I could and had fun, but he kept his distance. If I was honest, it bothered me. Our friendship meant a lot to me — he just got me and I missed that. I missed his smile, his tenderness. Okay, so he was the male equivalent of a slut, but he had a great personality. I wanted to hate him for adding to my bad week, for ignoring me, but I couldn't. Maybe I was just no good with guys?

My thoughts were interrupted abruptly as someone grabbed me and pulled me down the corridor and into the darkness, pushing me against a wall.
"You fuckin' slut!"
My eyes widened in alarm as I saw Ad's glazed expression and realised we were alone.
"You just showed me up in front of everyone and you're not gonna get away with it, Emma."
"And you think you can get away with what you did? You're a fake and you played me. What happened to the Adam that wanted a wife and kids, huh?"
He laughed, "I can't believe you swallowed that." His body pinned me against the wall and he yanked my hair back hard so I was forced to look at him.

I couldn't believe I had fallen for his lies. Why hadn't I seen him for what he was? My heart was pounding in alarm and fear. I had no idea what was going to happen.
"Let go of me, Adam," I said as sternly as I could as I struggled to get free. "Let go of me right now before…"

His mouth slammed down on mine. He was hurting me. I moved my head to try to shake him off but he brought his hands up to my face, trapping me in a vicelike grip.

I clawed at his back and brought my knee up between his legs.

"Ah!" he choked. "You fucking cunt!" He grabbed my hand and dragged me away from the wall and even deeper into the dark corridor.

I opened my mouth to scream as a hand grabbed my free arm and yanked hard, pulling me away and shielding me behind a body.

Scott.

Scott stalked up to Adam and punched him. Ad went straight to the floor but Scott went down after him, punching him again.

"Don't!" *Punch.* "You!" *Punch.* "Ever!" *Punch.* "Touch." He seized Ad by the shirt and pulled his face close to his. "Her again!" he roared, right into his face.

My hand flew over my open mouth, my heart pumping a thousand times a minute.

Scott was tense and his neck muscles were bulging to the point that I could see his veins. "Do you fuckin' hear me? Don't go near her again or I'll kill you." He shoved Ad away from him like he was some disgusting creature and stood up.

He turned to me, his chest heaving with great, angry breaths. His murderous eyes caught mine and I sucked in my breath. I had never seen him so full of hate.

He clenched my elbow and marched me out of the club through the back entrance.

Chapter Nineteen

Once we were outside he released me and aimed his furious glare at me. "Did he hurt you?" His voice was raspy, strained.

I shook my head with wide eyes, speechless.

He turned away jerkily and paced back and forth like a caged lion. "Motherfucking motherfucker," I heard him mutter a few times under his breath as he paced.

I wrapped my arms around myself, wishing he would calm down. I felt drained and shaky and cold. Scott was still pacing, his hands moving through his hair in agitation. I didn't know what to do or say.

He stopped abruptly with his back to me. I saw him take a deep breath, hold it for a few seconds and then exhale slowly, shakily.

"Scott?" I half-whispered, my voice trembling.

I didn't want to make him angrier. My plan of revenge had backfired on me and Scott had suffered for it, too. He had come to my rescue in a big way and I would be forever grateful to him. If he hadn't intervened when he did…A cold shiver ran through me. I didn't know what Adam would've done. To think that I had slept with him and spent so much time *alone* with him. My skin crawled at the thought of what he was capable of doing. I just wanted to go home and cry in the privacy of my bed.

When Scott didn't answer I spoke again. "I'm sorry, Scott," I whispered, "I'm so sorry." I shook my head and went to walk past him to go home but his hand shot out and he pulled me into him tightly.

He put his thick arms around me and buried his head in my neck. He held me until my shaking subsided and my body was warmed by his heat. I breathed him in. His smell comforted me. I felt safe. Safe was a word that I had never associated with Scott.

I don't know how long we stayed like that, but he finally pulled away and cupped my face.

"You don't have anything to be sorry for," he looked at me softly and brushed my hair off my forehead, "None of this was your fault Emma, do you understand?" His gaze was piercing mine, waiting for an answer.

I nodded, not trusting myself to speak.

"Do you know what could've happened in there? He could've..." he ground his jaw, "He could've hurt you so badly, babe. *Shit*, baby! Why did you rattle his cage like that?"

I lowered my lashes and tried to pull my face away but Scott held me gently and firmly, willing me not to hide my expression from him.

"I wanted to show him what it felt like to be humiliated." My voice was hoarse, clogged with tears. I closed my eyes and tried to lower my chin but Scott wouldn't let me hide and the sting in my eyes couldn't be denied. My mouth turned downwards and a sob escaped my lips as the tears came.

Scott's thumb darted out and wiped away the tears I was trying desperately to hold in. As more flowed he pulled me into him again and cradled me.

"I know it was s–stupid but he humiliated me!"

He sighed as his hold on me loosened. He took my cold hand in his hot one. "C'mon, lets go home."

We took a taxi back and Scott sent a text to Ash telling her that I had a headache but that he was with me.

He came into my apartment with me, led me to my bedroom and sat me on the edge of the bed. He knelt in front of me and took my heels off and then put me under the sheets and tucked me in.

"Scott?"

He looked up from what he was doing, his eyes soft, just how I loved them, his hair silky and thick and covering half of one eye.

My hand swept his hair back, "I missed you."

His eyes lit a little. "I missed you too, baby." He came to kneel beside the bed and stroked a gentle hand through my hair. "Do you want me to make you a hot cocoa?"

"No, I'm good but I…" I hesitated and let out a sigh. *Just say it!* "I really don't want you to leave me."

Scott sucked in a breath.

"I mean, can you just lay here with me? Just until I'm asleep." I didn't want to be alone tonight. What if Adam came in the night? He knew where we lived. He knew far too much about our lives, really, and I was frightened. I had had no idea that he could do something like that. I didn't know him at all.

"Of course, baby." He came around the bed and lay down next to me on his back. I got closer to him and put my head on his chest as his arm went around me.

We stayed like that, in silence, for a while. He had burst in like a knight in shining armour. I didn't know what to think anymore. Scott had got under my skin, and I had got under his a little, too. I missed him much more than I liked to admit, even to myself. There were no certainties when it came to love, no definites, just a lot of maybes, and I would be waiting for the day it ended. The thought of being heartbroken, the actual feeling of my emotions being so out of my control, was my darkest demon. I didn't want to end up like my mum. I wanted to avoid it at all costs — but what if the cost was just a different kind of unhappiness?

"Are you okay?" he asked suddenly, jolting me out of my thoughts.

"Yeah, I was just thinking."

"About what?" he asked as his hand came up to lie on mine, which was resting on his chest, over his heart. The steady thump was strong and soothing.

I looked down and saw crusted blood on his knuckles. "Scott, you're bleeding." I went to get up but he held me firm.

"It's not mine. What were you thinking?" he nudged.

I relaxed with a sigh. "About us," I said and saw him frown.

"What about us?" he whispered, his eyes searching.

"I was wondering if we're friends again."

He removed his arm, turned on his side so he was facing me and propped his head up. "Emma, I'm always your friend, but you know I want something more with you."

"Scott, I can't," I shook my head. I suppose I was secretly happy that he liked me that way but the fear of being broken like my mother was something that had been with me for far longer than the short time I had known him. "I'm sorry."

"Why," he pulled my face up to his, "Why, baby." He paused as my eyes widened. "What're you afraid of?"

"Nothing, I…I just…." I searched my feathery brain for an excuse but I couldn't come up with one, or lie blatantly to him while he was so focused on me. "I don't want to talk."

"Emma," Scott pleaded, "Tell me why. You can trust me."

I shook my head and looked away from him. "I don't want anything right now." That sounded stupid.

"You're lying to me. I'm not stupid, babe. I know when…" He stopped what he was about to say and breathed deeply. "You want me. You know it and I know it. Why are you fighting this?"

"Scott," I groaned, going to look away, but his hands came up to my face and he leaned over me.

"Stop it, Emma. Stop acting like all we have is friendship cos you know it's not. Look at me and tell me that I'm imagining this thing between us. If you can tell me that, to my face, then I promise I'll never bring it up again. I'll stop and move on." His gaze was scorching me, burning me from the inside out, the green of his eyes almost totally eclipsed by black.

Move on? That was exactly the kind of thing that made me fear giving in to Scott. He moved on almost every day. What made me so different? I knew that every girl that Scott took to his bed thought somewhere in their drunken or sober mind that maybe they could be the one to keep him. They all thought they would be Scott's first girlfriend. The trouble is that Scott isn't boyfriend material. I knew he had it in him but he just wouldn't settle and I didn't want to — no — I *refused* to be one of those girls that begged him to take them again — never.

Scott was already embedded in my heart, if I was honest with myself, and if I let it go any further I might just end up getting hurt. My mum's wan, unhappy face flitted behind my eyes and I hardened myself to him. When I got overwhelmed by my feelings, whether anger or hurt, I went overboard and it was as though I was watching myself react stupidly, without sense or a care for those I hurt in the process, but couldn't stop myself — like what had happened before mum moved us over here.

He was still watching me, waiting for me to speak, his jaw tight and his eyes focused and narrowed. *God, he's gorgeous!*
"Scott, you move on every day anyway," I teased but I didn't find it funny at all really.
He turned his face away from me, hiding his expression, and I wanted to pull him back. He never let me hide from him. "Does it bother you?" He studied me and waited for my answer, as though hanging on my every word.

"I think you're better than that. I happen to think you're pretty awesome actually, but you let yourself down. I don't understand why you sleep around. I don't think I ever will since you don't even seem to enjoy *doing* it." *Why did I just say that?* It was all true, though. He was awesome. When we argued, I hated it. When we were together, it was as though we pulled each other in like magnets whether we wanted to or not. I felt like I had known him for much longer than I had. He understood me somehow — he *knew* me.

"Only since you moved in." He waited for my reaction.
I frowned, "Since I moved in?"
"I haven't liked being with girls since you came."
I sighed, picking a bit of fluff off of his shirt. "Scott, you only want me because I've said no to you."
He sat up and grabbed me by the shoulders. "Is that what you think? Thats not the reason, Emma."
I shook my head. "It doesn't matter because I really need a friend right now. I want us to stay friends." I didn't think I could go through having sex again either. I cringed just thinking about it. "After everything that's happened with Adam and me the last week, I need a break."

"Did he hurt you?" he murmured, his breath held.
I knew what he was asking and I might as well be honest. It might help him change his mind about me if he knew I hated sex. "Yes, it hurt and I hated it." My cheeks burned. "I regretted it before it was over, and even more, I regretted that it was him." My eyes squinted with my scowl.
I looked at Scott and watched as anger flitted across his face. I wanted to forget about the whole thing.

Scott was silent for a long time. *What is he thinking?*
"Did you love him?"

I shook my head.

"Forget about him then."

Scott stayed until I fell asleep, but when I woke the next morning, he was gone.

Chapter Twenty

"He's telling everyone he got mugged outside Soundz by three huge men. Fucking asshole," Ash stomped with her mood. She was out for Adam's head.

It was Monday and I hadn't seen Ad yet and I didn't want to either. I wondered again how I could've been so blind to what he was really like, and I felt kind of stupid that I had been taken in by him. "I'll be happy if I never see him again. I still can't believe he did it."

We were walking to the cafeteria. I felt slightly nervous at the thought of seeing him again.

"I'm so sorry, Em. He did seem a bit up his own ass but I had no idea he would try something like that." Ash opened the cafeteria door and we walked in.

"It's okay. It's not your fault and nothing happened anyway. Scott got there before it got really ugly." I knew what would have happened if Scott hadn't intervened…

Speaking of Scott, he was sat at our usual table with Meg and Newton.

"There's our hero now." Ash faked a swoon but then froze. Her face turned red and her mouth curled.

Before I could stop her, Ash was marching over to Ad, who was watching her smugly. His face was one big bruise, which satisfied me — a lot.

Ash bunched her fists. "You fucking asshole!" The whole cafeteria came to a halt.

I ran to Ash's side and grabbed her left arm to drag her away. I saw Scott out of the corner of my eye, he was rising out of his seat and coming over, his face a wary mask.

"Come on, he's not worth it," I sneered at him.

"Fuck you!" Adam was talking to me now.

"Don't you *dare* talk to her that way. I bet everyone believes that story you spun but I want everyone to know what you're capable of." Ash tugged her arm out of mine as Ad stood up from his chair and squared up to her.

"Try it, bitch." He was about an inch away from Ash's face now, with his fists at his sides.

"Sit down, Adam, before you hurt yourself," Scott said from my side.

"Tell Ashley to get out of my face and I will."

Before I knew what was happening, Ash had pulled her arm back and let it swing full pelt at Ad's already bruised face.

"Ah!" he shouted in pain, "Cunt!"

Scott darted behind Ash, looped his arm around her tummy and pulled her behind him out of harm's way.

"You even blink in her direction again and I'll kill you!" Ash spat furious venom at him.

I looked around quickly. I didn't want Ash getting into trouble over this.

Scott was between Ad and Ash now, looking Adam squarely in the eye. "Sit down." Scott's authoritative voice brooked no argument.

"I get it," Ad said, "You want her for yourself."

Everyone looked at Scott in shock, which made Ad feel braver. "I've seen the way you look at her."

"Shut your mouth and leave," Scott growled.

"Do you hear that everyone?" Ad shouted at the top of his voice. "Scott's in love. Isn't that sweet?"

Everyone looked between me and Scott and I stared down at my toes, red faced. It wasn't true.

"You don't know what you're talking about," Scott denied.

"Don't be pissed that I nailed her first."

I gasped.

Scott looked at me with a menacing grin and then spun back to face Ad with a fist that connected with the underside of his jaw.

Ad roared in pain and Scott took my hand and led me calmly away from the cafeteria. We exited to the sound of applause and cheers.

He didn't say a word but just led me outside, stopping only when we reached the place where we had kissed.

He pulled me into him. "Are you okay, baby?"

I nodded and pulled away. "I'm okay. I can't understand what I ever saw in that disgusting excuse for a human." I scrunched my nose. "Everyone will think we're…" I cleared my throat, "You know."

"Is that a bad thing?"

"Yes, it's a bad thing! I don't want any more attention on me. Last week it was my virginity and now it's going to be this." I buried my face in my hands.

"It's not that bad, Em." Scott seemed offended. "You could do worse. You could still be with that loser."

I looked at him. "I just don't want to be talked about, and now everyone will think that we're secretly together and you are always with some fucking girl." Now this week would be another week full of whispers and stares.

"I got that." His voice was harsh now. "I know you don't want anyone or me," he swiped a hand through his hair. "You really know how to make a guy feel shitty."

"You don't need a confidence booster, Scott. There isn't a girl in this place that doesn't want to be with you."

"There's you."

"I…" I didn't know what to say. I didn't want to agree or disagree with him when he was in a mood like this.

"You what?"

"It doesn't matter." I crossed my arms and looked at him.

"You need to stay away from Adam," Scott said.

"I'll stay far away, don't worry."

"Good." Scott held out his hand. "C'mon, I'll walk you to your next class."

I looked at his hand and shook my head. "I don't want people to get the wrong idea about us, and they will after that," I nodded towards the cafeteria.

Scott sighed.

We started to walk. "I don't want to dent your reputation as a one-night man," I teased, not finding the funny side. It wasn't really funny — the way he was the total opposite of what I wanted or needed him to be.

Something occurred to me and I stopped, pulling on his arm. "You won't get into trouble for hitting him will you?"

He put his hands in his pockets and shrugged. "I don't care if I do, but I don't think he'll want it out what he almost did. You can still report him, you know."

"Hi, Scott."

I rolled my eyes as another fan came up to him.

"I saw you play the other night and I just wanted to say," she grabbed both his arms and turned him towards her and away from me, giving me a sly smile, "you were just fantastic."

"Thanks, glad you liked it." Scott seemed to love the attention and he put his arm around her shoulder.

Why did it feel like that had been for my benefit?

The girl smiled triumphantly in my direction and then ignored me completely. "I'm going to every gig from now on."

Rocked Under ~ Cora Hawkes

Ugh! She was really laying it on thick.

"That's what I like to hear, babe," Scott grinned at her beautifully and I felt a pang very close to jealousy deep in my gut.

"I'm just going to go on to class. See you later?" I asked.

"I think he'll be seeing *me* later," the brunette answered, screwing her nose and curling her mouth while eyeballing me from top to toe.

It annoyed the hell out of me that she thought that I wanted Scott and couldn't get him. Her rudeness grated on me so much that I wanted to snatch Scott out of her hands. Some girls were unbelievable, and she only made herself look stupid.

I frowned at her as she continued to give me her best death glare. Then, all of a sudden, a laugh escaped me. What did Scott see in girls like this? She was way over the top.

"What's funny?" She put a hand on her hip.

I couldn't help it — I giggled even more as she pouted like a spoiled little girl.

I shook my head and walked away. Scott was watching me but I didn't care. The giggles were upon me and if I stayed there, I knew they wouldn't go away

The week passed slowly and I didn't seen Ad at all, which was a good thing. People talked about Scott and me being together. I wasn't exactly Miss Popular right then, with all the girls who adored Scott out for my head. They thought I had taken him off the market but it wasn't true, and when asked I said it was just a rumour. Scott found the whole thing funny and wasn't helping by not being his usual flirty self.

I had a feeling he was doing it on purpose to add to the rumours. I supposed when I thought about it that, it wasn't really a bad rumour. I was being touchy by saying it really bothered me because it didn't, apart from all the abuse I was getting from girls

— well, not abuse, more envious stares and questions. Oh, the questions... "Is he a good kisser?"..."What's he like in bed?"

"Why can't you go back to being flirty Scott?" I huffed on Thursday after classes had ended for the day.

Scott put his arm around my shoulder and aimed his gorgeous smile my way. "I *am* flirting — with you."

"Oh, you're hilarious! You know what I mean." I removed his arm.

Scott's face dropped slightly for a split second and then his easy grin was back in place. "Okay, okay." A wicked grin spread over his face and I wondered what he was about to do.

Nothing could have prepared me... He grabbed the nearest girl in his arms and started to kiss her, full on the mouth — and on and on and on. It seemed to last forever and I watched in slow motion as Scott snogged the face off some little, red-headed beauty.

My heart kicked and a lump formed in my throat as I watched in shock as his hand crept down to her butt and squeezed, pulling her closer. He broke off abruptly and Redhead looked dazed.

"There, is that what you wanted?" His voice was husky and the girl was ignored.

I smiled, but I felt like my face was cracking, and I'm sure he could tell. "I..." I couldn't look at him any longer so I turned my face away. "Yeah," I replied in a small voice.

"Are you okay?" he asked and I looked at him for a moment.

"Yes," I said after a minute. "I have to go. I'll see you later." I rushed off with the burn of Scott's curious gaze on my back.

Much later, I was sitting at the usual table in Macy's. Ash, Newton and Meg were having a heated debate on whether Adam would leave me alone now. Why couldn't they stop talking about it? Ad had been absent since the scene in the cafeteria on Monday.

I was relieved, although I had an awful feeling that it wasn't over with him, not by a long shot.

From Under came on stage and Scott raised us a hand in greeting, his gaze staying longer on mine with a thoughtful look. I wished I could get into his head and see what he was thinking. I was near the stage dancing around while he sang and strummed on his guitar. The way he held the mic…His hands were the best hands I had seen on a man. Even his stance was sexy, masculine. I loved it when he sang to me, his gaze seeking out mine in a sea of hundreds of other eyes.

I was tipsy by the time he came off stage, He was immediately surrounded by six girls, all vying for his attention.
I knew how they felt and I wanted his attention on me. I frowned at my errant thought — I shouldn't have been thinking like that at all. I waited for him to come over to me like he usually did, but I waited and waited until I finally saw him pick one of the girls and lead her onto the dance floor. He didn't even look my way, not even once. I felt stupid, dumb for waiting for him and thinking that he would come. I had no claim on him. He didn't belong to me, he belonged to no one. Scott would never be any one woman's man.

I tried to remind myself that I didn't really want him and that I didn't wake up every day thinking about him or wonder where he was when I wasn't with him. But I was lying to myself. I was falling in love with him. I became still and a cold sensation crept down my back as I realised that I was actually being honest with myself. I had been on a path that led to heartbreak for a while now, and it had happened without me knowing.

Maybe I wasn't fully there yet, but I was going to be if I didn't do something. The past flashed through my mind in a succession of painful images and expressions and I gripped the edge of the bar as my heart hammered against my ribs in fear — fear of what would happen if I didn't take control now, fear of losing control out of pain and hurt, fear of hurting the people I loved.

I looked at Scott again briefly. He had his tongue down the girl's throat. Pain and jealousy created an overwhelming need to pull him away from her. I needed to get away. I wanted time alone to gather my thoughts. I went over to Ash and told her I had a headache and I was going home to get an early night. I didn't say goodbye to Scott and I didn't look back at him again as I made my way to the exit.

My phone buzzed as I lay in bed hours later, unable to sleep. I reached for it blindly, too lazy to move my head.

Scott: *R u ok? Ash said u have a headache.*

No kiss on the end, although I always sent him one on the end of my texts — but that was Scott all over, no emotion, just sex. I decided to ignore it. With any luck he would think I was asleep. I hated this. I hated that I wanted him but was too afraid to have him. Why was nothing ever simple for me? Now I was feeling sorry for myself — I loathed self-pity.
Another buzz. Another text message.

Scott: *I hope ur awake cos im comin down if u dont return my txt in 2 mins. Wanna know u got home safe!*

Me: *Im ok. In bed. C u 2moro.*

I left out the kiss. He never gave them back to me anyway.

Scott: *Sweet dreams!*

Rocked Under ~ Cora Hawkes

I was sure he wouldn't be dreaming or getting much sleep at all tonight. Agitation gripped me in its annoyingly firm hold and I turned onto my back to stare at the ceiling. I needed to stop thinking with my heart and start thinking about a practical way of avoiding falling for him completely, because this wasn't me — I didn't let my heart get to me over guys, ever. Maybe I was only delaying the inevitable? *No!* my mind screamed, *Do not go there — do not give in to it.* But it was hard.

Scott had everything going for him — looks, sex appeal, charisma. He was kind, could be tender and gentle at times. He was protective, a great musician, a loyal friend, and had great hair and eyes that a girl could look into forever. The list went on, so I concentrated instead on his bad points. He slept around and was afraid of commitment, those were the two bad things that counted as six. He was moody at times, he…I was running out of ideas already. I needed a distraction, something to set me on the right track again, because loving Scott would be the worst mistake I could ever make.

Chapter Twenty-one

The next day, things were almost back to normal. The rumour that Scott and I were having a thing had almost completely died, with Scott flirting last night with everything that had boobs. It was no great wonder. I say *almost* because I was now getting quite a few pitying looks from my fellow students. *Great!* I huffed and crossed my arms. I wasn't happy with Scott. I wasn't happy at all. But I would be okay, I told myself, and I repeated it over and over. Even though Scott had taken over most of my waking thoughts I could still pull myself out of this. I still had time.

Half the day was over and I hadn't seen him yet, but as I made my way to the cafeteria I knew that was about to change. It came sooner than I thought as I neared the cafeteria and saw Scott with a girl. He had her against the wall outside the door with his head buried in her neck. My heart missed a beat as a heavy weight settled in my stomach. I met the girls gaze. She grinned smugly at me and ran her fingers through his hair in a possessive way that rankled so much that my step faltered and she giggled at my near fall.

I wanted to go right up to her smug face and bash the grin off it, but that would mean I cared so I smiled politely as I pushed the cafeteria door open.
"Hi, Scott," I flung over my shoulder in the most average voice I could, just because she had pissed me off. I pathetically high-fived myself inwardly as I saw Scott pull away from the girl at the sound of my voice. I knew it was childish, but I didn't care. The bitch had thought she was getting one over on me.

"Hey, wait up." Scott grabbed my arm to slow me down. He turned me towards him." Are you feeling better?" He had a questioning frown on his face, showing his concern.

"Yes, thank you," I smiled up at him.

"You could've told me you were leaving early last night — I would've walked you back. Don't leave alone again."

He was telling me off now? Ordering me to *not* leave alone? Oh no — no way!

My back stiffened. He had no right to speak to me like he owned me, no right at all, and he needed to know that — this protective thing needed to stop. "Stop being so protective," my voice was sharper than usual, "You're my friend — you can advise, but you can't tell me what to do."

He frowned deeper into my eyes with his jaw tensing, "Sorry for caring."

"I don't belong to you. In fact, *no one* belongs to you," I sniped at him, and then felt bad. Why didn't I know when to keep my mouth shut?

"Are you mad at me?" His eyebrows shot up in surprise. "Are you mad at me because I've done what you asked me to do and gone back to being 'flirty' me?"

"I...No!" *Yes!* But I would never let him know and I wasn't supposed to slip up like that. *Oh, me and my big mouth!* I looked away, willing my cheeks not to glow as I noticed we were getting odd looks from a few of the other students.

"You wanna know what I think, Emma?"

"Not here, Scott." I pleaded with my eyes.

He closed his mouth into a straight, tight line and grabbed my elbow to take me to our usual table, which was empty.

We sat down and Scott studied me with a slight frown, his head lolling to the side slightly.

"What?" I asked. He was studying me like something he had never seen before.

"Why're you acting like this?"

"Like what?"
Scott shook his head and looked down. "I don't get you, babe."

We were interrupted as Meg sat down.

"Hey! Have you heard about the frat party?" Meg sat down excitedly. "I just spoke to Kyle Larson and he asked me to ask you," she looked at me pointedly, "to go!" She almost squealed.

Kyle Larson was a rich frat boy who I had noticed hanging around more and more lately. He seemed a nice enough guy but I had barely said two words to him in the time I had been there.

"I barely know him. Why does he want me to go?"

"Isn't it obvious?" Scott's voice was harsh.
I frowned at him and he stood quickly, "I'm getting my lunch."
"Wow, what's up his cute ass?" Meg asked as she watched him walk away. "Anyway, back to Kyle. He likes you, dummy!"

"Oh," I said as I looked down at my twiddling fingers. Kyle was a good-looking guy. I looked over at Scott, who was surveying me. I could feel him watching me, just like I always felt it, like a weird, messed-up sixth sense or something.

"*Oh?*" Meg mimicked. "Is that all you can say? He's smoking hot, Em! Are you *blind*? And he wants you to go so you're going, so I can go," she smiled sweetly, batting her eyelashes.

I chuckled in spite of my mood. "When is this party?" I asked, avoiding the subject of Kyle Larson completely for the moment, although I was girl enough to know he was handsome. He wasn't Scott, but he was nice in a totally different way. *Stop comparing!*

I looked over at Scott again and he was talking to another girl. She was taking all his smiles and intense stares. Jealousy was a savage bitch and she was biting me in the ass.

"Tonight. Ash and Newton aren't going so please, *please* say you'll come with me."

Rocked Under ~ Cora Hawkes

Wow. There was nothing like feeling second best, but then I supposed I could go. A bit of away time from Scott is what I needed and I would be going home for Christmas soon, so if I could make it to the end of the term then I would be okay.

"I'll be ready around eight," I told Meg and watched her bounce and clap in her seat. I frowned, knowing what she was up to. "Who are you looking forward to seeing then? New crush, Meg?" I asked.

"Maybe," she hedged while examining her fingernails.

Scott slipped back into his seat and put both elbows on the table.

"I persuaded her to go," Meg told Scott. "I would ask you too but I know you're at Macy's tonight aren't you?"

Scott's mouth tightened as he nodded and shifted his eyes to me.

"You know, Kyle's parents are rich. He's probably the richest guy here." She tried and failed to get me interested.

Kyle was probably a spoilt rich kid. I had known people like him all too well most of my life and knew that they were the worst sorts. I didn't want to stereotype, but when you live around rich people you realise that nothing is as it seems — friendships are usually fake and are there purely to keep up appearances while people stab each other in the back.

"Hey, baby." My ears hurt as I heard the sickly sweet voice and looked up.

The same girl Scott had been snogging in the hall was manoeuvring herself between Scott's legs, ready to dump herself onto his lap.

Scott looked at me and caught my scowl. He put his hands on her hips and pushed her off. "Go the fuck away." He swatted her away as though she was an annoying insect buzzing around him.

The girl's mouth opened and then closed. Maybe she was trying to tell him what a dick he was, but whatever she was about to say was swallowed as she changed her mind and stomped off.

Scott looked at me. The surprise on my face must have shown — I couldn't believe he had just turned her down.

I looked at Meg, who was shaking her head. "One day, Scott, you're going to fall in love and I hope she's the one to say no to you and makes you chase her forever. You're such a jerk sometimes."

Scott frowned and looked at me quickly before resting his gaze back on Meg. "She'd have to be some girl to make that happen."

I needed a plan. But it seemed that every time I had one I forgot it as soon as I saw Scott. It was like all logic and intelligence went out the window and all I could see or think about was him. If I felt like this about him now, what would I feel like if I was actually with him? And how would I feel when he betrayed me, which I knew would happen eventually with him? If I was anything like my mum, I would fall hard into a chasm of blankness and misery that it would take years to climb out of. That wasn't going to happen to me. *No way.*

"Emma!" I turned and saw Kyle jogging towards me after my last class. His almost-black hair was cropped short and dark, chocolate eyes sparkled with his smile. He stopped in front of me and I had to look up a good way to see his face.

"Hi! Kyle, right?"

"Yeah. Emma?" he asked and then rolled his eyes at himself. "Obviously you are because you turned when I called your name." He smiled and then actually blushed.

With his blush he got my full attention. This wasn't what I had been expecting at all. Usually guys like him were sure of themselves and confident — conceited. I giggled at his floundering.

"I…Uh…Are you coming tonight?" Hope lit his features.

I looked at him and studied his expression, trying to gauge his personality. He seemed genuine, but so had Adam. P*roceed with caution*, I told myself. "Yes. Thanks for inviting me along." *God!* I sounded so British.

"Great!" His whole face relaxed into an easy smile with twinkling puppy eyes. "See you later then."

I walked away with a faint grin on my face. He was really nice. He had a boyish quality about him that I found cute — an innocence that seemed so rare with rich kids. I would go tonight just to see where things went and at least have some fun.

Chapter Twenty-two

By the time we had arrived the party was already in full swing. The music blared out from speakers that were hanging from the ceiling and the house was filled wall-to-wall with people holding red plastic cups. Couples were making out on the stairs, ascending slowly towards the bedrooms.

We went to get a drink as soon as we got there. There were a few people I knew from my classes but most were juniors or seniors. I hoped Adam wasn't there. If he was, I was leaving. This was my first frat party and I intended to relish it. We queued for our drinks and finally got one each. For the next hour we chatted, mingled and drank.

"Hi!" Kyle was behind me and whispering near my ear.

I spun round and looked all the way up at him. He was as tall as Scott — *stop it, Emma!* "Hi, yourself," I grinned.

"Do you want to dance with me?" The way he asked so shyly had me saying yes instantly.

He put his arms around my waist and moved with me, but kept a distance between us that not a lot of guys would have done.

"You look amazing."

"How come you wanted me to come tonight?"

"I..I like you," he said simply. "You're different."

"Why didn't you ever talk to me then? You seem to talk to everyone else."

"I don't know," he looked away, "You seem so out of reach sometimes, you know, unattainable."

"Wow. I didn't realise I was that bad," I laughed.

"You're not bad, you're beautiful and you seem like a genuine person."

I thought about that for a moment and didn't like it when I thought about my feelings for Scott. Was I a genuine person? Or was I trying to plan my life based on safety instead of morals and values?

"What are you thinking?"

"Huh?"

"What has your eyebrows all drawn in like that?" He was studying me with those chocolate eyes.

"Nothing," I smiled, "This is a great party."

"Your accent is so good to listen to. Keep talking. Do you like it here?" he asked politely.

"I like it much better than home."

"Good, because we like you too," his toothy grin brightened his face.

I giggled and moved further into his arms.

An hour later I was merrily wiggling my butt with Meg on the space that was a make-shift dance floor. Kyle had left me but he was never far away.

"Who wants to play Spin the Bottle?" A guy's voice rose above the music.

"Come on, Em." Meg grabbed my hand and tugged me towards where the game was starting.

I giggled like a naughty school child when she sat me down next to her — it was a game that I hadn't participated in since I was a young teenager.

I looked for Kyle. Our eyes met and he came straight over to sit in on the game when he saw that I was playing.

I giggled again, my brain fuzzy from drink.

"Mind if I join in?"

I froze as I heard Scott's voice. *Bugger!* What was he doing here? I didn't think he'd been invited.

The girls squealed with delight while most of the guys groaned — but not Kyle, his cheeky grin was firmly in place and his eyes were twinkling at me again.

I smiled a hello to Scott and turned my attention to Kyle, although I was very conscious of Scott sitting there watching me.

There were nine girls and eleven guys sitting in a circle on the floor.

"The rules are simple — when the bottle picks you, you wait for it to pick your partner, and then both of you go to centre of the circle. The kiss must last for at least twenty seconds, and they must be real kisses. You can refuse a partner but there will be a dare if you do. Ready?"

I could feel a wave of anger hitting me and it was definitely coming from Scott. Why was he pissed off with me *now*? As far as I could tell, I hadn't done anything wrong except for being there.

The bottle was spinning and it stopped at a blonde girl sitting two away from me. The bottle spun again, picking her a partner. It was a guy I had never seen before. The blonde girl seemed a bit disappointed but she accepted without whining. They kissed thoroughly for a full twenty seconds to whistles and claps before breaking apart, red faced.

The game went on and I froze as the bottle landed on me and was then spun again to pick out my partner. It went around and around, letting fate decide who should or shouldn't kiss me. It slowed and stopped at Kyle. I gave Scott a sideways glance and saw that his jaw was grinding and he was glaring at Kyle.

Kyle was totally ecstatic and made his way to the centre of the circle.

He cupped my face, the way Scott had done, and brought his lips to mine.

"I've been waiting for this," he whispered just before his lips met mine in a surprisingly gentle caress. His tongue entered my mouth, stroking gently. In and out his tongue went, and I found I was liking it, so I deepened the kiss by running my fingers into his hair and pulling him closer. We went past the time limit and I heard people shouting at us to get a room.
We pulled apart.
"Wow," he breathed and smiled gently at me.

Scott looked outraged now and I swallowed, hoping that fate wouldn't be so cruel as to pair me with him.
The game started again and I kissed two other guys but none were like Kyle's kiss. Kyle also had a few more kisses, as did Scott. I didn't watch, but I knew he was watching me for a reaction. I didn't give him one.
Then, Fate was a bitch. The bottle landed on Scott, and then picked me for his partner.

I trembled slightly as I met his hard stare.
I matched him stare for stare. How dare he be angry with me for no good reason? I was just having fun, like he did all the time. I went to the centre of the circle to meet him. I plastered a smile on my face as I met his hard eyes.
His hands went into my hair, making shivers run along my spine, and I prepared myself for an angry kiss. I closed my eyes and I felt surprise as his lips met mine softly. Heat shot through me and I felt an overwhelming need to get closer to him. His lips were trembling slightly but his kiss was hardly there, like he was afraid I'd break or bolt or something, and it wasn't enough. I wanted him closer. I wanted more than what he was giving me.

The punishing softness went on and on until I felt coiled tightly and shook with the force of preventing myself from springing free. His tongue slipped into my mouth slowly and I groaned low in my throat. The vibration alerted me to the fact that I was losing it. I broke the kiss. He had purposely teased me and tried to make me lose it. I pulled away from him while dodging his stare as best as I could, but I failed. He was frowning slightly but smiled as everyone cheered. I put a plastic grin on my face and stood shakily.

"I'm out." I walked away to go get another, much-needed, drink. Once I had got one I rested against a wall, watching the general madness now that almost everyone was drunk. I looked into my cup, raised it to my lips and swallowed the whole lot.
"Are you okay?" Kyle stood in front of me.
"Yeah," I smiled. "Dance with me?"
He smiled, "You don't need to ask."
"Oh wait, I need another drink first."

Dancing with Kyle was comfortable and we were moving very close together. I knew Scott was there somewhere but my mind was woolly with drink and I no longer cared. I would think tomorrow.
All of a sudden, Kyle swooped down and caught my lips. His kiss was a statement of want and lust. I let him take me away into it and I noticed he was moving me off the dance floor and nearer to the stairs.

I felt hazy desire start to take hold of me as he caught me around my waist and pulled me close.
"You're so beautiful. I want you so much, but not like this, not while you're so drunk." I didn't want to hear it so I grabbed his face and pulled him in to me to try to make him forget his words. I needed this, I thought hazily. I needed this to forget about Scott.
I deepened our kiss and grabbed his butt to pull his hips into me.

"I know you want me, Kyle." My voice sounded slurred, my head was dizzy. I moaned as I kissed him again.

Suddenly I was being yanked away and before I knew it, Scott had punched Kyle and was dragging me out the door.

"What the *fuck* are you doing?" I screeched at him.

"Taking you home." His voice was tight, his face a mask of cold anger.

"I don't want to go! I want to go and see if Kyle's okay," I whined.

"Shut up, Emma."

"Let her go, Scott," I heard Kyle say. He had followed us out of the house.

"Go back inside, Larson." Scott was super-angry.

I didn't want Kyle to get hurt again because of me.

"Not without her!" He grabbed Scott by his shirt.

"You have three seconds to remove your hand, Larson," Scott growled.

"Kyle, it's fine," I said in a rush.

"No, it isn't, Em. He can't treat you this way." Kyle's temper was rising.

"It's okay. I'll be fine." I tried to placate him. The last thing I wanted was for them to fight over me. I wasn't worth it — if only they realised that.

"She's not yours, Scott. What gives you the right?"

"That's none of your business." Scott gritted his teeth.

"Please, Kyle. I'll see you tomorrow. Just go back inside. Scott's going to take me home."

"You trust *him?*" Kyle looked incredulous now.

"Yes," I looked down, "I do." I had just given away too much.

Kyle thought for a minute, dropped his hand from Scott's shirt and looked at me.

"I'll call you tomorrow." He looked at Scott. "If anything happens to her, I'll know." He looked at me one last time, then turned away.

Scott started pulling me along with him again.

"What the *hell*, Scott?" I shouted in frustration.

He walked me to a waiting taxi and bundled me inside.

He handed the driver some money and gave him our address. We sat in silence until we reached our building — but my mind was not quiet.

Chapter Twenty-three

He wouldn't let me go to my place so he took me up to his. He opened the door and turned the lights on low. I didn't sit but stood there watching him.

"Why did you do that?" I asked him, quietly now.

"You're wasted. I'm not gonna let any asshole touch you when you're like that."

"What gives you the right to decide who I sleep with and when?" I was right in his face. I was angry, frustrated with him, and I wanted him to stop being so protective.

"I happen to fuckin' care about you!" he shouted back at me.

"You care?" I laughed cruelly. "Don't make me laugh! You really showed me how much you cared tonight!" I was angry at him for not letting me forget him.

"Stop it, Emma!" He grabbed my arms and his eyes softened. "I stopped you from making a mistake, that's all."

"Oh right, so it's okay for you to sleep with anything with a vagina but it's not okay for me to sleep with one guy? What's *wrong* with you?" I took a breath and lowered my voice. "You don't own me, you're my friend, but I don't even know if you're that anymore," I finished quietly.

He dropped his hands and turned away from me. His hand went through his hair and he sighed. "You," he turned and pointed a finger at me, "are driving me fuckin' crazy." He started walking towards me.

"Stay away from me." I put a hand out to ward him off but he kept coming until the backs of my legs hit the couch and I tumbled over.

He bent down and put his hands either side of my head and brought his mouth close to mine. I leaned back further away from him but ended up almost lying down.

He came closer, lowering his body to mine. Fire shot through me as his body heat filled the gap between us and penetrated my cool skin. My heart raced while an ache started low down.

I bit my lip to keep myself from moaning in pleasure at his closeness and clenched my fists by my sides so I wouldn't touch him. I wanted to, badly.

"Why not me?" I heard him whisper.

His eyes held pain and need in them as they penetrated mine. It tore at me, but this could never happen.

"Why?" he urged, "Why do you let everyone else close but me? What're you afraid of?"

That was the second time he had asked me that question and I couldn't answer, only close my eyes against his overpowering need.

"I don't understand, Emma, I fuckin'...." he stopped abruptly, closed his eyes and shook his head. "I don't understand what's going on here. I don't understand you." He sighed and got up off me.

He turned his back to me and I sat up straight. I looked at his back and felt like a bitch again.

"Scott?" My whisper sounded loud in the silence. I wanted to console him but I knew I couldn't be the one to do it. This was how it was between us. We couldn't ever be friends now, there was too much there.

"I'm sorry." I stood then. I needed to leave. "I'm just gonna go." I felt sad and I had sobered up enough to feel his frustration.

I paused and looked at Scott's back for a minute. I felt an urge, so strong, to go to him, put my arms around him and say to hell with it all. He looked so lonely and sad.

I sighed and turned away. My feet started carrying me to the door.

"Fuck this." I heard the words and turned.

Scott stalked towards me with pure intent in his eyes. He grabbed me and slammed his mouth onto mine. He kissed me like a man who had gone without food. His tongue was duelling with mine in an age-old dance that had my head spinning and everything became unclear as I felt an overwhelming need rise up in me. He left my mouth to bury his head in the crook of my neck. My arms went around him to stop myself from falling to the floor.

My body was shaking with anticipation. He picked me up and carried me. His lips met mine again as he walked with me. The next moment I was laid on his bed, but I ignored it as his kiss slowed and gentled into a slow rhythm that melted my insides and curled my toes. He lowered his body over mine slowly, letting me get used to his weight. I felt him trembling ever so lightly at the restraint he was exerting.

"I want you so much," he whispered into my mouth while he moved his hips into mine. "Let me show you how it can be." His mouth rained kisses all over my face and eyes.

I groaned and held on to him. My heart was hammering against my chest. Heat pooled between my legs and I opened them to him.

"Please, baby, even if it's just once. I need you, now." His hands crept to the fastening on my top and I froze.

Just once? What was I doing?

"*Oh, God!*" I cried and he looked at me.

I watched as the passion in his eyes turned to hurt and then to anger. He stood abruptly.

"I'm sorry but I can't," I whispered and buried my face in my hands. I knew the tears would come soon. He wanted me just once.

Just once. There was no point in telling him that I wasn't a 'just once' kind of girl because he wouldn't change for me.

"You're sorry?" He turned and grabbed his hair in his fist. I looked at his back and I could see and feel the frustration, anger and rejection radiating from him. I knew in that moment that we could never be just friends. All we did was hurt one another and I had to stop it. For both of us, I had to put an end to what we had, even though I wasn't sure what that was.

I knew I loved him, but I wasn't sure what he was feeling and Scott hadn't said anything about how he felt. He just wasn't capable of being with one girl like I needed him to be — like I had to have. If we went further then I knew that, for me, there would be no consolation. For me there would be a lifetime of pain, a lifetime of comparing all the future men in my life to him.

Scott wasn't someone that I would get over, ever. The other girls he slept with didn't know the real Scott, they just saw a hot guy on a stage, a guy who gave them a good time in bed and a guy that they could brag about. But I knew the person behind the face and I knew that he was beautiful inside and out. His downfall was the fact that he couldn't stay with one girl. He couldn't be loyal. I knew what my future entailed and I wanted to be happy. I didn't want to fall into the same trap as my mum had. For myself and for her, I would do the right thing, the only thing I could do. I wanted to be able to show my stupid dad how it was supposed to be.

Scott turned to look at me and I sat up straighter to meet his gaze.

"You want this, too," he accused, his voice rough.

"No, Scott, I don't." I was pleased at the strength in my voice but I almost faltered when his expression changed to pain.

"You're driving me fuckin' crazy, babe. I don't know why you can't just…"

Rocked Under ~ Cora Hawkes

"Just what, Scott?" I paused, "Sleep with you? Add to the mile-long list of girls you've already had?" I sniped, starting an argument.

He looked shocked at my words.
"I could never be with you, Scott." I looked him straight in the eye, my throat squeezed painfully when I saw his brows draw together in pain. I hardened myself to it. This was for the best. "We will never be together so just stop this. I thought we could be friends but I was wrong. I don't know how I could make my feelings more obvious to you. I've told you that I'm not yours but you still treat me as if I am! It stops now. All this has got to stop."

Silence stretched as we stared each other down. I was almost shaking with the effort of keeping my gaze steady and hard.
"You're lying." He was right but he could never know that. "I know you are and this whole situation is fucked up." His hands made fists.
"Fucked up? You're the one that has a different girl here every night."
"How do you know? I'm actually not as bad as you think I am."
"Oh, please! Don't even try to tell me that I'm wrong."
"Don't lie to me and tell me that we have nothing because I see it in your face."

"Really? Why would I lie? Let's face it — if I really wanted you that way, I could've had you anytime." I cringed mentally. I sounded like a total bitch. It was okay if he hated me, it would make things easier, but hurting him was like hurting myself.
"I don't believe you. I *know* you. I *know* that this isn't you. I know you want me too. I know every expression. I know when you lie and I know when you're hiding something and," he squinted at me, "I know when you're afraid."

I looked away from him, this wasn't working out as well as I'd hoped it would. "I won't be with you because you sleep with anyone. You're not choosy about who you're with. You have no morals and I," I took a breath, "can do better."

He rocked backwards as if I'd slapped him hard. I kept my stony expression plastered to my face as if it was my lifeline, the only thing keeping me from crumbling.

I felt awful for hurting him. After the shock of what I'd just said, his face changed to a mask of cold disdain.

He started to open his mouth to say something but instead came at me so fast I flinched. I thought he would hit me.

He grabbed the tips of my shoulders and shook me in anger.

"Why'd you string me along?" he said through gritted teeth. "Why did you let me think that…?" He released me and stood over me. "You know what?" his eyes had turned colder than I'd ever seen them, like splintered emeralds encased in ice, "I fucking hate you." His voice held more contempt and conviction than I had ever heard from him. With a last glare he turned and slammed the door on his way out.

I sat there motionless, unable to move, unable to think, just numb, staring into space going over and over in my head the things that had been said, the different expressions on his face. I sat there for a long time, knowing that Scott would not be coming back for a good while.

He hated me and my insides felt squeezed and coiled, ready to release the pain that was bubbling and boiling just beneath my skin.

He hated me. He didn't really give a shit anyway, I told myself. It was probably all to get me on my back. My eyes stung as the first few tears streaked down my face and off my jaw. It was better this way but it hurt like hell. My body was still shaking with the force of my sobs when I heard the door open.

I froze and looked towards the door. A figure much like Scott's stood there looking back at me, frozen. It was Scott's dad. I scrambled to my feet.

"Hi," his voice was pleasant, "Are you one of Scott's friends?"
I nodded, "I was just leaving." My voice was raw and shaky.
Scott's dad frowned, "Are you okay?"
"Yeah, I…Scott's not here, he went out, so I'm gonna go."
"You're welcome to stay and wait for him, you know. I don't bite. Whats your name?" he smiled at me and his face was so much like Scott's that it was like a punch in the stomach. Scott would never smile at me like that again.
"It's Emma. I can't stay. It's late."
"Ah, British Emma," he smiled, "It's nice to finally meet you."

Finally meet me? Scott had told him about me? I made my way stiffly to the door and turned back to him. "It was nice to finally meet you too," I said, not forgetting my manners.

"Are you sure you're alright?" He watched me with curious eyes that were so much like Scott's.

"Yes, I'm fine…Um…Scott shouldn't be long." I opened the door and walked away with a quick 'bye'.

Chapter Twenty-four

A week later, I went home for Christmas. I hadn't seen Scott since the night I ended it our friendship, or whatever it was. I had been avoiding anything familiar with him. Ash had told me that he was drunk every night and sleeping around. I didn't want to hear it but I couldn't say anything to her about it. He had people back every night and he cranked the music up loud. I could hear girls giggling and then I'd hear them creep out the next morning. It hurt like hell, but I had done it — I had been the one to cut the ties, so I couldn't moan, and I had no right to any bad feelings but I still couldn't help it.

No one knew about Scott and I, so there was really nobody to talk to. I definitely couldn't off-load on Ash. I didn't want to admit that I had gone and done what I said I would never do and fall ass over tit for him. I tried to act normal, but I think Ash knew something was bothering me and was waiting for me to tell her myself.

Christmas came and went. One minute I was upset and hurt and the next guilt ripped through me at the thought of what I had said to him. I couldn't win with myself and I couldn't stop thinking about him. I spent a lot of time in my room just listening to music and constantly checking my phone for any messages from him, but there were none.

My mum came into my room a few days before I was set to return to college.
"Emma, are you alright?" Concern was in her voice.
"Yeah. Why do you ask?" I smiled.
"It's just you've been so down since you came home." She sat beside me on my bed.
"I'm fine, just tired." I smiled wryly.

"I know my little girl, Emma. I know you're upset and I have a feeling it's over a boy. Am I right?" Her gaze was penetrating mine and I couldn't lie.

"Not a boy, mum — a man," I corrected.
Her eyes widened. "How old is he, darling?"
"Twenty-two."
"Tell me about him." She took my hand in hers and waited patiently for me to spill.
I sighed and began to tell her. I told her pretty much everything from him being in a band to his reputation with girls, while she sat beside me, stroking my hand soothingly. Tears fell down my face when I told her that I loved him but I couldn't be with him because I didn't want to be hurt and betrayed by him — because it was not an *if* but a *when*.

Everything, all the details, came pouring out of me and afterwards it was as if the weight on my heart was lighter.
Mum was silent for a minute after I had stopped talking. She stared down at my hand while she stroked it in hers.
"This is my fault."
"No, Mum, it's not."

She raised a hand to stop me. "Emma," her hand went to my cheek and her eyes softened, "you shouldn't be afraid to fall in love. I know why it's frightening to you but I can tell you that your father and I, well, our situation was different. I chose to ignore what was happening instead of confronting him about it. I was so hurt that I didn't want to think about the answer he would give me. Do you understand? I buried my head in the sand because it was easier than facing the truth. In a way, my depression was partly my own doing."

"Mum, that's not true. It was his fault." I didn't want to hear her talk like this and blame herself for it.

"Let me speak." She was firm. "You can't blame your father for all of it. I had no family around me, no close friends that I could talk to and I didn't want to bother your aunt with any of it — she never wanted me to leave here for England so I was too ashamed to go to her when things went wrong." Her eyes became gentle again. "You have family around you and you're strong, Emma. Don't miss out on life because you're afraid of what might happen — that's no way to live, darling. We all need to love, whether we regret it or not and," she squeezed my hand, "you are no different from anyone else, my heart."

"Scott sounds as though he cares for you a great deal and he is probably frustrated and *confused* by your behaviour."

"I don't know, he's pretty bad when it comes to girls."

"But has he ever treated you badly?"

I shook my head, "Not really."

I looked at her. For the first time since I've been back, I *really* looked at her. Her lips were turned up at the corners and her dark-blue eyes were lighter, shinier. Her face had plumped out again and she had colour in her cheeks. Her blonde hair had been styled with lowlights.

"Wow, Mum! You look yummy."

She laughed, "*Yummy?*"

"Yeah," I smiled.

"So, can we enjoy our last few days together without you mooning over Scott Mason?"

I wasn't sure what I would do, but I would try to forget about him for now. Knowing the reasons behind my mum's depression helped me a lot, and I knew that I would never be alone — I would always have my family to back me up and pick me up if I needed it. I smiled inwardly as my fear started to shrink a little.

Rocked Under ~ Cora Hawkes

"So, do you think I should let him have his wicked way with me?"

She gasped. "Emma, I'm not giving you permission to go out and…Um…"

"Have sex," I filled in for her.

"Yes! I'm not saying that, but I don't want you to fear losing something that you don't have. Sometimes you have to take risks to be truly happy, and I took a big one with your father by moving us over there and I *was* very happy for a long time. He just changed so much…"

"Do you still love him?" I already knew the answer, but I wanted it confirmed.

"Yes, I do," she said quietly. "I love the person he used to be, I'll never stop loving that person and I know he's still in there somewhere."

"You can *forgive* him?" I was surprised.

"Forgiveness should be given to a person who needs it. Not only does it show compassion for that person but in a way, it sets them free to forgive themselves when they are ready to move on. You will understand one day, but keeping grudges isn't healthy."

I wrapped my arms around her and hugged her close. "Love you, Mum."

"I love you too, my heart."

The first day back I saw him. Ash and I had arrived back late the night before. The house had been in darkness and there had been no sign of Scott. Now, he was leaning against the wall outside the main building of campus, looking more gorgeous than I had ever seen him. His eyes were down looking into his phone and my pulse sped up as I realised I would have to walk straight past him to get into the building.

I seriously thought about turning around or hiding behind a bush but then scolded myself for being such a wimp. He hadn't spotted me yet, so I had about ten seconds to get my face and body right before he noticed me. I raised my head slightly and pushed my shoulders back as I walked by him as casually as I could manage.

Out of my peripheral vision I noticed his body stiffen.

I quickened my pace, but not too much — I didn't want him to think I was bothered by him at all.

Once I was about three metres beyond him, I let out a sigh and relaxed.

But it was short-lived. I felt a hand clamp around my wrist, Scott dragged me into the building and then hauled me into a utility closet just inside the double doors.

Once we were inside he shut the door, enveloping us in darkness.

"Hey!" I yanked my wrist away from him. "What do you think you're doing?" I couldn't see him, I couldn't see anything, but the smell of bleach hit my nostrils along with a trace of alcohol. Had Scott been drinking already?

"Would you turn the light on?" I kept a moody edge to my voice even though I didn't really feel it.

There was no answer and for a second I wondered if I was alone in there, but I could hear his breathing.

"Scott?" I asked, a bit unsure now.

I heard movement and the sound of his slightly laboured breath came closer. He was closing in on me and I had to keep it together. My body started trembling involuntarily in anticipation. After not having seen him for so long I was pathetically desperate for him — his touch, his smell, just *him*.

I gasped as a warm hand touched mine. I flinched at the contact as scorching heat zinged up my arm and set my heart on fire. My breath was shallow.

I backed up until I hit something cold and my hands went flat to the wall to stop myself from doing what I so wanted them to do.

"Stop it," I tried to say sternly but all that came out was a raspy whisper.

"Stop what, Emma?" he whispered back, closer to me than I had thought.

I heard movement again and my skin tingled and shook as I felt his body heat. He was standing right in front of me now, so close that I could feel his breath on my face.

Shit! Have to get out of here.

"I'm not touching you." His whispered voice came close to my ear and I shuddered as my breathing got deeper.

My skin sparked and I didn't trust myself with him — I had to leave quickly.

"I'm going," I announced and then tried to move sideways.

A loud smack echoed in the cramped space as his hand hit the wall beside my head and I froze. He now had me caged within his arms.

"Did you miss me, babe?" he whispered close to my mouth. I shuddered again.

"Scott, please…" I rasped my plea.

"*Please?*" he mimicked, his voice not so steady as his hands cupped my face firmly. "I like hearing you say that, baby."

My knees almost buckled as I felt the tip of his tongue drag softly, slowly over my lips. A whimper escaped my throat. I tried so hard to keep my shaking under control. My heart was hammering so loud and hard that I swore he could have felt it through my skin.

He chuckled low in his throat. "You like that, baby?"
"Why are you doing this?"
"Doing what, baby?" He dipped his head to my mouth again. This time he licked my lower lip in soft strokes that had me almost begging for his mouth to plunder mine deeply. On and on he teased me, with strokes that were barely there, until I was panting.

My hands flew off the wall and grabbed the belt loops of his jeans and pulled him closer.

Sense returned before I had pulled all the way and I went still. I turned my head away from him and his tempting mouth.

We stayed like that for a minute, getting our breath back.

"Why are you treating me like this? I thought you hated me."

"Who says I have to like you to want you? I don't like most the girls I let in my bed and you're no fuckin' different." I felt him shrug but his words cut me deeply.

My hands dropped from his hips and I shoved him away hard.

I heard him chuckle again.

"Stay the hell away from me, Scott."

"C'mon, you know you want it."

Why was he being like this? He had said he hated me, so why would he torment me like this? If he wanted to be like this then fine, I fumed. Two could play that game — why should I even care what he thought of me now?

He knew I didn't just sleep with anyone yet he was treating me like a slut. How dare he? I hated him — I. Fucking. Hated. Him.

"No, I don't." I shoved him out of the way and made it to the door, where I groped around for the handle, and was finally out.

Rocked Under ~ Cora Hawkes

Chapter Twenty-five

"Are you okay?" Ash came up looking flustered, eyes wide. I had been walking around in a daze since my run-in with Scott this morning.

"Yeah, why?" I frowned. Obviously something had happened.

She looked worried. "Come with me." She led me somewhere more private.

"What's wrong?" I didn't like the way she was acting.

"It's out. Everyone knows."

It took me a second to work out what she was going on about and then my hand flew to my mouth. "Oh my God!" I was stunned, I looked around me — people had been giving me odd looks all day. "How?"

"Adam," she sneered.

"Shit." My stomach clenched.

"Look, don't worry. Go home early and I'll meet you there soon, okay?" She put her hand on my shoulder, "It's not that big a deal so don't panic."

Knowing it would be for the best I walked home and it was like I was set on automatic. How could this have happened now? I should've known better than to believe I could leave it all in the past, that my regrets wouldn't follow me over here. Thoughts of moving again crossed my mind, but I couldn't and wouldn't, run forever. It had been a stupid mistake. Hadn't everyone done something that they had regretted?

I hadn't been home five minutes when someone knocked on the door. I ignored them — I didn't want to see anyone.

"Emma, I know you're in there."

Scott. The last person I wanted to see. "Go away!" I didn't want to see him just then, not after this morning.

"Please, Emma…" He banged again.

Something in his voice made me go to the door and open it.

He stood there, a mess. His hair was all over the place, like he'd been pulling at it, and he was pale.

"Have you come to…?"

Scott caught me close to him and held me tightly.

I relaxed into him but then stiffened as this morning came flooding back. Why was he being like this now? I tried to push him away.

"Get off of me, Scott!"

"No. I won't let you go," he growled.

He was angry? *Good!* "Why not?" I continued to push him away, "You hate me, remember? You go out of your way to make me feel like shit and then a few hours later expect a hug?" I beat at his chest with my fists. "You don't get to fucking touch me! You don't even fucking know me so get your bloody hands off me right now!" I pummelled him again and again, and he took it.

He wrapped his arms around me in a bear hug with my arms stuck to my sides. I struggled and struggled but he wouldn't let go. Eventually, after exhausting myself, my anger faded and I went limp. The silence stretched out between us. He released me slowly and I stepped back.

He was watching me with pain across his face. I wanted to wipe it away. Even after everything I wanted to make him smile, see his face light up like it used to. I was such a sucker for him and I hated that part of myself.

"I'm sorry for what I did earlier," he put his hand through his hair, "I don't know what the fuck I was thinking."

I nodded and looked away. "I suppose you heard about me too."

"Yeah. That's why I'm here. I came to see if you're okay, and obviously you're not."

"Have you watched it?" I looked down at my feet.

A finger lifted my chin until I was looking at him again. "Yeah, I watched it." His eyes were probing, searching for answers.

I sighed and closed my eyes. "Is it bad?"

He frowned in surprise. "You haven't seen it?"
"No, I could never bring myself to."
"What happened?"
"How much do you know?" I tried to lower my face again, but he wouldn't let me.

"I know that you're filthy rich," he smiled and wiggled his brows.

A laugh escaped my lips. The sound surprising me. How could I laugh just then? When was the last time I had even *heard* my laugh?

"You can trust me, babe. I won't judge you. You said that I don't know you, but that's not true. I know who you are *now,* and to me that matters more. It's the person you are inside that counts, and you're beautiful. You're beautiful outside, too, but that's not what's got to me," He put a hand over my heart, "This has."

I could see the sincerity in his eyes and heard it in his voice. My lips trembled. He saw it and moved his hand from my heart to rub his thumb along my bottom lip.

His eyes gazed into mine and the familiar heat rippled under my skin. My breath became shallow. He moved his hand again and cupped the side of my face, but he had that pained expression again and dropped his hand into my lap, curling it around my hands. Disappointment had never been so cruel as it was then, but I closed the lid on it. His words had touched me. Nobody had ever said anything like that to me before and I realised that even though

Scott and I hadn't always got on, he had always been there when I'd needed him.

He might not have loved me but he cared about me a great deal, and that lifted my spirits to a high, which was the last thing I had expected right then.

"Baby, what happened?" he asked with gentleness, careful not to push too hard.

I looked down at our clasped hands. "The night that video was taken I had just found my dad in his apartment, snorting coke in his underwear with some tart, who was also in her underwear. She was closer to my age than his." I hesitated and looked up at Scott.

"Jesus. Go on, baby," he nudged.

"My dad is big news over there." I shook my head, "I'm not going into the boring details, but I was so angry that I wanted to hurt him like he'd hurt my mum and I…I…*Oh God!*" my hands came up to my face, "I don't even want to say what I did."

Scott pulled my hands away and turned me to look at him. "Emma, you saw your dad cheating on your mum. That's something no son or daughter should have to go through, so don't you dare hide your face. It's not you that should feel ashamed. He sounds like an asshole." His eyes burned into mine, conveying what he felt towards my father.

"My dad wasn't always such a bastard. He used to be the best dad," I smiled faintly, but it was bittersweet, "and I was his little princess. I remember a time when he used to be my hero and nobody could compare to him. He met my mum here, you know. They got married, had me, and my dad is British so he wanted to move back over there…"

"You were born here?" Scott seemed surprised.

"Yeah, didn't I tell you that?"

He shook his head.

"Anyway, we lived on the outskirts of London and everything was fine until he stopped coming home some nights and started to stay at his apartment in the city. I was ten so I didn't really think much of it, but I remember that I missed him coming home, you know?"

Scott nodded.

"That went on for a couple of years and by the time my twelfth birthday came around, my parents were arguing all the time in private, but in public we had to put on the perfect family act." My mouth curled at the memory of it. The only time my dad showed me and my mum any affection during that time was when we were at a party or a charity event.

"Mum got lonely and slipped into depression. As time went on, he stopped caring and coming home completely. Mum was a mess and stopped going out. She cried a lot and I was so *angry* with him for having caused it. Looking back, I realised that she must have known he was messing around for years before that night. But she loved him, so she stayed, thinking that things would go back to the way they used to be. Dad would come home once in a blue moon. There would be pictures of him in the papers with beautiful young women on his arm. When my mum asked, he would get angry and say that she was looking into things too deeply."

"I wasn't the best daughter either. I left her almost every weekend once I turned sixteen to go out and get pissed." I looked down. "I couldn't stand to be around her like that and she wouldn't help herself. She loved him and loves him still. She stopped caring about me through her depression and I was basically on my own. I hated him for what he had done to her, and I'd had enough of it."

"One night I drove to his apartment to have it out with him, but when I walked in I found them together, snorting coke and drinking and...Um..."

"You don't have to say it, babe."

"I remember the look on the woman's face and I just wanted to *kill* her." I closed my eyes and felt Scott squeeze my hand in support.

"I remember shouting at him, calling him a bastard, and then I ran. He called after me but I ignored him. I'll never forget the shock on his face. I instantly wanted revenge."

A sob broke from my throat. "I wasn't thinking rationally — I never do when I'm angry. I went into the most exclusive club in London, where I was known, and got off my face. I scored some coke and did it right in front of everyone while calling my dad a cheating bastard. I was wrecked, totally wasted, and danced like a fucking stripper — well, you saw it, didn't you?" Tears flowed freely down my face.

"I thought, if he can misbehave then so can I. I had spent most of my life being told how to act and to speak in public like a lady, but I wanted him to know that I'd had enough, and that mum and I wouldn't be pretending anymore. In my anger, I let a guy record me snorting that crap. I hated it but I wanted to show him that I wasn't his little princess anymore."

Scott seemed totally unsurprised by it all.

"The next day it was everywhere, in the papers, online, and I was literally the talk of Britain. My reputation as the perfect daughter died that night and I...I was *glad*. My mum went nuts, so I told her what had happened and why I had done it. In a way, it was a blessing in disguise, because it made her see that she needed to do something. She banned him from coming to see us at the house and divorced him on grounds of adultery, took half of everything, and moved us over here."

"I realise now that he had a cocaine habit, but he could've been honest with us, we could've helped him. My mum spent years trapped by her love for this one man who was making both of us miserable."

Scott wiped my tears away again and held me tight. "Baby, I'm sorry you had to go through that. I wish I could've been there for you."

"Scott?" I said in a small voice as I looked up at him.

"What, baby?"

"I'm so glad that you're here. I mean, I know we haven't been on the best of terms lately but I'm happy you don't hate me."

He shook his head, "I could never hate you." His voice was low and rough as his eyes pinned mine. "Never."

Chapter Twenty-six

February came around and excitement fizzed within me as I got ready to go to Macy's to watch Scott's gig. He had been my rock recently so the least I could do was keep my promise to get out of the apartment tonight and actually listen to some of his new stuff. The thought of seeing him on stage after so long had me shaking as I applied my make-up.

I hadn't been out in weeks, not since it all come out — and it had all been thanks to Adam and his detective work. Scott had gone after him for it and we heard that he had got transferred somewhere else, which pleased me. Scott never talked about what had happened, but I know he had threatened him and told him to leave me alone. It must have been a pretty good threat.

So while I was sort of hiding I spent most of my time catching up with work, reading and watching movies, while I came to terms with everything. Since leaving England, I hadn't let myself think about anything in depth, but since I'-d talked to my mum I had started to see things differently. My feelings towards my dad had changed somehow.

I'd spent the last weeks thinking things through from an adult's perspective, instead of through the eyes of a hurt child. Things were never black and white and I had realised that, in his own way, my dad had hidden his habit from us through shame. Maybe he hadn't stayed away because he didn't love us but because he *did*. My memories of him before all the shit happened were of a family man who loved his wife and his daughter.

I remembered he used to tuck me into my bed at night and read to me softly until I was asleep. I remembered the moments when he would look at me through soft, dark, coffee eyes that were full of love. There were so many things I remembered that conflicted strongly with the man he was today. I knew I needed to talk to him, and one day I would, but just…Not yet.

Ash and I arrived at Macy's and went straight to our usual table. Newton and meg had been waiting for us. As friends of Scott's, we would always have this table to ourselves. When Scott came on stage there was the usual buzz. Girls screamed his name as they rushed to the front in a frenzied battle to be the one who caught his attention first. He stood there, much like he had on his first night, silhouetted against the spotlight. He was silent. Still. A hush came over the audience while they waited for him to start.

When he did, my heart leaped into my throat — he looked directly at me with a sexy smile and a wink. Eyes turned towards me, girls watched me with unveiled envy. His gaze trapped mine and I suddenly felt as though we were the only two people in the room. It was like he was a different person on stage. As though he felt braver, like anything could and would happen.

I looked away but only because the stares I was getting were making me uneasy. I sneaked a peek back at Scott but he was still watching me as he sang his ballad. I glowered at him, shaking my head, and I knew he'd got the message as he grinned and looked away. I finished my drink and got up to dance. I stayed towards the back and started swaying, moving with the music, letting it guide my body.

Scott's eyes touched me every now and then but I didn't mind. Every time Scott was on stage it was like falling under his spell all over again, and I loved and hated that feeling all at once. When he finished the set he came over to me and planted a kiss on my cheek. This was a new thing with him — he kissed me now, but it was always in a friendly way.

"You actually came out from your fuckin' cave!" He slung his arm around my shoulders, his eyes twinkling.

"I told you I would." I looked up into his handsome face, taking in every fine detail.
"You wanna dance?"
"I'm going to get a drink. Later?"
He nodded and let me go.
A while later I saw him dancing with someone. I watched him and every now and then he would glance at me and then look away. I didn't know why he felt so protective of me, but a part of me revelled in the feeling of being safe and having someone there to watch my back. I'd never had that before. Most of the friends I had had back home had been handpicked by my dad because of their parents' social status.

A man came up behind the girl Scott was dancing with and pulled her away from him. I stopped dancing. The girl struggled against his hold and Scott stepped in, trying to pull the girl back to him. Fear licked the back of my neck. The guy came close to Scott and punched him in the stomach, winding him. My hand went to my mouth as Scott doubled over and I watched the guy walk away, leaving the girl stroking Scott's back. Scott looked up, looking for the guy and started after him towards the exit, with angry strides, his fists curled tightly at his sides.

I ran to find Newton, spotting him after just seconds, I pegged it towards him, shoving sweaty bodies out of my way.
"Newton!" I screamed at the top of my lungs as I neared him, "Scott's in a fight outside. You gotta come. Now!"
Newton, Bone and Alan pushed past me and ran for the exit with me hot on their heels. I had a bad feeling, a sick weight in my stomach.

Outside there were only people hanging around but we heard grunts coming from the alley. We ran towards the sound and saw Scott on the ground, curled into ball, while three men laid into him. They were kicking him repeatedly while he was down. I wanted to throw up at the sight of him, so helpless, as they beat him.

"Scott!" I screamed in panic.
"Get the fuck off him!" Bone shouted as he went for the biggest man and tore him away by his shirt, throwing a punch with his other hand.
A brawl started between the six guys, but I was more worried about Scott. I ran over to him and fell on my knees next to his still body.
News stories of people dying after having been punched in the wrong spot on the head came back to me as I looked at his bloody form. "Oh no, *Scott!*" Tears flowed down my cheeks. He was curled up and I touched his head. Blood was everywhere so I couldn't tell where he was hurt.

"Scott?" I shook him, "Scott, oh God! Please wake up!" My heart stopped and then sprinted off again at an alarming rate. I couldn't breathe and blood rushed in my ears. He wasn't moving. I started to shake as I put my fingers to the side of his neck and felt his strong pulse. The relief was so sharp and swift that a wail escaped my lips. He was unconscious. I pulled my phone out and dialled 999, only to hang up, furious at my mistake, and call 911 for an ambulance. The fight was still going on around me.

After hanging up, I ran my fingers through his hair and cried. What if he didn't wake up? What if he went into a coma? What if his brain had been damaged? What if I never saw him smile again? If I had to live without him looking at me as though I was his everything again I thought I would crumble.

Chaos surrounded us as I lifted his head gently off the cold concrete onto my lap.

I sniffed. "Please be okay."
A low groan escaped his lips. "Emma…"
I froze, unable to believe he had said my name. "It's okay, don't move. An ambulance is on the way."
"No…" He tried to move.
I placed my palms on his chest. "Don't move. Please just stay still until help comes, okay?"
He groaned, "Fuck, they got me good." His voice was hoarse and sounded pained.

"It was three against one. You had no chance with those odds, you idiot." I chided softly.
He tried to laugh but ended up grabbing his ribs and gasping as pain seared through him.
My spirits were lifting the more he spoke. He didn't seem to have brain damage and he could move. Sirens could be heard in the distance just as Newton and Bone fell on their knees next to us, with Alan standing behind.
"Dude, you look like shit!" Bone cringed.
"Thanks." Scott mumbled in reply, but his eyes were on me.

The ambulance arrived and carted Scott off to the hospital. I wanted to go, but Scott refused to let me lose any sleep because he had been injured in a fight that was his own fault. I went home but couldn't sleep anyway. I kept thinking that it could have been worse than it was. It disturbed me deeply, and whenever I closed my eyes things replayed in my mind over and over. In the end, I did fall asleep, but I kept jerking awake with the sensation of falling.

Chapter Twenty-seven

Scott got away with a minor concussion, two broken ribs, a split lip, and a body covered of bruises and scrapes. To put it mildly, he came home looking like shit. A week later, I knocked on his door after my classes.

Scott opened the door in a pair of ripped jeans that sat low on his hips and nothing else. My gaze skimmed his body. His bruises were starting to fade and he looked a hell of a lot better than he had done a week ago.

My eyes moved lower to his navel and the dark line of hair that disappeared elusively beneath his jeans. My heart started to race and my mouth went slack. Bloody hell, even busted and bruised he was sexy.

"Babe, are you coming in?" he rasped and then cleared his throat.

My eyes darted to his and my cheeks grew warm. "Uh yeah. Hi!" I forced a smile to my lips and took a slow breath to slow my heart rate.

His eyes darkened as his brows lowered and his head went to the side. My stomach fluttered and I swallowed loudly. "What?" I asked in a low voice that didn't sound like mine.

He shook his head and turned around, walking into his apartment. "How was your day?"

I was relieved that he had asked that instead of teasing me about ogling him. "It was good. How was yours?"

I knew what he was going to say before the words left his mouth. "Better now you're here, Florence." He turned and bestowed a cute, cheeky grin on me.

He was referring to Florence Nightingale — and he had said that to me every day this week. I'd been here every day since he left the hospital. We spent most of the time watching movies and listening to music. Since he had to rest, I kept him company. He also had the time to help me with my work, like he had said he would ages ago in exchange for his piano lessons, but had never seemed to get the chance to do.

He passed me a hot cocoa — made the way I like it with marshmallows and cream — which he had waiting for me.
I smiled my thanks. "How are you feeling?"
"Fuckin' bored." He crossed his arms and frowned.
I laughed, "You look like a sulky little boy." I took a sip and closed my eyes, "Mmm…Yum!"
"It's not funny!" I could see his lips twitching, "But it will be tonight when I make you watch the scary movie I've got for us."
I put my hand up. "No way, Scott! I already told you — I don't do scary movies."

"You are tonight, and it's the new one about the girl that gets possessed." He turned and headed into the kitchen. *Great! I'm going to make a total ass out of myself.* I hated scary movies. I didn't really mind gore or zombies or vampires or other silly things — it was the paranormal ones that got me. And they didn't just get to me — they *terrified* me.

We settled down on the couch after having eaten and Scott put the film on. We sat with the popcorn between us as we always did, like there was this unspoken rule about keeping space between us at all times. There was always this atmosphere around us, warning us not to go too far. He knew that I was attracted to him and I think he must have known that I cared about him. He didn't know that I was in love with him though, and if he ever found out, I'd be devastated.

Scott didn't do love. He didn't do commitment. And I knew that and had accepted it. Maybe he wanted more, but at the end of it all, he would grow bored of me and toss me away like he did all of them. No. I'd rather have him this way than have him break my heart and leave me in pieces. We couldn't have any relationship after that. I looked sideways at him, he was so handsome. Even just lounging around in scruffy jeans he was hot. He had a presence, an aura of masculinity that nobody I knew could contend with.

I turned back to the TV as the movie started. I pulled a cushion onto my lap in case of emergency and tried to mentally prepare myself for my first spooky movie I'd seen in eight years.

Twenty minutes in and I was curled into a ball and flinching wildly with the cushion in front of my face for the bits that I didn't want to see.

"You're really that scared?" Scott was laughing.

I nodded, wide-eyed.

He chuckled, "Come here." He lifted his arm.

I scooted next to him and curled into him while his arm came around me.

"Don't worry, I'll keep you safe." He was finding this hilarious while I was seriously scared!

"Thanks a bloody bunch."

Some time during the ordeal I found myself in his lap with my arms clamped around him tightly. When had that happened? Embarrassed, I lifted my head to see if he had noticed and found myself staring into his eyes. His breathing was heavy and his jaw was clenched. How long had he been watching me? His darkening eyes lured me in and I couldn't look away. My heart kicked against my ribs. My lips parted so I could breathe easier. His eyes touched on my mouth and then flicked back up again. He moved and placed his hands under my arms to pull me up onto his lap so I was straddling him properly.

My hands instinctively went to his ripped bare chest. His eyes flared while I froze for a moment, unable to believe that I had touched him so intimately and that I could feel him hard beneath the rigid part of his jeans. His pupils were dilating right there for me to see. His lids grew heavy and his heart thumped hungrily beneath my hand. He was magnificent. As I went to move my hands, one of his came up quickly and caught it, placing it back over his heart. His eyes bored into me as though he was trying to tell me something.

I gasped. My pulse was racing all over the place and the butterflies wanted out of my stomach. I was so aware of him, of his stiffness beneath me, of his heart beating under my hand, of his smell. Most of all though, it was his eyes — they burned into mine, searing me, scarring me forever. His other hand came up and stroked my hair away from my face and then came to rest on my cheek. A gentle look entered his eyes and his thumb stroked my bottom lip ever so slowly.

I closed my eyes and took a deep breath. This couldn't happen now. But I wanted it to with every atom in me. My body craved him, like he was its missing piece, but my mind wouldn't allow it. My skin was flushed and tingling — sensitive — as I felt his erection growing even bigger. I wanted to test the length. I yearned to move myself along him.

The thought sent erotic images of us flicking through my head and warm heat burst in my lower belly. My head fell back and he moved his hand from my cheek to the back of my head with his other splayed along my back to support me. My palms still rested against his chest. I needed him so badly and I was losing the will to fight it.

Scott leaned forwards and at the same time shifted himself beneath me. I flinched as a spark shot through me from him rubbing me where I needed it most. My lips parted in a moan and my palms went up to grip his shoulders.

His lips touched my neck and I was gone. I started moving myself against him, unashamedly taking what I needed from him.

I was moaning and Scott was breathing heavily, almost growling as his lips caressed my neck. His hands came to rest on my hips. His jaw clenched as his dark eyes watched me slake myself on him.

Back and forth I went, faster and then slower. I circled my hips into him, hitting the right spot. A gasp escaped me and I sped up to reach the point I needed to.

Scott put a hand between us, the pad of his thumb resting on my clit over my jeans as I tried frantically to end it.

"I got you." His thumb started to move in circles as his other hand went around my back. "Lean back, baby." His voice was ragged.

I did as I was told because it was too late for me to stop now. I needed release and it was building quickly.

"Ah, Scott." I couldn't help it — I actually had no control over myself.

He groaned and licked my open lips. "Fuck, I want inside of you so bad."

With those words, my release exploded out of me with a shout. My body contracted so tightly that it was almost painful. Scott pulled me back into his hips to ride it out as the sensation gripped me and shook me.

"Fuck, baby, *fuck!*" Scott leaned back against the sofa. "Emma," Scott gasped. His hands gripped my hips tight. My eyes shot open. Scott was leaned back against the sofa with his eyes closed breathing deeply.

Shame came crashing through me almost straight away. "*Oh God!*" I scrambled off him and to the far side of the sofa so fast that he didn't have a chance to catch me. My hands came up over my face and I was shaking. "I'm so sorry. I didn't mean for that to happen, I just…"

"No, baby, don't be sorry." His hands covered mine and pulled them away from my face but I couldn't look at him. "Look at me."

I turned my face towards him and looked at him reluctantly. He was hunched in front of me on the floor. His eyes were soft.

"Why are you sorry?"

Why? Because I didn't want to lead him on. I didn't want him to think that we were together. "It shouldn't have happened." I looked away again when he frowned.

"But it did happen and I know why, even if you're not ready to admit it to yourself." His hand came up and moved my face back to his.

I didn't want to hear him say it. "I don't want to talk about this, Scott." I brushed his hand away. "It was an accident and I'm sorry okay. Can we drop it? I like us as friends."

Scott stood up and walked over to the balcony doors. He stood with his back to me, his arms crossed. "What's so bad about the thought of *us*? I want you, you want me, and you can fuckin' deny it all you want but I know the truth." He turned around and started walking towards me.

"I know the way you watch me. You're always watching me." He inched closer. "I see the look on your face when I'm with someone else and I know what it is because I had the same look on my face when I saw you with Adam and Kyle."

I stood before he could reach me. The intent in his eyes made it clear that he wasn't going to stop. I went around the sofa and stepped backwards with every slow step he took my way.

"The way you care and look after me. I recognise that, too. I remember the night in the alley when I had that fight. You were crying for me."

"Of course I care," I threw my arms in the air, "You're my friend, Scott."

"It's not fuckin' friendship, Emma!" he boomed, making me flinch.

"You're probably the best friend I have here and I don't want to lose that just because *you* want a fucking fuck buddy!" I yelled back.

"That's not true!" he fought back, his face darkening.

"Why do you have to try and get every girl you meet into bed then? What is *wrong* with you?" My chest was rising and falling sharply as I stared him down.

He looked away then and buried his fists in his pockets.

I knew I was being nasty but I'd had enough. "If you're willing to chuck our friendship away for one night in the sack then you can't respect or care about me at all, so what exactly do you feel for me Scott? Is it really friendship or is all this some ploy to get me into your bed because you can't any other way!" I took a deep breath and stared at him, spitting fire.

"What I *feel* for you?" Scott's expression was incredulous.

"Yes. *Please* tell me because I don't know what to think anymore when you have a different girl here almost every fucking night and then get rid of them in the morning. You really expect me to believe that I'm going to be any different?"

He was quiet for a moment and I wished I could read his mind as his expression grew pensive.

"Answer me a question first." His voice was soft. "Are you scared because of what happened between your parents?"

Cold tingles went up my spine and I could only look away.

He came closer until I was backed against the closed door and he stopped inches from me.

His eyes bored into mine. "The look on your face tells me I'm right." His fingers grazed my cheek. "I'm sorry for the hurt your dad caused your mom and," he paused and took a breath, "I'm sorry your mom hurt *you* in the process of her pain and made you afraid."

He implied that my mum hadn't been a good one and that hurt. Anger came to my rescue. "You don't know what you're talking about." I got closer to him, right in his face. He knew nothing about what my mum had been through. "You have no idea about me, or my parents, so keep them the hell out of this. You don't know me!" My fists were clenched at my sides and I was breathing heavily.

He grabbed the tops of my arms and squeezed. "And why is that?" he shouted, his neck straining with the force of his words. "You keep everything hidden away. I had to find out about your past from a fuckin' video on the Internet!" He shook his head in defeat. "I take what I can goddamn get with you but you only give me tiny amounts of yourself." His tight grip loosened and a hand came up again to my face.

His face relaxed. "I've committed every part of you to memory, did you know that?" A pained expression entered his eyes. "You're so fucking beautiful that sometimes I can't see straight." His other hand came up to my face. "I want you so bad, I can't take this shit. The first night we met, it was like being hit by a tornado all over again. You entering my life was a huge event and you shook and shifted everything for me. I want you to be mine and," he paused, "I want to be yours."

I went to turn my face away but he wouldn't let me hide, he never did. His words touched something deep within me and I couldn't ignore them, but it was hard to let go of the fear. I was a coward — too frightened to take a chance on him. I needed to think, I needed to get away from him, clear my head, figure out what I wanted.

"When I saw you with Adam I wanted to rip his fuckin' head off," he sighed heavily.

"When you slept with him, I hurt like crazy and it still kills me to think of you with him. The thought of you with anyone else…" he swallowed and shook his head as he looked away from me. He closed his eyes and breathed in deeply, slowly. "I can't take this shit, babe. I'm stuck. I feel as though I'm trudging through waist-deep mud with you." His voice broke and he turned away from me abruptly. His hands went through his hair as he sighed.

"Scott." I took a step forward but stopped.

"Don't, Emma." He turned around. The pain in his eyes tore through me and I wanted to comfort him but I couldn't.

"Don't say what I know you're going to. I can't hear that shit right now."

I couldn't let this happen. I didn't trust it. In my heart I wanted him, I believed him, but my head was telling me to be cautious, to be aware of what I would be setting myself up for — an eternal walk down Heartbreak Lane, a world of hurt and pain and wanting and wishing and regrets.

"Scott, if you really want me so much, then why do you still mess around with other girls? How can you expect me to believe anything you've just said when I see you with girls all the time?" I clasped my hands in front of me and looked down at them.

"Shit, babe. If only you knew…"
"Knew what?"

He looked away and I thought I saw a faint red tinge in his cheeks. "Nothing."

Then it hit me — hit by a tornado all over again. *All over again?* My God! I didn't know he'd been hit by a tornado. "When did you get hit by a tornado?"

He frowned, "Huh?"

"You said, 'hit by a tornado *all over again*'."

His face cleared as understanding dawned in his eyes. "I was — Tornado Emma hit me twice."

It was my turn to be confused now.

"Macy's wasn't the first time we met."

"What? I don't remember." I was surprised.

He sighed and shook his head. "Just forget I said anything. Let's forget this whole fuckin' night and its mess along with it." He stormed away into the kitchen, leaving me standing there wondering if things had just changed for good.

I slipped out the door without saying goodnight and wandered down the stairs, unseeing, lost in my thoughts. I couldn't remember having met him before Macy's. No matter how hard I searched my memories, it just wasn't there. When I first met him, it was as though I had seen him somewhere before so maybe I had been right. I considered asking Ash about it, but I didn't want her getting involved.

"You 'kay?"

I jumped. Ash was huddled on the sofa with a blanket and a movie. "Yeah, I'm good. What are you watching?" I looked at the screen and didn't even need her to answer — this was one movie that I could watch over and over.

"*Legends of the Fall*. He's so effing gorgeous," she swooned.

I rolled my eyes at her mooning. "As much as I love this film, I'm going to bed. Nighty-night."

"You're boring," Ash called as I left the lounge.

Rocked Under ~ Cora Hawkes

Chapter Twenty-eight

"Damn, girl! You look *hawt!*" Ash stood in the doorway admiring my outfit for the night while I added the finishing touches. I was wearing a white strapless dress that had a gold loop between my breasts. The white satin hung open down to my navel. The soft drapes then hugged my figure just above my backside and held the very tips of my thighs — and that's where it ended. My hair was up in a twist with a few wisps coming down here and there. Gold flat sandals finished the look.

I smiled and looked her over. "Thanks, you too." Ash was wearing a daring red dress that was backless and short.
It was Valentine's Day and everyone was getting dressed up extra special for Valentine's Night at Macy's. From Under would be covering old power ballads for the night. I wasn't in the right frame of mind for it at all. After having messed it up the other night with Scott I wanted to cry sick. Things had gone backwards between us. We had both tried hard to ignore what had happened — it was as though we were both striving for a normal friendship.

He had started bringing girls back again and it hurt. Apparently he knew what it did to me, he had said so last week, so why would he be hurting me on purpose? How could he do that after all the things he said to me? It was all utter bullshit. What else could it be? I knew I had no right to be angry with him because I kept refusing him. I wanted to be snarky with him. *Is this ever going to end?*

"Ready to go? Want to get there early."
"Yeah, two seconds." I looked around for my purse.
Maybe it was too late for me. Maybe I should sleep with him and let him get out of my system once and for all. I treasured our

friendship but was it worth this? Would our friendship last *anyway*?

When we got there, I went straight to the bar. Everything was going round in my head and I wanted to forget for a while. Alcohol wasn't a complete cure, but it was a darn good temporary one because I knew that once Scott came off stage he would be in the arms of someone else, and after his words last week I really didn't want to see it without having anything to soften the blow.

After downing two shots I snaked through bodies to our usual table with the first round.
Meg whistled. "Wow! How is it possible to look hotter than you usually do?" Meg grinned.
Ash pulled me down next to her, "Are you okay?"
No! "Yeah, I'm fine. Why?"
"You don't seem like yourself lately and you looked a little uptight at the bar," she said.
"I've been tired," I shrugged and turned away.
"I guess you've had a lot of late nights recently with Sco…" She stopped mid-sentence and looked at me as though she had seen a ghost.

"What?" I had to ask as she was staring at me like I had three eyes.
Her head went to the side questioningly. "Emma, has something been going on with you and Scott?"
The question shocked me. Nobody had really guessed anything was happening with Scott, so I was taken aback. I looked away. Would it be so bad if I told her about it? Wasn't she over him now? She seemed to be. I looked back at her and sighed as I nodded.
"Oh, Em! Why didn't you tell me?" Her gaze softened and pity was written all over her face.

"I really don't want to talk about this now, Ash."

"Have you slept with him?"

"No!" I denied. "Can we talk about it later?"

She put her hand over mine and squeezed it comfortingly. "Of course."

From Under came on stage and I took a deep breath to steady my heart at the sight of him. He was gorgeous. His hair was super-glossy tonight and he was wearing a new shirt which hugged his chest. Fluttering started in my stomach as I watched him while he was unaware. The way his hands softly gripped the microphone, the way his mouth moved against it, had me almost panting. Again I mused, maybe I should sleep with him to get him out of my system. Maybe that's what I needed to move on, and him too. *Stop it, Emma!* I shook myself hard — that wasn't going to happen.

There was a slow, lazy beat to his song. The crowd was thick with lovers rubbing against one another and singles doing their hardest to be noticed. I began swaying my hips slowly as I got into his slow ballad, not interested in getting attention — I only wanted to dance. I closed my eyes and let the music do its thing to my body and my senses.

It wasn't long before warm hands touched my hips gently. My mouth turned down slightly but I kept my eyes closed as I began to imagine Scott's hands there. My breath hitched as I day dreamed about Scott's hands doing what these hands were doing — rubbing up and down my sides slowly, setting my nerve endings alight with sensation. A head came down to my shoulder and I shuddered as I felt the imaginary Scott there. I turned my head towards his and wrapped my arms around his neck to keep him close. His hands were all over me, swiping my belly low down.

Scott's voice stumbled mid-lyric and my eyes shot open. He was watching me and the pain I saw on his face made a lump form in my throat. His voice had deepened huskily, as though his throat was closing. I felt like shit — guilty and ashamed with myself all at once. I was a bitch and I wanted this guy's hands off me. It didn't matter that Scott had put me through the same torment — my conscience wouldn't let me not give a crap.

The man's hand drifted down and grabbed my behind. I turned around and pushed him away. His face fell but he let me go.

I turned and found Scott's dejected eyes still on me as he sang. I couldn't watch any more. I turned away with my head down. I wanted him and it made no difference that my rational brain warned me away. I loved him, and at the end of the day, I was miserable without him. I missed him every minute of every day, even if I hated him, even when he was with someone else.

I was pathetic. The time we had spent together after he had been beaten up had been bliss, and I wanted that back. Eventually Scott announced the last song and the familiar sound of *Give In To Me* by *Michael Jackson* filled the room. The crowd erupted with cheers. I watched from the now-empty table as the song began.

Scott didn't smile. He looked strained as he melded his eyes with mine and his hands fisted the microphone tightly. He sang to me. His voice poured out like I had never heard it before. It was like he was feeling every word, like it had come from his soul. He didn't release me from his intense hold all through the song. Every lyric hit me in the heart. He was angry with me, he was hurting, I could feel it in every syllable. The song closed and Scott turned away from me, mumbling a pathetic thank you before going off stage. He wasn't his usual self and it was my doing.

Rocked Under ~ Cora Hawkes

This was doing neither of us any good, we were hurting each other too much. I went to the bar and ordered a couple more shots. An hour and a few more shots later I was back on the floor, dancing alone while almost everyone else had dates. I didn't give a shit. I wanted to be alone. I deserved to be alone. I spotted Scott dancing with a gorgeous, busty blonde. Scott was behind her, his eyes were on me as his lips trailed down to her neck. His hand massaged her breasts and his other trailed down to cup her between her legs. His eyes half-closed on me when he started to stroke her gently.

Searing pain lanced through me and I felt my face crumple, too upset to even try to hide it. I spun as the tears came and ran through the crowd as fast as my wobbly legs would let me. I wanted to scream at Scott for making me feel what I was feeling. I needed to get out the door Scott had shown me, out into the alley, for some privacy. I almost made it. As I put my hand on the door handle and started to pull the door open a hand slammed it shut again from behind me, I was spun around and slammed against the wall.

Scott loomed over me, I lowered my head so he wouldn't see me cry but he just forced my face to his.
"You fuckin' did this to us, Emma, so why the hell are you crying, *dammit?*" he shouted at me.
I put my hands over my face as I cried harder. I wanted him to leave me alone, to just leave me with my tears in private. I didn't want him to see me weak like that.
"No!" he yelled again, "You don't get to hide your face from me. I want to see every raw bit of pain on your face."

What followed was a fight to get my hands out of his — his iron grip was hurting me. When I managed to pull a hand free, I slapped him — hard.

He reeled back and froze in shock. I sobbed, grabbed the door handle and ran as fast as I could to get outside.

"Emma!" He was on me before I knew it.

He plucked me from behind. "Leave me alone!" I fought against his hold but he carried me into the band's back room, kicked the door closed and stopped. His arm was like a clamp around my waist, keeping me from moving.

I fought and kicked at his legs but it was no use.

"Stop it, Emma!"

But I couldn't stop. I was fighting against him, us, my feelings, his, everything.

"I hate you!" I screamed and dug my nails into the hand around my waist.

He spun me around to face him and shook me hard. "No, you don't. When are you gonna open your beautiful fuckin' eyes and see?" he shouted back.

His words dragged up mental pictures of him with various girls. "I've seen all I need to see!" My face was burning with the anger I felt. "You wanted to see me in pain and you did it. I deserve it, but it's over. I'm leaving! I'm leaving this building, I'm leaving this bloody town and I'm fucking leaving you!"

His face fell. He let go of me abruptly and I turned my back while I got my breath back and calmed down. My heart was thumping so hard that I could hear it.

"I wish I'd never met you." My quiet rasp shook.

I heard him come closer until I could feel his warmth on my back. His closeness was excruciating and exquisite at the same time. After all this, I just wanted him to touch me, I wanted him to comfort me. I felt his big warm hand stoke my bare back slowly. I shuddered as his other hand snaked around and pressed my lower tummy setting a thick pulse between my legs.

Rocked Under ~ Cora Hawkes

"You don't mean that," he whispered close to me.

He pressed his open mouth against my shoulder blade and nibbled gently as he kissed. His hand on my belly pressed deeper. My head went back as a whimper escaped my lips. "Yes, I do, Scott. You hurt me," I sniffed, "all the fucking time." I wanted to reach behind and touch him desperately but I wouldn't allow myself to.

I felt his lips on my neck now, kissing slow and hard, his hands on me getting tighter, moving slowly all over my tummy and sides. He was all over me.

"Baby, I can't take this anymore." He was breathless and shaky. "Please, no more."

"No," I moaned, "I just saw you touch her. I don't want your hands on me."

But he didn't take his hands away. His touch was needy, wrenching a deep craving within me that started in my chest and spread outwards through my body, making it his.

"You're torturing me, babe." His hands rubbed down the sides of my hips. "All I think about is *you*," he groaned into my neck, eliciting a shudder, "and I can't stop." He shook his head. "I've tried so fuckin' hard to be your friend, but I can't do it. You know we can't anymore, Emma."

He spun me around to face him. I had a second to look at him and my heart sang at the violent want in his expression before his lips crashed down on mine. His lips were hard and desperate and slow all rolled into one. He groaned into my mouth and it was almost my undoing. His tongue plunged in and out and he felt so good. I wanted things to be perfect, for us but they weren't — there was too much to overcome, too much crap between us. This wouldn't work but, God, I wanted him so badly. I had never loved him more.

He gripped my hips and pulled me into him hard and fast as his mouth continued it exploration. His hands wandered down to squeeze my butt and then up to graze my breasts.

I tore my mouth away from his. "Scott, please! I can't do this."

"Yes, you can," he groaned into my neck. His eyes had blackened as his pupils dilated, eclipsing his irises. He stayed like that for a moment trying to dampen the heat between us, his lips were rubbing softly, slowly, behind my ear. His breath wasn't calm, though, and after a second I heard a quick hiss of inhalation as he lost the battle to keep his last thread of control.

His mouth slammed down onto mine and I knew there was no way out. His tongue opened my mouth savagely, his lips showing no mercy. He had never kissed me this intensely. I was losing myself. My thoughts of refusing — fighting — were flitting away and were turning instead to him, his hands on my body. He gripped my ass firmly and lifted me. He was carrying me to the couch, his mouth still attached to mine, and I couldn't think. I had no time.

He laid me down carefully and stood over me, watching me as his nostrils flared with his deep breaths. I knew he was giving me a way out from the hopeless look haunting his eyes.

"Scott, I can't," I whispered, my eyes never leaving his.

"Why?" His voice was a rough sound.

"I'm scared. I'm so scared." I pleaded with my eyes for him to understand.

His hands went into his pockets. "You're scared of me, but you slept with *Adam?*"

"It's not like that."

"Like hell it isn't," he roared, the muscles in his neck growing.

He turned his back quickly and I watched with guilt as his hands went into his hair, balling into fists.

Rocked Under ~ Cora Hawkes

"Fuck," he muttered. "Fuck it!" he yelled and punched the wall.
I jumped upright on the couch.
He placed his hands against the wall and rested his forehead on it. His breath was heaving and guilt crushed me. I didn't want to see him like this — he looked defeated, lost and so sad.

I wanted to explain. "Scott…"
"Just fuckin' go." He turned to face me. "Go! Now." He looked strained and my heart went out to him.
I had really hurt him this time. I wanted to take the pain away, erase that look from his face. I walked forward on shaky legs until I stood by him.
He went stiff and frowned before turning his head to the side and away from me.
I reached one hand up to cup his cheek. "Let me explain why," I whispered.

He looked down at me, his brows drawn, his mouth tight. "Take your hand off me and get the fuck out," he sneered in a thick, strained voice that sounded unlike him.
It was like someone had punched me in the stomach — a physical pain. I removed my hand and left as fast as I could, my eyes stinging with the first sign of tears.

Hours later, I had been sleeping when a loud thud that came from upstairs woke me.
"Noooooo!" It was painful and gut-wrenching, and it came from Scott's apartment.
Like I was on automatic, I jumped out of bed, pulled my pyjamas on quickly and ran up the stairs two at a time. I went straight into his apartment without knocking. I went through to the lounge, not knowing what I was going to find.

Scott was crouched on his knees on the floor sobbing uncontrollably, his shoulders quaking with the force of it. "No! It's not real!"

My heart skipped a beat as fear shot through me, "Scott?" I went to my knees beside him, "What's happened?"

He didn't answer me but just kept moaning 'no' over and over. I looked around for clues to what could have happened. I saw a mess — it looked like the place had been ransacked. I also saw an empty whisky bottle on the floor not far from him.

"Scott?" I stroked his hair gently, trying to soothe him.

He flinched and looked up at me as though he had only just noticed I was here. His eyes were bloodshot and puffy. His whole face was wet with tears. Anguish was in every line of his face as he stared at me like a lost little boy.

"He's gone," his voice cracked out.

Before he could bury his head again I gently cupped his face. "Who's gone?" My heart was in my throat and sickness swirled within my stomach.

"My dad — he's dead." Scott closed his eyes tight.

I gasped and my hand closed over my mouth as tears started to sting my eyes. "My God, Scott." My heart broke for him. I knew how much he loved his dad — he was all he had left. I got down closer to him and put my arms around him tight. He turned and buried his head in my chest while I cradled him like a child. "I'm so sorry." It sounded lame but what else could I say? There was nothing that anyone could have said to make this easier for him — nothing.

"He's gone. I'll never see him again. He's all I have."

I held onto him while he cried his heart out. His hands were holding onto me like I was his lifeline. Eventually, after what seemed like an hour, his crying became quieter. In that time he had vomited twice in the toilet.

"Come on, let's get you into bed for now. You need to rest. You can't face anything tomorrow until you rest."

I helped him up from the bathroom floor, where we had ended up, and into his bedroom. I took off his jeans and shirt before helping him into bed.

"Do you want me to get you anything?"

He was very quiet now, staring into space with eyes that looked heavy and swollen.

He shook his head. "Stay. Don't leave me."

I went to him. "I'm here, Scott, and I'm not going anywhere until you want me to." I stroked his face. He was tired and all cried out for now but I knew this was just the beginning of his grief.

I wanted to take his pain away from him. The thought of him having nobody was more than I could handle and I vowed that I would be there for him from now on. I loved him and I wouldn't let him be alone now.

I got into bed next to him and he turned towards me. I held his hand and stroked his hair like my dad used to do to me to lull me off to sleep. He lifted my hand to his lips and kissed it sweetly. Tenderness overtook the sadness in his eyes for a second as he looked at me. I leaned forward and kissed his cheek. He squeezed my hand like he wanted more but grief and booze overtook him, exhausting him, and he passed out cold. I watched him for a long time after he fell asleep. His features were creased and I smoothed the lines from his forehead.

"I love you," I whispered. There was no more denying it or hiding from it — I needed him in my life and he needed me.

Chapter Twenty-nine

"How is he?" I asked Newton. It was now nearing the end of March and I hadn't seen or heard from Scott since the morning after he had found out that his dad had died.

"He's not in a good way, Em." The concern in Newton's eyes was worrying.

"What do you mean?"

"I talked to him last night and he was distant, you know, not really there." He frowned as if trying to work out why his friend would be like that with him.

"But did he say he was okay?"

"Yeah, that's just it. He said he was cool, but he sounded pissed at the same time."

"Did you ask him when he's coming back?"

"He doesn't know yet, says he needs more time and he's got his dad's shit to sort."

I huffed moodily. "Where is he? Why won't you tell me?"

Scott didn't want anyone to know where he was. He didn't want to speak to or see anyone except Newton.

"He wants to be left alone. Just give him some time."

The morning after Valentine's Day, I had awakened to Scott rifling through his drawers, shoving things into a suitcase, mumbling to himself and rubbing his eyes.

"How are you?" I had asked, my voice still thick with sleep.

He hadn't looked at me and had just carried on with what he was doing. "You should go." His voice was scratchy and he looked pale and withdrawn, with puffy, bloodshot eyes.

I had wanted to comfort him but I could tell that he was still angry with me and had far more important things on his mind. Did he remember last night?

"Are you going away?" I had hoped not.

Rocked Under ~ Cora Hawkes

"I'm going for a while, yeah." He still hadn't looked at me.

I hadn't wanted him to go. And why wouldn't he look at me? "Scott, please look at me," I had asked in a soft voice.

He had stopped what he was doing. His hands had gripped the cabinet and he had leaned on it, lowering his head and shaking it. "I can't do this now." He had taken a deep shuddering breath. "I…" He had shaken his head, swallowing the words. "Please go." His scratchy voice had been barely there but I had heard it.

My heart had broken. Tears had threatened to come but I had no right to cry, none at all.

I had wanted to put my arms around him, tell him it would all be okay, but I had known that he didn't want me there.

I had got up and hesitated. "I'm here if you need anything, or if you need to talk."

He had nodded but he still hadn't turned to look at me.

As I had reached the door I had looked back. He had watched me leave with a sadness on his face that wouldn't be erased from my mind easily. It was as though he had been saying goodbye to me. I hadn't been able to shake the feeling of finality.

"Earth to Emma," Newton was waving a hand in front of my face.

I blinked back to the present. "Sorry, what were you saying?"

Newton shook his head, "It wasn't important, *Dweeb*."

Ash joined us a few moments later, with her hair wrapped in a towel after her shower. She and I had had a long talk a few days after Scott left — after I had spent days crying over him and the way he had looked at me the last time I had seen him. Ash had cornered me in my room with tea and biscuits. She had sat down next to me and opened her arms sympathetically, "Come here, honey."

I hadn't known whether it was her gentle voice or her sympathy but I had started sobbing on her shoulder like a baby.

"What's going on? Why've you been crying so much? Don't tell me it's nothing, I won't accept that this time." She had been firm.

"I love him, Ash. I went and fell in love with him."

"Oh, honey," she had hugged me tighter.

"Why does it have to be him?" I had sniffed, "You know what he's like, Ash. He can't be what I need."

"Does he know?"

"That I love him?"

She had nodded.

"No. I don't want him to find out either."

"I won't say anything, but," she had paused and I had looked at her, "I think he feels the same way about you."

I had pulled away from her shoulder and looked at her. "Has he said anything?" I had wiped my nose on my sleeve.

"No, but Newton has."

My eyes had widened and before I could say anything she had carried on.

"Scott hasn't said anything but Newton has. He knows Scott more than anyone and he thinks that Scott has some deep feelings for you. He knows that Scott watches you all the time and he asks questions about where you are and who you're with. Newton's never seen him like it and I must say that I haven't either." She had frowned. "I don't know why I didn't notice earlier but it's obvious really."

To me that hadn't meant much. It had only meant that he wanted me. "That doesn't mean he loves me. He just wants me so much because he hasn't got me yet. I'm a challenge to him. When did you ask Newton anyway?"

Ash hadn't looked sure. "Only last night, because I was worried about you and I remembered what you had said at Macy's the other night."

I had shaken my head. "It doesn't matter anyway, it's never going to happen for us."

"Why not? Do you know how many girls want to be in your position?"

"That's just it, Ash," my shoulders had slumped, "One day he'll get bored of me and move on. I don't think my heart could take it."

"Yes, it can. You have to take risks if you're ever going to be happy, and a relationship is always a risk."

"I know that and you're right — I know you are. But I expected to fall in love with someone totally different from my dad, you know?"

"Emma, it doesn't matter who you're with — anyone can break your heart."

I had known she was right. "How can I trust him when all he does is sleep around?"

"Perhaps he hasn't found the right lady." She had teased.

A ghost of a smile had played at my lips and then disappeared. "It doesn't matter now anyway. He doesn't want me anymore." That final look had come back to haunt me. It was like an image that had been branded in my mind and I had known that I'd never forget it. In the three days after he'd left, I hadn't had a call or text from him. It had only driven home what I already thought.

"Why do you say that?"

I had told her about our last time at Macy's and what had happened afterwards and in the morning when he had left.

She had stayed silent for a while, considering what I had said, a frown marring her features. "Just give him time. Things will work out in the end."

I was brought back to the present again by Ash.

"You 'kay?" Ash asked me as she sat down with Newton and I at the dining table and picked up the coffee I had made for her.

"Yeah, I'm fine." My fake smile came out but it was useless — Ash had got to know it well lately.

"Have you heard anything?" she asked.

I shook my head. Still no word from him. It had been five weeks now. Did he ever think about me? I thought about him constantly. He was my first and last thought in the day.

The rest of the day went by in a blur as I spent most of the time debating whether or not to send him a message. That night I stared at my phone and then started writing a text, only to delete it and retype it a different way. I repeated that process a lot before I eventually pressed send.

Me: *How r u? xx*

I had decided to keep it short. I asked the main question I wanted to know and kept everything else out of it.

Sixteen minutes later, my phone alerted me to a text.

Scott: *Good.*

He didn't want to talk to me. I stared at the screen for what seemed like ages. That was it then. He didn't want me anymore. I had been right about that look he had had on his face when I had left him.

I couldn't blame him. I deserved this. I had left it too long. A heavy weight settled in my chest as my vision blurred.

I curled up on my bed with my phone still clutched in my hand as I cried over him for the last time.

The next morning I sat at the table with a cup of tea in my hand and the laptop in front of me. I'd made my decision and now I had to tell Ash.

"Morning." She sat next to me with a coffee. She frowned, "What's wrong?"

"I'm looking for a new apartment. I can't live here anymore." I looked at her. "I'm going to start looking today."

"Okay, but you know Scott could come back at any time so we might not get moved in time."

"I know that and it doesn't matter. I want to get the ball rolling now."

"Okay, I'll help you look. And you're not leaving me here, I'm coming with you, so any viewings have got to include me." she smiled.

Chapter Thirty

"Wow, I love this, and look at the view. Oh my *God*, there's a *jacuzzi*!" Ash squealed as she danced from room to room.

Over the last month we had viewed so many apartments, and there had always been something wrong with them.

I laughed and turned to the owner. "I think we'll take it."

"That's great. It'll be ready in around five weeks. Does that suit you?"

It didn't but I couldn't risk another month of looking so I agreed and put a deposit down.

As soon as we got in the car Ash was on the phone to Newton telling him that we'd found a place. My heart flipped. Ash was lucky to have someone she could call, someone who loved her to bits. I sent a text to Kyle and got a near instant reply.

Kyle: *Thats gr8 news! Wanna celebrate? x*

We went out that night to celebrate at Macy's. I hadn't been out in weeks. Macy's wasn't the same without Scott there and it definitely wasn't as busy. Halfway through the night, Ash and I were dancing with Kyle when we noticed a commotion by the entrance. We tried to get up on tip toes but it was hard when you'd had a few and people were dancing all around you.

"What's going on?" Ash asked me as I was taller by an inch.

"I can't see anything but big heads," I said, annoyed.

"Come on." She looked at Kyle, "Back in a sec." She took hold of my hand and tugged me towards the tight ball of people at the door.

I really couldn't care less who it was. "Someone famous maybe?"

She frowned, "Not in here. Wait here while I check it out." She weaved through the bodies until I couldn't see her anymore. Damn Ash and her nosey nose!

I didn't care who it was, I wanted to dance.
She came back a moment later, her eyes finding mine.
"Who is it then?"
She looked down at her feet and then back up to me with wide eyes. "Scott's back."
I froze and my heart thudded painfully against my ribs. *Oh no!* I didn't want to see him. I looked towards the crowd and saw him emerge from the parting bodies. He looked thinner. He was pale and his smile was strained as he greeted everyone who was welcoming him back. I had missed him for months and now panic took hold and froze me to the spot. He was walking this way.

"Oh my God, Ash, *help me*! I don't think I can see him yet."
"It's okay, Em. Just act natural, okay?"
Act natural? That was easy for her to say but I was shaking like a chihuahua on ice. He was still the only guy in the room that the girls gawked at — he still had that dangerous edge to him. I looked away until he was standing right in front of us.
"Scott, how are you?" Ash went forward and hugged him.
Traitor.
"I'm okay, Ash." He gently pulled her off.

Something wasn't right with him. He seemed distant, exactly as Newton had described him. He had an edge of quiet anger about him that hadn't been there before — it wasn't obvious but I could see it. I felt it.
He looked at me. His eyes made contact with mine. I flinched at the pain and anger I saw hidden in their depths, but in an instant it had been cleverly masked and just an echo of it remained. As a bad cut left a scar on skin, the pain he had experienced would be

forever ingrained in his eyes, like a brand. He looked behind me as I felt a hand rest on my shoulder and I turned to see Kyle, giving me support, but it didn't help.

Scott's lips tightened. "Emma," he greeted me, his voice low.
"Hi!" I cleared the frog in my throat.
His eyes travelled down to my mouth and he smirked before walking off and leaving us standing there, wondering what had happened to the Scott we all knew and loved.

"I'm going. I can't stay here." It was obvious that he didn't want to have anything to do with me. A ping pong ball-sized lump formed in my throat.
Ash was frowning after Scott. "Yeah, I'll come with," she said as she continued to study his retreating figure.
Ash went to tell Newton that we were leaving and told me to meet her outside.
"Are you good?" Kyle asked, eyeing me with concern.
I nodded. "I just wasn't ready for that."
"It'll get easier, sweet." Kyle touched my hand and squeezed.
Kyle was the only person apart from Ash, Newton and Meg who I had told about Scott. "I hope so. Are you staying or going?"
"What do you want me to do?" he asked.
I smiled, "Whatever you want to do."
"I think I'm gonna call it a night."

Kyle walked me outside and waited with me until Ash came out.
"Newton wanted to stay and catch up with Scott," Ash shrugged.
"I'll call you tomorrow." Kyle leaned in to kiss me on the cheek and then left.
"He really likes you, Em." Ash's eyes followed Kyle's backside as he walked away.

"I know he does," I sighed. I wished it could have been Kyle.

"Scott's different." *He hates me.*
"Mm…" She looked back at Macy's as we strolled home. "It'll take a while for him to get over it."
"He looks like he's taking it very badly. I'm worried about him." I didn't know why. All I'd heard from him was one measly one-worded text message, which was a reply to one I had already sent so it didn't really count.
"I'll speak to Newton tomorrow, find out what he knows."

Later I was woken by the front door slamming and a high-pitched squeal. I stopped breathing. Scott had brought a girl home. Tears threatened my eyes again. I couldn't do this. I couldn't lie here and listen to them upstairs. How could he be so cruel? I blinked my eyes and rolled over to look at the alarm clock on my bedside table. 02.47 it read. I got up and went to the kitchen for a drink. Ash was still asleep and blissfully oblivious to it all.

I poured myself a glass of water and went back to bed.
As I got under the covers, music started pouring through the ceiling from his stereo and I knew that I wouldn't be getting much sleep, if any.
I put the pillow over my head and tried to sleep but my heart was sick and tired of it and I wanted him to be the Scott I knew. I went to sleep crying, mourning the person he used to be.

Morning came after a night of tossing and turning. The dreams in between dozing and waking were the worst. I had dreamed in graphic detail of Scott with someone else every time I had closed my eyes. I had woken up crying after every one of them. I went through morning classes almost snarling at everyone. When lunch came I grabbed an energy drink — which I never did — and a slice of chocolate cake to have after lunch for the sugar rush.

I sat at our usual table and hoped that fate would be kind and Scott wouldn't come in. I didn't even know if he was coming back.

"What's up with you?" Newton sat opposite me.

"Nothing. Why?"

"You look seriously pissed off."

"I didn't sleep well," I almost grunted.

I wanted to ask him about Scott, but this wasn't the place or the time — he had just walked in with a girl stuck to his side. She slithered around him like a snake.

I frowned and concentrated on my lunch, which was even less appealing now. *Please don't come over here, please don't come over here*, I repeated in my head, hoping my will would work on him.

"He's coming over, Em. Ignore him if he's a dick," Newton whispered.

I could only bob my head in understanding. I took a breath, straightened my back, schooled my mien into one of indifference and looked up.

The girl was from one of my classes and she was looking straight at me and smiling. *Bitch.* I smiled back, hoping my face didn't break.

I dug into my lunch unenthusiastically — it tasted like nothing but I needed to do something with my hands and eyes.

"Dude, get your slug off the table," Newton moaned.

I looked up. Scott had sat down and placed her on the table in front of him. He was watching me. He was doing this on purpose.

"Fuck you, asshole," Scott's girl spat at Newton.

"You're a real lady, aren't you?" Newton returned.

The girl turned to Scott. "Are you gonna let him talk to me that way?"

"Leave her, Newton. You don't mind do you, Emma?" Scott's eyes were glassy.

I couldn't believe he was actually asking me if she could sit with us while he fondled her in front of me.

"Scott," Newton warned him, "leave her alone."

Scott focused on Newton, his eyes squinting. "Why do you care?"

What the hell is wrong *with him?*

Newton leaned forward so he was close to Scott. "You're being a dick and she doesn't deserve this, so back the fuck off."

I'd had enough. If Scott wanted to be a twat, then fine, but I wasn't going to sit there and watch Newton argue with his best friend over me. I was grateful to him for trying to help, but I didn't want them to fall out over me.

"Wait, did you two…?" The girl waved a hand between Scott and I and laughed.

Scott looked at me and smiled with a cruel twist to his lips before looking back at the girl. "No, she's too prissy for me."

My throat thickened. Why is he doing this?

"That's not what I heard," her voice went down to a whisper, "I saw that video." She giggled.

"Scott!" Newton raised his voice.

I had had enough. I pushed my chair back and stood, anger pulsing through me. The bitch was going to get it any second. *How dare she?* How could *he*? I hated him. I wanted to knock his head off right there in front of everyone.

"Don't bother, Newton. The only kind girl he'll ever be good enough for is sitting right in front of him." I looked at Scott and saw his jaw grinding.

Good — I at least made him angry if nothing else.

"Fuck off, bitch!" The girl stood too and was shooting arrows through her eyes, but I just smiled.

"*Fuck off, Bitch?*" I mimicked and forced a laugh. "If you want a slanging match with me, I suggest you broaden your vocabulary considerably before uttering another word and giving me further reason to believe that you came from a settlement of inbred idiots."

The girl turned pink under her thick layer of foundation.

"Do yourself a favour and sit down." I shook my head. "You won't win with me," I spat.

She was burning red now but I didn't care. As far as I was concerned she deserved it — she had laughed at something that was personal, something that was a part of my past that I wanted to forget. Scott knew how much I hurt over that. I shot him a look of pure venom.

Scott's mouth was a tight line, his eyes dull as he looked away from me. I wanted to slap him so hard for being like this with me, for treating me like I didn't matter. Did I mean *anything* to him? Obviously fucking not.

The shit of it was that I loved him. I felt my lips tug down as my eyes had that familiar sting. I went to walk away but Newton grabbed my hand to stop me. Out of the corner of my eye I saw Scott's gaze zero in on the touch. "You haven't eaten anything," Newton chided.

"I'm not really hungry." I looked at Scott, "I didn't sleep well last night."

"Scott, she needs to eat so go have your lunch somewhere else if you're gonna be a fucking asshole." Newton wouldn't let go of me even though I tugged at my hand.

Scott's eyes narrowed on us.

"I'm not hungry." This was getting silly. Newton meant well, but couldn't he see that I wanted to go before I blubbed in front of everyone?

Scott sighed. "Sit down and eat, Emma."

We were getting odd looks from everyone and I noticed Kyle was on his way over. I sat down.

"Hey!" Kyle's warm smile was exactly what I needed right then.

"Hey, you." I tried to be cheerful but it came out cracked.

He sat down beside me and flung an arm around my shoulders with a frown. He looked at Scott and then back to me. He knew something was up. "You wanna get some lunch with me?"

"Now?"

"Yeah. Come on, my treat."

Relief swept through me. "That sounds good."

I stood again. Scott's eyes were on me but I refused to look at him again.

I said bye to Newton and walked away.

"She doesn't fuckin' deserve that," I heard Newton say as we walked away. "What happened to you, man?"

Chapter Thirty-one

I had been seeing a lot of Kyle since Scott had left. He was one of those people who was easy to be with, even if you hadn't spoken in ages — you could just jump right into conversation as though you talked every day. That's what I liked about him. He was into me but he knew I wasn't looking for that kind of thing. And he knew that Scott and I had had something but he never asked any questions — obviously, that wasn't the case anymore.

"Are you okay, sweet? You looked uncomfortable back there."
"I am now," I smiled and he let it drop.
We had a nice lunch and I actually laughed. He was so funny sometimes. He made me feel good. Why couldn't I love him? He was so nice and he never tried to take things further than friendship.

Two weeks went by and it was the same almost every night — loud music and girls. That had meant no sleep for me, although Ash slept peacefully through it as she was a heavy sleeper. I was struggling with everything from course work to eating. Weeks of barely sleeping had got to me. I barely saw Scott, for which I was grateful. When I did see him, it was never pleasant — he blanked me and I was afraid of feeling what he made me feel in the cafeteria.

He hated me and I didn't understand why, and there was no way in hell that I was going to confront him about it. My mood was all over the place — one minute I was angry, the other upset, which probably had a lot to do with my lack of sleep. That night, though, I had had enough. It was almost four in the morning and I was raging. For the last few hours I had lain in bed seething at the noise coming from his apartment — and the fact that he didn't give a shit about Ash and I pissed me off even more.

He flaunted girls in front of me whenever he got the chance and I was sick, *so bloody sick,* of it all. I threw the blanket off me and marched upstairs in my pyjama shorts and tank top. I didn't care. My anger carried me quickly and adrenaline pumped through me.

I got to his door and thought, *fuck it, I'm not knocking.* If he could invade my life, why couldn't I do the same? I walked straight in. I went through to the living room and froze. It was as though someone had taken my breath and wouldn't give it back. I couldn't breathe. Scott was lying naked on top of an equally naked girl on the sofa. Her legs were parted wide to accommodate him as he moved rapidly over her, going into her.

His dark head was buried in her neck while one of his hands held her face away from him. I couldn't watch any more — the pain erupting in my chest was too much. I lowered my gaze and paused as I caught sight of the coffee table. On it was an old DVD with white lines of powder on it and a rolled up bank note next to it. I knew it was cocaine straight away. I looked back at them. The girl was moaning now. She opened her glazed eyes and saw me.

She pushed at Scott's chest, he frowned at her and she nodded at me. Scott's lust-filled, hard eyes looked at me and I couldn't look away. Realisation and shock slowly dawned in his features. I stood there wide-eyed, unblinking — unbelieving that I was witnessing the horrible scene in front of me for the second time in my life. I squeezed my eyes closed as the two meshed together in my head.

My heart was beating so hard and fast that I put a hand over it to touch the pain. I was breathing heavily and cool air hit the trails of my tears, cooling me faintly. I opened my eyes. Scott had put jeans on and was coming towards me. I didn't even need to think — I turned on my heels and ran.

"Emma!" he bellowed as he came after me, his voice rough.

I couldn't face him now. Everything was swirling around in my head — parts of the night I had caught my dad with another woman and bits of what I had just seen. I was losing my mind. I needed to sleep. I needed to be away from this house. I *needed* to be away from Scott.

It seemed like forever until I reached his door and ran out of it. My foot caught on a ruckle in the carpet and I couldn't get my balance. I was going down. The floor was coming for my face. Perhaps I would be knocked out for a little while — forget the hurt.

He caught me around the waist just in time and pulled me up.

"Get *away!*" I fought out of his arms but he seized me again and trapped me against the wall.

"What the fuck are you doing up here?" he shouted, anger rolling off him. His hands were on my shoulders shaking me. I couldn't bear for him to touch me — not with that girl still so fresh on his skin, not with cocaine running through his veins.

I closed my eyes against his angry stare and breathed for a moment. I just needed to be strong for a little longer. I *would not* give him the pleasure of letting him know how much he'd upset me. *Be strong, girlie.* I felt my mouth turn down in disgust as his hands were on me. "Don't touch me," I whispered. I opened my eyes and let my disgust and disappointment out.

He took his hands away from me quickly and put them through his hair. "Fuck, Emma!" His face was haggard and there was pain in his eyes as he looked at me.

I looked away. "I can't sleep. Can you just keep the music down?"

"Is that why you came up?" He studied my face for a hidden answer.

I nodded. "Just keep it down for a few weeks and then you'll have the place to yourself."

I turned my back on him and went down the stairs but he followed me into my apartment. He took my hand but I yanked it away. "Don't fucking *touch* me." My voice was forceful enough to make him stop.

"Just leave."

"What are you talking about? Why will I have the place to myself?" His voice was hoarse.

"We've found another apartment. We leave in three weeks."

He crossed his arms and looked down.

I left him and went into my room and closed the door. I didn't care if I had just left him in my apartment. I just wanted to be away from him. I couldn't stand to look at him.

He was using drugs. Tears ran down my cheeks and into my hair. He was lost. I knew first-hand how that could change someone. I wanted to scream at him for doing it to himself. Even though I tried hard not to care, I did. I still loved him and everything he had done lately had hurt my heart. My head started to pound and I cried harder as memories of better times for us came back to me in full colour.

Chapter Thirty-two

I woke feeling nauseous. My body felt as though flames were licking me from the inside out and I was hurting everywhere. I tried to lift my head but that hurt, too, so I stayed where I was and drifted back to sleep.

The next time I woke it was to something ice-cold on my forehead. I groaned and tried to shake it off. Opening an eye, I realised Ash was testing my temperature.

"She's burning up." Her voice seemed far away and strange to my ears. "Looks like flu." I didn't know who she was talking to and I didn't care.

I felt terrible. The sun was coming through the blinds. My eyelids fluttered as the bright light felt like needles being poked into my eyes.

"Emma? Sit up and take these painkillers." Ash put a cold hand behind my head.

"No!" My voice was distant to me like I was talking from inside a bubble.

I groaned hoarsely. Everything hurt so much, every joint, every muscle.

Then something cold got stuck in my ear and arms held me down as I tried to get it out.

"Jesus Christ! It's one-oh-five," a guy's voice said.

Newton? What is he doing here in my room?

"I'm calling the doctor," Ash said. I could hear the worry in her voice.

"No. I want to sleep."

"She's out of it, babe. Just call him and I'll keep an eye on her."

A heard a distant thud.

"Who's that?" Newton asked.

Ash mumbled something and then the room was quiet apart from my rapid breathing. What seemed like an hour later I heard a commotion coming closer.

"I'm not lying, Scott, she's sick."

"Ash, I saw her five hours ago and she was fine so don't fuckin' lie to me. I need to talk to her." Scott was there too.

"Five hours ago?" Ash said.

It must have still been early.

"God, what's wrong with her?" Scott said.

I didn't want him to see me like this. I started crying and turned onto my side. I was so cold.

"Flu, probably. I came in an hour ago and found her like this. She's got a temperature of one-oh-five."

I still couldn't open my eyes. My head was pounding and so sore. My scalp even felt sore. Warmer hands were suddenly on me. I knew instinctively that they were Scott's. He lifted me into his arms and I moaned at the pain in my head and body.

"Okay, baby, I got you." His voice was soothing but I caught a hint of shakiness in it.

"What're you doing?" Ash said, concern in her voice.

"Have you checked her for a fuckin' rash?" he growled and pulled my top up.

I moaned and tried to push his hands away but it was no use — I was too weak to fight.

"Why do you care, Scott? The way you've treated her since you got back is disgusting." Ash was angry.

I could imagine she had her fists balled and was turning pink. A giggle escaped my lips.

I felt Scott stiffen beneath me and wondered why he would care.

"She can't sleep because of you and she barely eats! This is *your* fucking fault and I goddamn *warned* you to stay away from her." Ash was getting hysterical.

Scott sat me up and leaned me forward. His fingers ran over my back "Get me a glass." he ordered.

There was a pause and then a gasp.

"Oh God, I didn't think," Ash whispered.

"Ash! Glass. Now!" Scott repeated.

Everything was fuzzy. Was I dreaming this? What a funny dream to have. Like Scott would give a shit about me. I was really losing it. *Was last night a dream too?* I giggled.

"Baby, I'm so sorry. I'm so fucking sorry." His voice broke as though he was crying. He squeezed me close to him and kissed my forehead.

Scott's crying? Okay, I really am losing it. I giggled again and then winced and cried more. I didn't know why I was crying but I was far away from myself.

I felt weird. I wanted it to go away. I needed to sleep. A coldness was laid against the skin on my back going right through me, and I bucked. Strong arms held me still. Scott's strong, uncaring arms, which had been wrapped around girl after girl. I sobbed louder — at least, I thought it was.

"Call 911, Ash."

I heard Ash in a panic on the phone, crying. "Oh my God! I need an ambulance…My cousin…She…"

"Ash?" I rasped. I wanted to comfort her.

"She's okay, baby. Just relax."

I felt as though I was slipping away. My body started to shake uncontrollably from within and it wouldn't stop. My eyes shot open in fear. *What is happening to me? I'm dying!*

Rocked Under ~ Cora Hawkes

Scott's eyes were wide as he held me. "Emma, no!" Scott shouted before everything went black and a deep peace blanketed me.

I had flashes of bits and pieces but I couldn't tell one minute from the next or what order those moments went in.

My eyes opened and I knew straight away that I was in hospital. I had tubes attached to me.

The door opened quietly and Ash walked in. She had a coffee and she was typing something on her phone. Her blonde hair was tied back with wisps falling down around her ashen face, making her eyes look sunken and tired. Her clothes were rumpled, too. I frowned — Ash was always so neat.

She glanced at me and back to her phone. Then she froze and slowly looked up. "You're awake!" A relieved grin spread across her face and tears made her eyes glisten. She pocketed her phone, put her coffee down and came to me.

I tried to smile but everything felt alien to me.

She sat down on the bed beside me. "How are you feeling? You gave us such a scare." She put her hand to my forehead in concern and tears rolled down her cheeks and her lips trembled. "I'm so happy you're okay." She took my hand and sniffed. "You nearly died, Em. I..." she squeezed her eyes for a moment and took a deep breath, "I nearly lost you."

I tried to smile but it felt like it came out wrong. I remembered Ash calling an ambulance in a panic, like I had dreamed it. My memories were surreal, like I had been drunk or tripping out.

"I..." My throat was so dry that I found it hard to talk.

"Here," a straw was shoved between my lips, "Sip it slowly or you'll bring it back up." Her voice was still shaking. "You haven't had anything in your stomach for days."

I did as I was told. The cold liquid felt blissful as it slid down my parched throat. My head went back to my pillow and I smiled at her gratefully.

"I'm feeling better." My voice was raspy. "What happened?"

"You went down with bacterial meningitis three days ago. You've been out of it since."

I frowned. "Am I okay?"

She smiled. "Yes, Emma. As soon as you got here, they gave you antibiotics," she pointed to the tube in my hand. "The first twenty-four hours were..." she looked at me, "I don't even want to think about the time we spent waiting for you to respond to what they gave you, but you did and you've been catching up on your sleep since." She tried to sound light but I could tell she had been deeply afraid for me.

I covered her hand. "I'm sorry I worried you."

She stroked my hair and shook her head as if to say *forget it*. "I'm going to tell the nurse you're awake so she can check you over. I'll be right back."

"Okay."

I'd missed three days. I thought back to the last *clear* thing I remembered. I had walked in on Scott having sex with a girl. I squeezed my eyes shut but it didn't stop the mental movie playing. The way Scott was rocking into her made me want to cry. And then having seen the cocaine on the table — I hadn't even known he used it. The shame on his face when he had seen me — or maybe I was imagining that part because there was no part of the Scott that I knew left in him.

He had shown me a polar opposite of himself — I had never seen that part of him. Anger swirled in my stomach, making me feel sick. Maybe the Scott I thought was real wasn't real at all. But I didn't truly believe that — I couldn't. The pain in his eyes when he had caught me on the stairs told me that he wasn't happy. He wasn't over his dad's death — he was hiding from it.

My mum came back in with Ash and a nurse.
"Mum!"
She came over to me, her lips wobbling. "Oh, my heart! I love you so much. I was so worried about you." She wrapped me up in a big hug and kissed me all over my face as she smoothed my hair.

I smiled and put my arms around her as best I could with the tubes still attached to me.

"How long have you been here?"
"Ash called me when you came in and I've been here since."
The nurse then took over and ushered mum and Ash out of the room while she checked me over. She told me that I was lucky that I had friends who knew what to look for as she went about her task.

Mum and Ash stayed until I ordered them to go home and get some rest. It was pointless them staying when I planned on sleeping as much as I could, and I was gradually feeling better as the day wore on. They reluctantly left me with a promise of returning first thing in the morning.

That same night, the nurse announced that I had another visitor. I sat up a bit straighter. Maybe it was Scott? Who else could it be? I finger combed my hair quickly, rubbed the sleep out of my eyes and made sure I had no embarrassing bits on show. The door opened and my heart jumped into my throat. The person I had least expected was standing in the doorway — my dad.

He came in slowly, with hesitant steps. "How are you feeling?" he said, standing beside my bed.

He looked older. His black hair was littered with grey. His eyes were drawn with purple bags and wrinkles. He no longer stood tall, he had a slight slump to his once proud shoulders. He had aged so much since I saw him last.

"What are you doing here, Dad?" I tried to sound strong but I couldn't, I was too weak.

He looked down. "Your mother called me a few days ago." Then his sad eyes met mine again. "I had to come, Emma. You are my daughter."

I humphed. "Now you care?"

He pulled a chair close. "May I?"

I nodded.

"Emma, I want to apologise for what happened."

"You have no right to show up here and ask me to forgive you." Then I felt my brows rise as I remembered my mum's words about forgiveness. I looked at him, did he really need it? Was he desperate?

"I know that," he bent his head, "I know that I did a lot of things that hurt you and your mother terribly, but I love you both more than you can know." He looked up. "I was ashamed. I couldn't tell your mother that I had fallen into something that I couldn't climb out of." He paused and looked lost in thought.

I looked at his hands, they were shaking slightly. Pity for him — my father, the one who had hurt my mum so badly — rushed into me.

"Your mother is the greatest thing to have entered my life." He looked at his hands. "I don't know if you remember, but I cherished her every day. When things went wrong and…"

"You became addicted to cocaine," I finished for him.

He looked at me sadly and nodded. "I was ashamed, Emma, and I didn't want her to know that I had made a massive mistake. I felt like dirt on the bottom of her shoe — I wasn't worthy of her. So I stayed away and lied about working late, so she didn't have to witness it. I tried to give it up — numerous times — but I couldn't do it. Whenever I did come home, she would wonder where I had been and we argued."

"Yes. I was there, remember?"

"I was never angry with her, I was angry with myself for making such a mess of things. Once I started to lose her, I sunk even lower, and the rest you know about." He sighed heavily, as though a weight had been placed on him. "When you and your mother left I was so distraught that I checked into a rehabilitation clinic, where I stayed for three months and got myself straight again. I love you and your mother more than anything in this world and I'm willing to do whatever it takes to make us right again. I love you, princess, and I miss you so much and I'm more sorry than you can ever know." Tears shone in his eyes.

I looked down at my clasped hands. I had been right. He did love us. Maybe I knew, deep down, that he had loved us all along. He had always been such a great dad and I did love him. It was time to let go. I was ready. I couldn't keep my anger festering away inside me forever and I didn't want to. I wanted him to be the caring, happy man that he once was.

"I'll understand if you can't forgive me, Emma, because what I did and how I treated you both is inexcusable, but I *do* love you. I just wanted you to know that." He sighed. "I have sat in a hotel room for the last couple of days just waiting to hear how you were. When your mother called me in a state saying that you had been rushed to hospital and they didn't know if you would make it through, I flew straight over here." He shook his head and looked down, his lips rolling in as tears threatened to overflow. "It was the longest flight of my life and I kept thinking that I would be too late, that I would lose you — my beautiful daughter — without making things right with you, without holding you in my arms and telling you that I…" he broke right in front of me.

Tears rolled down my cheeks, "I've missed you, Dad."

Rocked Under ~ Cora Hawkes

Chapter Thirty-three

After getting the okay from the doctor a couple of days later I was allowed home. Everyone I knew had visited me in the time that I had been there. My dad had visited me every night and brought me crossword puzzles to keep me occupied — it was so typical of him and it felt good to know that he hadn't changed too much. One of the nurses said that he had called every few hours since I had been admitted and it had solidified my choice to forgive him. He had listened to me talk about my life and taken in every detail. It had been nice just to see him smile again.

I had asked my mum about Dad and she told me that he was going back with her to stay while he was over here. She was very close-mouthed about it, but the dull glow that I was used to seeing had changed and morphed into a bright light that had her eyes twinkling again.
They had wanted to take me home with them but I had refused. I didn't want to be clucked over, I wanted to be left alone. In two weeks we would be moving and I had to get packed. Mum wasn't happy about it but she let it alone when I gave her my I'm a big girl now stare.

Ash picked me up and helped me into the car like I was a delicate child. I was feeling loads better — still weak, but I was told that would pass shortly. I hadn't mentioned Scott at all since I had woken up but I wanted to ask if he was okay. Had he even asked about me? Did he give a shit?

"How's Scott?" Ash stilled but didn't look at me, instead keeping her eyes on the road.
"He's okay, I guess." She turned her head away from me and pretended to be interested in something out the window. She was

lying. I knew my cousin and I knew that she turned her head away when she lied.

"Ash, I know when you're flibbing." She smiled a little at our old word for fibbing.

She sighed. "He's not good, Em. But don't worry about him now, we need to get you to full strength first."

I looked down at my hands. "Has he even asked about me?"

She looked shocked. "Don't you know?"

Oh no! What now? "No, I don't know anything! I've been in the hospital for the last week if you hadn't noticed."

"Emma, Scott stayed at the hospital for three days while you slept. He refused to leave and only left when you woke up and the nurse had done your vitals."

Shock went through me and my eyes widened. "Why would he do that?"

"The morning I found you he burst in wanting to see you, to talk to you. When I told him that you were sick, he wouldn't believe me — he said that he'd seen you hours before and you weren't sick at all." She gave me a questioning look and I looked down again. "He went into your room and saw you and I swear it was like he *knew*. It was weird, but if he hadn't have checked you for a rash and found the spots on your back, we wouldn't have called an ambulance when we did."

The words *and you could've died* were left unspoken between us but they hung in the air like a poltergeist and made me uncomfortable.

Baby, I'm so sorry. I'm so fucking sorry. I kind of remembered him saying it to me as I lay in his arms.

"I had no idea. I thought he didn't care."

"Emma, that guy loves you. He's a total mess."

I didn't believe her so I kept quiet for the rest of the short drive home.

Ash led me straight to the couch to lay me down. I could tell that if she was ever a nurse, she'd be a bossy one. She already had everything I would need on the coffee table, which she had moved next to where I was supposed to lie — books, tissues, a selection of my favourite DVDs, munch, laptop, remotes and more.

"Wow, thanks," I smiled in gratitude, "You're awesome."

She beamed. "Hey, you're my favourite cousin. Can't have you being sick for long."

I laughed. I was her *only* cousin. She had been at the hospital with me every day for a week and I was so grateful to her for caring so much. She had gone a bit nuts when I had told her about my dad. She thought he would hurt us again, but I needed to let go of my anger and give him a second chance. Didn't everyone deserve that? It wasn't as though he had killed or raped anybody. He had just lost his way — okay, he had lost his way *big* time, but still…

"Where's Newton? You and him are usually inseparable."

"Oh, he knows that I'm with you so he doesn't mind." She swiped her hand through the air like it was nothing, but I felt guilty.

"Go out with him tonight. Spend some time together. I'll be fine here and I can call you if I'm not."

"No way, Em! I'm not leaving you on your first night home." She straightened her back. "You just got out of hospital after being in a serious condition." She was firm, but I was determined to get her out of the apartment so she could spend time with Newton.

"Look. I could do with some time alone. After spending a week in that place, I feel violated. You don't have to be late and you have a phone…"

"Cell, Emma. It's a cell over here," she interrupted.

"You have a *cell* and so does Newton," she was about to argue, "and Scott's upstairs unless he's playing tonight."

She considered it for a moment. "You promise to call if you want or need me?"

"Of course I will, but I'll be fine."

"Okay, but you better answer if I call."

"Of course I will."

As soon as Ash was out the door I went to have a shower. I needed to get the stench of hospital off me. I stepped under the warm spray and lifted my head, letting the water run over my face.

I noticed that I had lost more weight — my ribs were faintly noticeable, my collarbone protruded more, but I didn't look like a stick yet.

"Emma!" I heard a muffled shout.

I quickly turned the shower off and jumped out, only to realise that I had forgotten to grab a towel on the way in.

Shit! "Who's there?"

"It's me. Are you okay in there?" Scott was behind the door now.

My heart started thumping wildly when I heard his voice and I became breathless. I was still weak and my body started to shake from the cold seeping into the steamy room from the poor-quality window.

I wasn't ready to face him yet — not after what had happened. "What're you d–doing here, Scott?" My teeth started chattering.

"I'm checking on you — Ash told me to."

I rolled my eyes, that girl was a menace.

"I'm f–fine. Can you go now?"

"I'm not going anywhere until I've seen that your good with my own eyes, so you can come out, or I'm coming in."

Bloody hell! "Can you get m–me a couple of towels then? I forgot. They're in the closet." How lame did I sound? He was probably thinking that I had done it on purpose or something.

He opened the door a crack a minute later and poked two towels through, letting more cold air at my wet skin.

"Thanks." I put a towel around myself and wrapped up my hair with shaking hands as I prepared to walk out of there with nothing on but a towel that covered me from the top of my boobs to the middle of my thighs.

I opened the door and even more cool air hit me. I started to shiver uncontrollably.

"Jesus, Em. You're shaking all over the place."

I looked up at his panicked expression and was knocked sideways again by how attractive he was. He looked rough, but he still managed to be the best-looking guy I had ever met.

"M–my b–body is s–still weak, b–but I'm okay."

Scott came towards me and scooped me up and bundled me in his arms.

I gasped. "Put m–me down."

"You're freezing your fuckin' ass off."

I had nothing on but a towel and Scott was carrying me. Not only was I embarrassed for looking like a washed-out rag but now he had my almost-naked body in his arms. I wanted to become invisible. Straight away his warmth seeped into me, easing my shivering, but I would never have admitted it.

He took me to my room, placed me on the edge of my bed gently and let go of me, taking his warmth with him.

"Where's your warm bed clothes?" He looked around him.

No way was he doing what I think he planned on doing. "I can get d–dressed on my own." I tried to sound firm but my voice was weak. "I don't n–need your help."

"The hell you don't!" he growled suddenly. "Where are they?"

I shrank back from him and pointed over to my bottom drawer. I was too tired and cold to argue back even though I wanted to.

He pulled out the first warm things he put his hands on and came back to me.

"I promise I won't look, but you need to drop the towel so I can put these on you."

"Nice t–try, asshole." As if I was going let him to do that.

"You either do it or I'll do it for you. You should be chilling out, not fuckin' showering." His mouth was a thin line. "You want me to call Ash and tell her that you're not resting?" His green eyes brooked no argument — he was resolute and I knew that he wasn't bluffing.

I huffed. "You'd better not look."

As I lowered the towel to my waist, Scott kept his eyes on mine while I tried to keep my face indifferent. I wanted to cringe and squirm with my whole heart. Scott Mason was dressing me! *What if my body isn't as sexy as the other girls he's been with? I wonder if he compares them like I do?*

He lifted my fleece pyjama top and put it over my head. His eyes were darkening and I knew that he was trying very hard to keep his eyes glued to mine.

Why do I even care what he thinks anyway? I. Don't. Bloody. Care.

But I did. I *cared* what he thought about my body — what he thought about me.

I pushed my arms through and then Scott — without looking — found the hem and barely missed touching my breast which sent a jolt of liquid heat through me as he pulled it down the rest of the way over my stomach.

My skin became warm and my face heated in an instant.
He picked up the flannel bottoms next as I expelled my breath. *Oh, God!* "I need to stand up." *So embarrassing!*
He moved away and helped me stand. Once again, he kept his eyes on mine as I lowered the towel hesitantly to the floor.
I could hear him breathing deeply and I started to tremble. I knew it had nothing to do with my body recovering and more to do with Scott and the way he was looking at me with open hunger, which he tried, and failed, to conceal fully.

He opened my pyjama bottoms with both hands so I could step into them. I put my hand on his bare arm for support as I slipped my legs inside. He pulled them up slowly, his hands gliding up the outside of my thighs, over my hips, sending sparks on a collision course with the deepest part of me. And all the while, his eyes had never left mine.
"Thanks." My voice was breathy and I stepped away from him and swayed on my feet.

"Jesus, babe. You need to rest." He picked me up again, carried me into the lounge and sat with me in his lap. I went to move but he held me tight and wouldn't let me go.
"I'm fine now. You don't need to stay." I tried to move off him again and he let me.
I got under the blanket as he stood.
"Emma, about the other night…"
"I don't want to talk about it, I really don't." I shook my head.
He sighed.

"We'll be gone in two weeks and you can do what the hell you want. You can sleep with the whole fucking town and do all the drugs in the world." I looked away to hide the fact that it upset me. Why would I want to talk about it? I wanted to forget what had happened, not relive seeing him fucking another girl like that after everything he had said to me. When he had come back he had been a Scott that I didn't know — there had been no softness to him. He was a stranger.

Those two weeks had been a hell of hurt and anger and I hadn't known why. I guessed a part of his behaviour had been to do with drugs, but that couldn't have been the *only* reason. I knew first-hand how cocaine affected someone — how it twisted them and how addicting it could be. How could he do it? Why did I let him get to me so much? Oh yeah — it was because of a little thing called *love*. Loving a person was arming them.

"Don't keep looking away from me." He sat down next to me and gently turned my face towards him. "I'm sorry you saw what you did. I haven't used it since that night and I won't be going there again. It just made all my problems worse."
"Please, Scott, not now. I don't care about it. You're sorry and that's — great." I did care.

He looked upset then and put his head in his hands. I felt bad. I didn't want to hurt him — I just didn't want to *be* hurt anymore.
"I know you're hurting and I'm so sorry that your dad died and left you," my voice was gentle, "but I can't do this with you anymore. When you were gone, I missed you — but you didn't call *once*. I wanted to be there for you. I was worried and you must have known that I would be. We were friends if nothing else, Scott!"

He gripped his forehead before running his hands over his face and looking at me.

My tone hardened. "The way you have treated me since you've been back, like you hated me," I paused when he looked away again, "I didn't deserve that. I really don't understand why you singled me out — out of everyone — and chose to hate me…"

His nostrils flared. "I told you before, I could never hate you."

"You confuse the shit out of me all the time. You say all this stuff to me and then the next time I see you, you're with someone else?" I took a breath. "Which, by the way, I *know* you did purposely to hurt me. So what the hell do you expect me to think?"

"You need to calm down. You've been really sick and…"

"The only thing *to* think was that you were talking bullshit." I stopped my rant and breathed.

He studied me for a moment. "Everything I said that night, I meant. That was the first time I'd ever said that to anyone and you rejected me again and then a-fuckin'-gain!" He frowned and clasped his hands together. "You won't fuckin' be with me and it kills me. It's like my hands are tied up and I can't reach you, I can't even touch you." He stood unexpectedly and turned his back to me. His shoulders were slumped and his head hung down on his neck. "It's fuckin' with my head. You have the most readable fuckin' eyes that I have ever known and I see that you feel something for me, but you fight it."

My throat tightened and he turned to face me.

"Why do you fight it so much? Be honest with me." His eyes were begging me and I couldn't deny him.

He deserved the truth. "I'm scared. I'm scared to be with you because you'll get bored with me and move on. You could have anyone and you have girls throwing themselves at you *all* the time."

He crossed his arms and looked down at his toes.

"I can't live like that. I really couldn't watch it if we were together."

He dropped to his knees in front of me and gripped my face. His eyes pierced mine and I could see the need shining through them.

I closed my eyes tight, not wanting to see it.

"Let me have you," his voice was gravelly, my heart squeezed, "I'll show you I don't want anyone else."

The night before I had gone into hospital was fresh in my mind, the images not yet grainy, unblemished, and the hurt was no less. "I can't now."

He deflated in front of me and then stood, looking down at me with glossy, dejected eyes.

"I'm sorry."

He shook his head slowly. "Don't be. You deserve better than me anyway. I was a fuckin' idiot to think that I had a chance."

What was he talking about? "It's not about you being good enough — it's about me and it's *my* fault."

He smiled but sadness tainted his features. "You don't need to say that."

An awkward silence started and I groped for something to say but nothing came. There was actually a lot that was left unsaid but I knew I would always keep it to myself.

Scott raised his hand to grip the back of his neck. "Do you need me to get you anything before I go?"

"No, I'm fine. Thanks, though."

"I'm sorry for being a dick to you when I got back — it won't happen again. I want you in my life any way I can get you and if that means letting go, then I'll do it — I'll never bring it up again." He pocketed his hands. "I prefer your company to anyone else's and if I had to go back to spending all my time listening to Newton moon over Ash, I might go fuckin' nuts." He was making light of things, but I knew better.

I laughed and the sound was unexpected. "You never told me that you and Ash…Um…"

"It's in the past and forgotten," he cringed.

"She rented me that new comedy to try and cheer me up. I was going to put it on. Do you want to stay for it?"

Scott smiled, his white, even teeth showing. "Sure."

Scott disappeared into the kitchen and came back with a mug of hot cocoa with marshmallows and cream before putting the movie on and sitting with my feet in his lap.

Chapter Thirty-four

A week of recovery went by and, finally, I went to class for the first time since I'd fallen ill. Ash deserved a medal for putting up with me — I didn't make a nice patient at all but she got me better and cheered me up the best she could.

I was walking to lunch when hands started tickling me under my arms from behind. I squealed loudly, making everyone turn their heads in our direction. I swung around to see who it was.

Kyle stood there with a cheeky grin on his face.
I laughed.
He put an arm around my shoulders as we continued to walk. "How are you? You look back to your ravishing old self again."

A wide smile split my face. "Thanks, and yes, feeling much better."

"Good enough to come out tonight?"

"Where?"

"A bunch of us are going to Soundz and I know you won't refuse because I happen to know that you love to dance."

I laughed again. "Is that right? Who told you that bit of top-secret information?"

Kyle opened the door and walked us into the cafeteria.

"Ah, I have eyes and ears everywhere. I'll tell you in exchange for a kiss." He closed his eyes and puckered his lips.

I laughed harder and my heart lightened. "Thanks, but I'll leave it top secret."

He clutched his chest and feigned heartbreak. "Oh, my heart doesn't take rejection from your beautiful lips well."

We went towards my usual table and I noticed Scott sitting there on his own right away.

He turned as though he knew I was thinking about him and caught my eye. He glanced from me to Kyle, to his arm around my shoulder and then back to me again.

"I don't think Scott likes me touching you," Kyle whispered.

Scott smiled and raised a hand in greeting.

He was really trying. Over the last week he'd popped in a few times to check on me and ended up staying until late.

We had watched movies and he'd cooked for me while Ash had been busy with classes. I had told him that he didn't have to keep me company but he just said that he was repaying the favour.

I had asked him how he was dealing with his dad's death on one of the nights that Ash had gone out with Newton.

"I'm okay. I miss him. I miss the thought of him being *here*." He had then looked down at his hands. "It's been hard to accept that all I will ever have of him is memories and his things."

I had put a hand over his. "I'm sorry you lost him. He seemed like a really nice guy."

He had looked at me and smiled faintly. "He was the best and he didn't deserve to go like that — not at his age." He had looked sad again. He had been looking at me but his eyes had been distant, as though he was reliving a memory. After a moment he had snapped back to me. He'd looked at our joined hands and squeezed as he shook his head. "I miss him so much." His voice had broken and I had flinched as he had stood up agitatedly, turning his back to me.

He'd been trying so hard to keep his tears in. Tears had welled up in my own eyes just watching him, but I'd pushed them back and stood up. I'd moved close to him and put my arms around his waist, resting my head against his back, which shook with silent sobs.

I had circled around to face him. His jaw had tensed, his lips tightened and eyes closed tight.

"Don't!" His voice had been a deep, broken appeal and he had tried to turn away from me again.

I had cupped his cheeks before he could make it. "Scott, it's okay," I had said softly, "It's okay to cry."

It had been like a dam breaking. He had hauled me into his arms, buried his face in my neck and held on while great powerful sobs racked him. His legs had been taken from under him and we had both fallen down on our knees.

We had been a heap on the floor and I had held him while he let his pain out. I had run my hands through his hair and whispered to him while his heart broke for a father that he had loved — who had been taken from him so unexpectedly.

"He didn't deserve to die. He was so fuckin' good." He had squeezed me harder. "I must have been a fuckin' disappointment to him but he loved me anyway." He had barely been able to get his words past his lips.

I had pulled away to look at him and wiped his tears. "I see a lot of good in you and so do Ash and Newton and Meg. So don't ever think that."

His sobs had eventually dwindled and he was quiet for a long time. We had moved to the sofa where he laid his head in my lap. I had stroked his dark, silky hair until we both fell asleep. When I woke up, he had gone and a blanket had been tucked carefully around me.

My mind snapped back to the cafeteria. "Don't be silly. He doesn't care one way or the other — he's probably having an off day." I had known different but I had wanted to save Scott's face. I felt protective of him. He'd been through enough and he was alone in the world with no family. I couldn't imagine how he felt.

I moved away from Kyle and he dropped his arm with a frown. "So, you *are* worried about what he thinks."

"Not at all. Um…About tonight — I'll be there. What time shall I meet you?" He didn't notice my swift change of subject.

"I'll pick you up on the way. Nine okay with you?"

"I'll see you at nine." I smiled widely at him.

I walked over to where Scott was sitting and plopped myself down next to him.

"Hey, you okay?" I asked as I nudged his shoulder with mine.

"Yeah. Good morning, babe?" He smiled but it barely touched his eyes.

"Yeah. Beats being stuck at home."

"What did Kyle want?" he nodded in Kyle's direction.

"He wants me to go to Soundz tonight since I haven't been out in a while." I hoped he didn't think it was a date.

"Don't you think you should take it easy for a while longer?" He was frowning.

"I feel fine and I want to get out of the apartment."

He looked down at his hands.

Speaking of getting out of the house… "When are you starting with the band again? Macy's isn't the same without you," I smiled.

"Tomorrow night — with a two-hour rehearsal before to blow away the cobwebs."

"What cobwebs? Scott, you were born to play and sing."

He smiled and when he did his eyes twinkled this time. "Come and watch and you'll see how rusty I am."

"Fine, but you don't have anything to worry about. Have you got the tour all sorted?" I didn't want him to go away for three months while he toured. I selfishly wanted him to stay. I was going to miss the hell out of him.

"Yeah, we leave in about two weeks." He didn't look excited about it.

"Oh," I smiled.

"So, who else is going tonight?"

Uh oh! "I'm not sure. He said a bunch of them are going."

He nodded and looked away. His jaw hardened.

I put my hand on his arm. "Scott, Kyle and I are just friends."

He looked at my hand before looking at me. "You don't need to explain shit to me, Emma. I can handle it."

I tilted my head close to his. "I wanted to," I said in a low voice.

He looked at me. A crease appeared between his brows and he let his gaze hold mine. His pupils grew and his eyes morphed into inky pools of want. His lips parted a little and my eyes followed. My breath faltered. The desire in his eyes was so raw and intense that I gasped as a twinge of need throbbed between my legs.

Scott's jaw clenched and his chair scraped noisily as he stood.

"Gotta go. See you later." He grabbed his bag and left.

The familiar noise of the cafeteria came rushing back as I watched him bolt out the door. I looked down at my hands. Why had he left like that? It was as though I had *scared* him.

My face heated as I shifted in my chair to try to put out the desire that Scott had ignited down there. He was turning me on with a bloody look now. What was *wrong* with me? I wasn't that desperate, was I? I pulled my lunch out of my bag. I wasn't hungry now but I had to look after myself after what had happened. I didn't want to get sick ever again.

Chapter Thirty-five

"Are you sure you don't want to come with?" I asked Ash as I got ready. I was wearing my black skinny jeans with a pair of heels and a deep red halter top. I left my hair curly and down — it fell down my back past my bra strap. A bit of make-up and some kohl finished the look.

"No. Newton's coming round to give me a hand packing but he'll probably end up watching me do it." She watched me get ready as she sucked on a lollipop.

"I'll have to make a start on my stuff soon — it should only take a night to do."

She nodded.

There was a knock on the door. "That'll be Newton." She jumped up and bounded to the door like an excited puppy.

I envied her. She had someone that she loved. She wasn't afraid to jump in. But then I suppose Newton had never been a womaniser — he was a decent guy for Ash and she loved him to bits.

My mind wandered back to earlier, going over — more like fantasising — what had happened for the hundredth time today. I still couldn't figure out why Scott had left like that. I remembered his eyes, the hunger in them, and closed my eyes as I let myself dream about what it would be like to be with him. I knew he'd be good in bed — he had had enough practise. My eyes opened as I thought about all the girls he had been with. I didn't want to go there. That road hurt too much.

"Emma!" Ash was shouting, "Kyle's here!"

Then it hit me — I hadn't seen Scott with anyone since I'd got ill.

For the first time in ages I was having a good time. I was dancing with Kyle and it felt wonderful to be out. He had that special something that some people have — the ability to light up a room and the people in it. Right then, a warm tingly feeling erupted inside me, making me throw my head back and laugh whole heartedly.

He pulled me into him and bent to my ear, "Drink?"
I nodded.
He went to the bar and left me dancing. I had the funny feeling that I was being watched, for the second time since I had arrived, but I ignored it. Guys tried to dance with me but I brushed them off. I didn't want to know — I just wanted to have fun with my friend for once without having to think about guys.

I let myself go and moved my body as though it was only me and I was back home, in my room, dancing in front of my mirror. The music was good tonight and reminded me of the happier times I had had back home. The DJ played new and old together, which could get anyone moving.
"Here."
I whirled around and found Kyle holding two shots for me.

I thanked him with a smile and a cheeky wink and downed them one after another. He took the empty glasses from me and slipped a bottle of water into my hand, making me pout.
He came close, "Don't look at me like that, you need to stay hydrated."
I nodded and was touched that he cared. My eyes widened as the DJ started to play a remix of *Feeling This Way* by Conductor and The Cowboy.

"I love this song!" I grabbed him and pulled him to me. I turned in his arms so that my back was to his chest and we danced.

I waved my arms in the air and raised my head. Kyle was moving with me but he wasn't crossing the line. I wished that I could love him. He was everything that a girl could need and he had a wicked sense of humour that tickled me in all the right places. But he wasn't Scott.

Kyle moved his hands to my waist but I didn't mind — I knew he wouldn't take it further. The song was one of my all-time favourites to dance to and I let my body get into the familiar groove as I sang loudly and, probably, very badly. I had that feeling again, that I was being watched. I did a quick scan and saw Scott leaning against the far wall watching me.

My heart jumped into my throat. He was standing there like a dark phantom with his hands tucked into his front pockets. His head was lowered as he watched me. He knew I had seen him but he didn't care or try to look away. He watched me as though it was his right, without shame or inhibition. He was pure male and I wanted him. There was no two ways about it — I felt as though he was mine and I had for a long time now.

The reason I was so hurt when I saw him with other girls was the same reason I couldn't stop thinking about him — I loved him. Soon he would be leaving for From Under's tour and I knew that I would miss the hell out of him. I would be miserable, waiting for a call, wondering who he was with — could I put myself through that? The question was — would I put myself through that just to save myself from being hurt?

I watched him watching me. The words I sang dried up on my lips as the words blurred, meshed together. Desire curled low down and it had nothing to do with the person I was dancing with. I hadn't seen Scott with a girl since that awful night before I had gone into hospital. Maybe he had changed. *Could* he love me?

Surely he would have told me — he had had so many chances to say it over the last week.

It was no good. I wanted him. I *needed* him. It was useless fighting it when we would both be unhappy. He needed someone just then and I wanted to be that someone. I loved him and I only wanted him. At the end of it all, I would rather live knowing love and regret than die not knowing how it felt.

My mum's words came back to me — *You have family around you and you're strong, Emma. Don't miss out on life because you're afraid of what might happen — that's no way to live, darling. We all need to love, whether we regret it or not, and you are no different from anyone else, my heart. Scott sounds as though he cares for you a great deal and he is probably frustrated and* confused *by your behaviour* — I knew I had been kidding myself all this time. I had thought that I would never get hurt — that I could go through life with a security blanket around my shoulders, but I was hurting anyway.

The song ended and I told Kyle that I was going to the ladies and I would find him later. I walked through the crowd towards Scott, slowly, savouring every look that crossed his face as he watched me come nearer. He looked away and I stumbled. Why would he look away? I carried on regardless of his indifference.

I took his hand when I was close enough but he shook it off. I frowned.

"Go back to Kyle," he spat at me.

I flinched. "I told you — Kyle and I are *friends.*"

He laughed cruelly. "Yeah?" his amusement died, "Like we're *friends?*"

I frowned. Why was he being like this again? "Have you been...?" I was about to say drinking.

"You know what? Don't answer that — I don't fuckin' care." He turned his head away from me.

Did he really not give a shit? I wouldn't believe that. I went close to him. "Please, dance with me?"

He looked down at me for moment. His eyes quickly masked his hunger and his jaw clenched. "Don't play with me, Emma."

That wasn't the answer I had expected. "You don't want to dance with me?"

He shook his head.

That stung. How did I let him know? How did I tell him that I had changed my mind after all I'd put him through — after all my rejections? "Why are you here?"

"To keep a fuckin' eye on you. Why do you think?" His eyebrows pulled together as his eyes widened faintly. He looked away from me.

"You came to watch out for me but you won't dance with me, even though I want you to?"

He came forward and grabbed my upper arms. "You and me — it's never gonna happen. I get it. But it doesn't mean you can rub salt in the wound." He shook his head like he regretted having said it and released me.

"I'm n…"

"Just go back to your fuckin' fairy boy." He walked away into the crowd and left me before I could say a word.

Hypocrite. That's the only word I could think of as I watched him walk away like he had a dildo shoved in his ass and I remembered every time that I had had to watch him with someone else. He knew Kyle and I were just friends but when he was with someone, I knew he would be taking her home. So, he thought it was okay for him because he was a man or something? Anger spiked within me, making my blood boil and my face start to burn.

He had rejected me because I had danced with Kyle and he had touched my waist. That was nothing compared to what I had witnessed a couple of weeks ago, when I had caught Scott at it with some dirty, drugged-up slapper. It was about time he knew what I had been through.

I marched out onto the floor, asking myself again why I let him upset me and push my bitch button. I started to dance with the best-looking guy I could find. I got his attention almost immediately and he put his hands on my waist. I egged him on by running my hands up to his neck. His hands went lower and were resting just above my backside.

I hoped Scott was watching this. I hated him right then. No, I didn't hate him — I wanted him to come and get me. But how dare he get so worked up about a dance when he had done so much more?
I went up on tip toes and kissed the guy on the mouth. His hands went straight to my ass and squeezed as he pulled me into him. I would be so pissed if I found out that Scott wasn't watching this and I had let this guy molest me for no good reason.

I pulled away from him and went to find another guy but I saw Kyle and took the opportunity to tell him that I was going soon to get my head down — I told him I was tired. He offered to take me but I said I would get a taxi. He hugged me and told me to call if I needed anything. He was so sweet, a nice person through and through.

The second guy I found was someone I vaguely knew from school. He wasn't as forward so I moved onto the next, and that's when I saw Scott. He looked dangerous and a little thrill went down my spine. His body was bunched, the muscles in his arms flexing as his fists clenched. His eyes were slits as he warned me not to go too far with this guy.

The third guy turned me around and thrust his hips into my ass while his hands fondled my breasts painfully. Scott was watching so I played along but I hated it — he made me feel cheap and dirty. The guy just wouldn't stop touching me. He put his hand on my tummy and slid his hand down low so he was cupping me through my jeans. My eyes widened and as I spun around to tell him to stop a fist flew past my face and smashed into the guy's jaw. He stumbled back with a wide-eyed, dazed look.

Scott gripped my arm tightly and my wide eyes looked into his furious green ones. Scott hauled me away and didn't stop until we were hidden under the staircase.

He caged me in so I couldn't go anywhere. "What the *fuck* are you doing?" he shouted so loudly that I didn't need to be close to hear him. His neck was corded and his fists were ready to fly — prepared to fight anyone that got in his way.

"I was dancing! You wouldn't dance with me and I didn't want to dance alone. *Why* did you hit him?" I yelled back at him, but I knew the answer. I felt like a bitch for secretly revelling in the thought of Scott getting jealous.

"Are you seriously asking me why?" his eyes bulged, "You didn't want his hands on you, that's fuckin' why!"

"How do you know what I want?" My hands went to his chest and pushed but he wouldn't budge.

"It doesn't fuckin' matter, you're not dancing again tonight." He sounded decided and he pushed his chest closer to me to drive home the fact that he was bigger and stronger than me.

"Yes, I am!" I went to walk past him but he scooped his arm around my waist. His other hand went into my scalp where it clutched a handful of my hair and pulled so I was looking up at him as he rose to his full height.

"Let go of me."

He looked down at me darkly. "You're not going back out there," he growled, "You're better than that. I won't let someone else touch you because you want to hit back at me. I'm not worth it."

I gasped.

"*Fuck!* Why are you doing this to me?" he shouted.

I relaxed in his hold and reached a hand up to his face, my own softening. "Isn't it obvious?"

He closed his eyes, let me go and stepped back shoving his hands in his pockets. "No, it's not."

He let me *go*? I didn't understand. Last week he was saying how much he wanted me and then in that moment, when I had tried to show him what I wanted, he let go? I closed the distance between us. I slipped my hand around the back of his head and brought it down to mine.

Our lips joined and I felt Scott stiffen, but as I moved my lips over his slowly, softly, he relaxed. My hand slid up into his glossy hair while my other went around his back. His hand cupped my cheek affectionately as his lips took the lead and we begun a slow, deep dance that went on and on until my heart was swelling, overflowing with love for him.

My lips were released and he placed gentle kisses on my cheeks, down my neck, hitting the sensitive part on the way.

I slipped my hands under his shirt and skimmed over his back, every muscle defined. "Scott," I moaned as he nipped me tenderly.

Without warning, he gently moved me away from him and held me at arm's length. His eyes were wide as he stared at me in shock.

I frowned. Why had he stopped us?

"Fuck sake, babe," a hurt expression crossed his face, "This has got to stop."

Rejection was like a slap across my already heated cheeks. I stepped back from him. Everything crashed in — where we were, the people around us, the music.

His expression was one I hadn't seen before — hard to read. I looked down. *He had rejected me again?* I had made my move and he didn't want me. I felt embarrassed all of a sudden. I clasped my hands together.

I looked up at him. "You don't want me," I stated.

Surprise flared in his eyes, his hands came out of his pockets and he took a stilted step towards me. "I don't know where I fuckin' stand with you — I never have. All the times you've blown me off — all the fuckin' shit you put me through…" His eyes burned into mine.

He was right, I couldn't just change my mind like that. What shit had I put him through, anyway? I sighed. We had put each other through it, each of us at fault in our own way. I couldn't unwrap the cotton wool from my heart and he couldn't stop sleeping around, even though he wanted me at the same time.

I looked at him. His frown was in place, his anger still there. "I'm taking you home."

"I'm not going home, Scott. Go without me." I wanted to be away from him now.

"No fuckin' way am I leaving you here, *goddamnit!*" he gripped my wrist.

"Get your hands off me," I said firmly. I was the worst kind of brat but I wanted space from him. Being blanked like that had hurt and I wouldn't, *couldn't,* let him see that.

He dropped his hand and looked at me like I had grown another head.

I stared him down before brushing his body with mine as I went back out onto the dance floor. I went with the music, raising my arms above my head and swinging my hips as I sensed his hungry gaze caress me. *Touch Me* by Rui Da Silva started playing. I opened my eyes and found Scott's blazing with need. Every part of him was pure male aggressiveness. I sensed a violent hunger flare in him as he crossed his arms and lowered his head without taking his eyes from me.

I was caught in his stare, in our own need. I loved him so much that I couldn't breathe. Without realising, I begged him with my eyes to come to me. I needed him so badly that I ached painfully with it. I danced on but when he didn't come over, pain clawed inside my chest and my throat thickened.

Then he pushed away from where he was leaning and came towards me.

He pulled me into him roughly as his stormy, green eyes glittered down into mine. I didn't have a second to catch my breath before his lips met mine. His tongue stroked mine firmly and frantically. He gripped me tighter, his hands digging into my back, but I welcomed it. That was where I belonged — in his arms. I felt safe there, he would never let anything happen to me.

His hand went into my hair and pulled me away from him. "Is this what you wanted, Emma? To drive me over the fuckin' edge?" he rasped loudly above the music.

I let my gaze wander over his face — the face I had come to love so much more than I had ever thought possible.

"Don't look at me like that," he closed his eyes tight, "I hate you right now." His nostrils were flaring and his jaw clenched.

Rocked Under ~ Cora Hawkes

His words slashed through me and broke me. I looked away from him, wanting to hide my face from the pain that I knew was painted across it.

This wasn't working out how I had wanted it to — he was too angry with me to give me what I wanted. If there was going to be a first time for us, I didn't want it to be out of anger.
I struggled out of his hold. "I'm going home."

Chapter Thirty-six

As we entered our communal hall, Scott dropped my hand as though it would poison him.

He had followed me out of Soundz, taken my hand forcefully and almost marched us home. The silent walk had been awkward and tense, with many sighs.

"Go to bed." He turned his back on me, about to go upstairs without saying goodnight.

"I'm a big girl. Don't tell me what to do." How dare he talk to me like a child? Was that how he saw me?

He spun around to face me and stepped nearer, his frown in place and his mouth pursed. "You're a big girl? What was that about tonight then?" He came closer. "You don't think, do you? Any one of those guys could've taken you and it would've been your own fuckin' fault for acting like a hooker. *Fuck*, you even tried to come on to *me!*"

I looked down at my feet — it was true and he had every right to be annoyed with me.

His hand caught my chin tightly and pulled it to him. "Don't *do* that!"

I jerked my head to the side so he couldn't see my shame. *You have the most readable eyes that I have ever known.*

"You did it on purpose." His voice was gruff, defeated. He turned and went upstairs.

I hadn't done it to hurt him — I had tried to tell him that I loved him but it had all gone wrong. His rejection had been too much for me and I'd fucked up. When it came to him I was impulsive, and I knew I was, but I had always been that way when I had been hurt.

Rocked Under ~ Cora Hawkes

I marched up the stairs after him a few minutes later. I had decided what to do and I knew that I should apologise. I didn't want to hurt him — I fucking loved him, and when he hurt, I did. I went into his apartment without knocking. The sound of *Nothing Else Matters* by Metallica reached my ears. It was dark apart from a lone floor lamp, which stood in the corner of his living room. Scott's silhouette rested by the balcony doors. His hands were buried deep in his front pockets and his head was down.

He didn't move when I came in, and when I shut the door he didn't look around or even flinch.
"I'm not in the mood, Emma. If I were you, I would leave."
His quiet warning unnerved me, but I needed to do this. My heart was hammering in my chest painfully as I walked slowly towards him. "I'm sorry. The last thing I want to do is hurt you but I don't understand you. The other guys…I just wanted you to know a part of how I've been feeling when I've had to see *you* with other girls, and…"
He turned swiftly and paced angrily towards me. "Well, let me tell you that you did a good fuckin' job!" He grabbed my arms painfully and my eyes widened in alarm. "I'm hurting so much I'm fuckin' sick with it — I'm tired of feeling like this!" The muscles in his neck were corded, his lips curled back.

I could see pain in his eyes and I wanted to erase it more than anything.
I reached my hand up to his face but he flinched and let go of my arms, turning his back on me once again.
"Get out — I'm done with this." His voice was stilted, gruff.
Tears pricked my eyes. "No."
"Leave, before I lose my goddamn temper."
I took a shaky breath. "I'm not leaving you." How could I have left at that moment? I had made my choice and I was sticking to it.

I knew he didn't mean any of what he had said and I knew he would never harm me physically.

"I said, fuckin' leave!" He turned as he shouted at me.

I shook my head and we stood facing each other, our breath heaving. He stood there at war with himself and I watched, with my heart pounding, in fascination. I saw the exact moment that he lost it — his jaw clenched and he pinned me with dark eyes.

He strode over to me and jerked me into him forcefully. His mouth went to mine angrily as he moved me back, trapping me, but he didn't need to — I was going nowhere.

My arms came around him and I pressed myself into him, wanting to get closer. His tongue went in and out without mercy as his hands clasped my face. His hips went into mine, thrusting. I moaned low in my throat and stroked my hands through his hair.

All of a sudden, he stopped and placed his forehead on mine. His eyes were hidden behind his lids and he rasped air into him. "Go, Emma. I'm not strong enough to stop this again. I just watched you get mauled by fuckin' strangers. Every instinct in me is telling me that you're mine and to erase them from your body."

I let my hands slip under his shirt and roam over his contoured back. He moaned and shuddered — the sound was the most erotic thing I had ever heard.

"Emma, don't," he groaned, grabbing my hands away from him and pinning them above my head. His eyes were full of desire and pain. He banged my hands against the wall again, lightly. "Stop."

I whimpered, "Scott." My voice was breathless as I tried to wriggle my hands free — the need to touch him was unbearable.

Rocked Under ~ Cora Hawkes

He frowned and watched me for a moment, his eyes changing tone. As though coming to a decision, he lowered his mouth to mine slowly, hesitantly, waiting for me to refuse him. His lips brushed mine softly before he took them away, making me whimper my need for him again.
"I don't want you to stop." I could weep with how much I wanted him.

A confused look entered his expression. "Emma…" He took a shaky breath and looked away.
I wanted him. I couldn't fight this anymore and I didn't want to. I couldn't bear to be away from him for months again while he went on tour — I couldn't do it. I was ready for him, ready to love him.
He swung his head back to me, his eyes intense and sad. "I can't do this with you."

"Scott, please," I begged as my hands went to his shoulders. I pulled his head closer. "I need this, I can't get you out of my head. I want it to stop."
His hands clinched my waist. "We can't. I'm not what you need but, fuck," he squeezed my waist, "I wish I could be."
"You're everything I need and all I can think about is what you would feel like inside me!" I raised my voice and put my lips on his forcefully.

For a split second he froze, then, with a low growl, he clutched me to him and surrendered. His mouth devoured mine. The days' stubble scraped over my sensitive skin. His hands travelled over my butt, where he took a breath and hauled me up quickly. I wrapped my legs around his waist and his mouth came back to mine. I felt him, hard, ready for me, and I couldn't stop the jerk of my hips as I rubbed myself on him and moaned into his mouth. He put his head back and hissed as air rushed through his teeth.

He crushed my ass and moved me against him slowly, teasing me. I hissed and held him tight as his hardness hit me through the ridge of his jeans, again and again. I was coming apart.

He watched me, his lips parted, and his tongue darted out to dampen his kissed lips.

His mouth came down to my neck as we started to move to his bedroom, kicking the door closed as we went through it. I was lowered onto the bed but I didn't take my arms and legs from around him until his body pushed me into the mattress. The feel of him there, between my legs, his mouth on my neck, was where I needed him to be.

He eased himself up onto his knees to look down at me as I lay with my head on his pillow. His hand stroked me slowly from my neck, between my breasts, over my stomach and right down to where I ached for him the most. He cupped me — I gasped and jerked my hips, the intense pleasure too much for me — too sensitive, I was too aware of him, of myself, of everything. His eyes held mine as he circled my clit with his thumb.

I bucked as a piercing need ripped through me again. "Scott!"

His eyes widened and his jaw clenched. He came at me, his mouth was on mine hard. I heard him growling. His hands were everywhere, his smell, his presence cloaked me in a way that I had never known.

Suddenly he was pulling me up and taking my top away from me, and then his came off too. His mouth smashed against mine again. He took my tongue into his mouth. My heart was hammering and I couldn't stay still.

He stripped the rest of our clothes off until we had nothing left between us but skin. He was huge. His erection stood proud and tall. A deep-seated hunger bloomed inside me, threatening to take over my body unless I gave it what it desired. I looked at his muscles bunched up and tense with his need, his tattoos a multitude of colours and indecipherable swirls that swam before my hazy eyes. I was itching to touch him there, on his chest. I sat up and let my hands wander over him while he shuddered.

My hands drifted down to his abdomen. I watched him watching me.
He was everything that I knew he would be and more. There was nothing feminine about him — every inch was pure, male perfection. I knelt in front of him on the bed so we were roughly the same height as I ran my hands everywhere. I dipped low and watched him suck in a breath, then moved away again, up his torso, over his nipples.

He grabbed the back of my head and massaged with his fingers in a scratchy motion while I explored him.
I let my hand stroke low until I accidentally brushed his erection.
He gasped and his hand tightened around my nape. "Emma, *fuck*, I'm losing it." He closed his eyes tight as he concentrated on his breathing.
I moaned as excitement throbbed through me. I felt empowered, bold even. I put my thumb into my mouth to wet it, then put it to the tip of his cock and rubbed him slowly. He was velvety soft there, and I wanted to lick it so badly.

"*Shit!*" He jerked violently and before I knew it I was on my back and he was upright on his knees between my legs, panting. "Baby, carry on doing that and I won't last another minute." He pulled a condom out from the inside of his pillow, tore the packet open and put it on quickly.

He bent his head and kissed my stomach tenderly, sending sparks up through me that made me bow up off the bed.

"Scott!"

"Shh, baby." He kissed and licked his way up slowly. He came to my breasts and his mouth went over a nipple. He sucked and licked, giving each bud equal amounts of attention. I was going crazy for him, I was throbbing deeply — it was almost painful.

My arms went around his back and I forced him down to me. I felt the tip of him driving me mad as it gently nudged me where I needed it the most.

"Scott, please."

He watched me writhing on the bed for him. My hair was a mess, I felt hot everywhere and the throbbing ache I felt was too much — I needed attention. I moved my hands downwards, past my stomach, and touched myself to ease the ache.

I was so sensitive that a loud sigh escaped my lips as my eyes latched onto his.

His eyes widened faintly and he reared back into an upright position on his knees. "Ah, Emma," Scott groaned as he watched me touch myself, his eyes darkening beyond belief.

He reached down to himself and gripped his cock. With his eyes watching my fingers play over my clit, he started to stroke himself slowly, back and forth, hard and slow.

"Scott." I gasped at the erotic sight before me and my fingers quickened on myself as I watched his lips part in a growl so deep in his throat that he sounded wild.

His other hand came up to fondle his balls while he pumped away. "Ah, fuck," he ground out as the pleasure he was giving himself took over.

I was going to come just by watching him please himself like that. I was close, so close to exploding.

He moved towards me with his hand full of himself. He nudged my hand away with his free hand and then brought the tip of his cock to me. He slid it up and down my folds in unhurried sweeps, wringing me out until it was too much.

"Oh, God!" My hands dug into the sheet beside me as he continued his torment. My legs were trembling all over and I closed my eyes tight. *I'm going to die!*

"You're so wet, baby," he groaned as he slid himself down towards my opening and nudged himself inside a little before sliding back up to my clit. "So sweet, so fuckin' stunning."

I needed him inside me now. A sob of pure frustration escaped from me, "Scott, I need you to…"

He stopped and leaned down over me, "Not yet, baby." He kissed me deeply into the pillow. He kissed me until I was calmer and then looked at me tenderly as he stroked my cheek. There was something in his eyes that I had only seen a handful of times since I had known him. His eyes were soft, but there was more there. "You okay?"

I nodded and wrapped my legs around him to get closer and I moaned his name when I felt his erection pushing against me.

He started to buck slowly against me, letting the tip enter me and then slide up to my clit, only to repeat the teasing again and again. His head dipped down and took my mouth in a kiss that started gentle but built and built until we were desperate. He drew me out, making me go to the limit until I couldn't wait anymore. My body was throbbing painfully. I craved him inside me, deep, filling me. It was torture, but it was the sweetest torture imaginable.

I broke away from our kiss and grabbed his butt to pull him into me. "Please…" I begged him with my eyes.

He was panting, his cheeks were red and sweat dripped from his forehead.

He sat back and pulled me on top of him so that I was straddling him. His hands held my hips firmly as he moved me over him.

I took over and rubbed myself against him hard. I moved my hips in circles and then back and forth. I was breathing hard, groans were escaping my lips.

He was panting now as he watched my face. "That's it, baby." His hands grasped my ass hard and he squeezed. Air hissed into his mouth, "Emma, ah, baby."

He laid me back down and let his fingers go down there. He slowly stroked me, sending me wild with heat. My body was rushing towards its release so fast that when he flicked me just once, I came apart, and he quickly inserted fingers into me.

"Scott!" I cried out loudly as my body convulsed around his fingers.

He reared up over me, his hands holding him up on either side of my head. "I'm here, baby." He positioned himself at my entrance. "You ready?" His eyes bored into mine.

"Yes."

He entered me slowly until he was buried deep. He felt huge, but I was ready for him. He started moving and as he did I felt myself building for release again. He was readying me for another wonderful fall into ecstasy.

"You're beautiful, baby," he shook, "so beautiful." His mouth came down for a gentle kiss, his tongue mimicked the thrust of his hips.

He came all the way out of me and then nudged into me again, but this time he only went partly inside and carried on doing that until I screamed for him to fill me.

Rocked Under ~ Cora Hawkes

He thrust harder and faster — I was almost there.

He reared back onto his knees and lifted my hips to him. He entered me again, in and out until I was sobbing for my release.

"Baby, look at me." His fingers went to my clit while he thrust himself into me, stroking me just where I needed him to.

He cried out as I did while we came together. I bucked but he didn't let go of me. My heart melted as he held me through it, stoking it, lengthening the pleasure for me.

He dropped his head in the crook of my neck and gathered me in his arms as though he didn't want me to let go. "I'm so fuckin' in love with you, babe."

Chapter Thirty-seven

His voice was painful, as though the admission was ripped from his soul. His words shocked me and moved me and thrilled me all at the same time. My body was sated and humming with pleasure. *He loves me?* My chest swelled and overflowed, sending a warm, content feeling buzzing through me. It was like coming after home having been away for a long, long time.

He was still lying on top of me and he was still inside me. I turned my head to look at him but he wasn't moving, and he hadn't moved since he had spoken those words. His breath was getting steadier, his body was calming inside of me. *Had I heard him right?*

"Scott?" I whispered.

He rose up on his elbows to look at me. His eyes were the colour of the darkest moss, full of lingering desire and that look again. "Are you okay?" his voice was like sandpaper.

I frowned. I was sure he had told me that he loved me. Or did he tell all the girls that when he was finished with them? I continued to stare at him, trying to get some clue from him.

"Did you just tell me you loved me?" I whispered, worry that I hadn't heard him properly was clear in my voice.

His brows creased and his eyes held regret in them. He closed his eyes tight and clenched his jaw hard. After taking a deep breath, he rolled off me and stood. He walked into the bathroom, giving me a perfect view of his behind, without a word or a backward glance.

I frowned at the door, tears threatening, but I wouldn't cry — I couldn't cry here. He had rocked my world, given me the best sex I could ever have imagined and told me he loved me, only to take it back? That was definitely regret I saw on his face and I would never forget it for as long as I lived. Was I not good? Did he think I was bad in bed?

Humiliation made me move and get up. I quickly wrapped a sheet around my nakedness. My skin was still sensitive and thrumming from our lovemaking. I stood outside the closed bathroom door. I didn't know what to do. Should I confront him, or just leave? I stood there for a moment longer, debating whether I should burst in there and give him hell for treating me like his other girls and leaving me.

Decided, I yanked the bathroom door open and paused as steam enveloped me. Scott stood in his large walk-in shower, which spanned a whole wall. His hands lay flat against the wall as he leaned with his head down. Water flowed over his head and ran out of his hair to skim his beautiful body. He looked so good when he was wet that I almost moaned. He turned his head and looked at me, pain in every shadow of his expression.

I flinched. "What's wrong?"
He shook his head and looked away.
My throat started to close. I had been so happy only moments ago and now everything was falling out of place again. More fucking misery. "Please say something because I don't know what I'm doing. You can't say something like that to me and then just…," I flung my arm out, "Just leave me!" My eyes were starting to blur from the tears I had been keeping in.

He looked at me hard before straightening up and pacing towards me slowly, his gaze locked onto me. His hand came to mine while his other pulled the sheet away from around my breasts, baring me again, before he led me into the shower with him. The warm spray tingled as it hit my skin. I was hyper-aware of Scott's nakedness in front of me, so close that I could almost lick the water from his skin. His expression held tenderness and that odd look was there again. He bent his head and brought his lips to mine in a sweet kiss that told me something was shifting between us again.

He cupped both my cheeks and released my lips to gaze at me intensely. "I love you, Emma," he croaked as though his throat was also tight. His head shook. "I can't hide it or run from it anymore." His face creased. "It's fuckin' crushing me and I feel like I'm gonna break."
My breath whooshed out of me and my heart stopped.
"It's always been you. I'm incapable of loving anyone else. It's you or no one." He brought his body into contact with mine. "I would be so good to you, babe. Please, just give me a shot at making you happy."

My heart wanted to burst from my ribs, it beat so fast as it rejoiced over Scott's words. I reached my hand up and swept his wet hair off his forehead. I smiled but my lips wobbled. "Scott, you already have made me happy by saying those words, because, I love you too, and I'm not willing to fight this anymore. I want you in any way that I can have you because I'm miserable without you." I took a breath. "God, I thought that you regretted saying it when you came in here like that."

He frowned, then his face cleared. "I thought you didn't want to hear it."
My brows lifted. "I've wanted to hear those words more than anything, and when you said them, I couldn't believe it. I love you so much it's been hurting."
He caught hold of me and turned me so my back was against tile. His eyes shone with love and desire as he pressed his body to mine. I delighted at the touch of his warm, wet skin against mine.

His lips collided with mine and talking was over as he devoured me.

One of his hands rested on my waist while the other was against the wall beside my head. His feet gently nudged mine apart and he slid his cock between my swollen lips unhurriedly.

My head fell back as I cried out. He was slow, teasing and tormenting me, and I could do nothing but hold his gaze while he watched me come again, his name leaving my lips in a loud moan.

He slipped himself inside me and continued to tease me with his unrushed strokes that wouldn't speed up.

His eyes were fixed on mine, his jaw was clenched with his restraint as he watched me writhe against the wall, my fists bunched, when his leisurely pace became too much.

"Scott, please…"

"What do you want, baby?" he rasped.

My hands flew to his ass and squeezed as I tried to tell him what I needed.

"Tell me, Emma. Tell me what you need," he groaned. "Say it!"

"Please, I want…," I moaned again as his cock came out fully and then slipped all the way back in.

"Come on, baby. *Tell* me." He watched me struggle with dark eyes and I knew he was barely holding it together. His hand left the wall and stroked down my side and then up to my breasts making everything more intense.

When I couldn't take anymore, I lost it. "Harder!" I shouted in frustration, "I need it harder!"

He gripped my waist with both hands and drove into me. His lips parted and his lids became heavy.

He pumped harder and faster. Our bodies were slapping together under the spray of warm water.

I screamed out his name when my release came and we slid to the floor together, spent and sated.

Scott threaded his fingers through mine and lifted our hands to stare at them.

We were lying in bed, my head on his shoulder. It felt so right.

"I first saw you years ago, you know."

The quiet confession had me turning my head in surprise. He had told me that he had met me before but he hadn't told me when and I still couldn't remember.

"You were thirteen. I knew straight away that you were different from other girls. I couldn't stop thinking about you after that night."

My eyes bulged. "Thirteen?"

"You were over here visiting Ash and you came to one of my house parties with her." He smiled to himself.

I could remember the party but not much after my first couple of drinks. My mum and I had flown over for Easter, without my dad for the first time, and I had been upset that he had missed it. We had always gone together, as a family. My mum was depressed and I had needed to get out so Ash had brought me with her, promising my mum that she would look after me, but I had ended up very drunk and throwing up. I barely remembered the party. To think he had seen me like that was really embarrassing.

"I remember," I cringed, "I was drunk."

"Yeah, some asshole mixed tequila in with your drinks." He looked at me. "I was in the bathroom changing and when I came out you were lying on my bed, crying so quietly that I didn't notice you at first. I didn't know who you were but when I sat next to you, you started to tell me what an idiot your dad was and then I knew who you were from your accent."

He brought my hand to his lips and kissed my palm with smiling lips. "You were so fuckin' young and I was sixteen. I thought you were the prettiest girl I had ever seen. You crawled onto my lap and put your arms around me and you stopped crying. You looked at me for a minute and then kissed me, and I don't mean a chaste, kiss-your-mom kind of kiss — you actually *kissed* me," he chuckled.

"Oh, God, please don't tell me any more." My cheeks heated. I did remember something but it was very vague, too far away to be clear. To think that I had kissed Scott before was weird. I had no recollection of it.

"You were a fuckin' sweet angel and I wanted to kiss you back so much, but, you were so young and drunk, so I couldn't — I couldn't take advantage of you that way," he groaned.

"I'm sorry." I wasn't really though. A thought occurred to me and I laughed. "Oh, no way!"

"What?" he asked.

"I had my first kiss a few days after my fourteenth birthday, behind the bike sheds at school." I looked at him in mock shock, "I'm sorry, but you had my first kiss that night." A big grin spread across my face.

He laughed. "Don't be sorry, babe, it's how we met and I'll never forget it. You were so wasted. I got Ash and, with help, she took you home, where I heard that you blew chunks everywhere." He laughed again. "Ash got into loads of shit with her mum, and later I explained that someone had spiked your drink and got her off the hook."

"Hey, I was thirteen," I smiled.

He looked at me with love in his eyes and pulled me closer to him for a deep kiss that took my breath away. "For a long time afterwards I waited for any mention of you from Ash and didn't happen that often. When I first saw you at Macy's I didn't know for sure that it was you, but you reminded me of thirteen-year-old you and I had to have you. Does that make sense?"

"Yeah. I've changed quite a bit since I was thirteen."

"I didn't realise it was actually you until you spoke." He kissed my hand again. "Ash warned me away from you before you arrived, said if I so much as looked at you wrong, then our friendship was at an end. She said you'd been hurt enough already, so I didn't know what to do." He sighed. "I became your friend, but it was so fuckin' hard. I started to fall in love with you straight away and there wasn't a fuckin' thing that I could do to stop it."

"Scott, you don't have to explain, because I've struggled too." I swallowed and looked at him. "It's been so hard to watch you with other girls and I couldn't understand why you did it."

He took a breath and threaded his fingers through mine. "Babe, I tried to forget about us and get over you — I fuckin' tried. Those girls don't mean anything to me and they never did." He looked away with a hint of sadness touching his mouth. "I get lonely and I can't stand it all the time. Since you came here, I've imagined that they...," he swallowed, "I imagined that I was with you instead of them."

I gasped and thought about the number of times I had imagined his hands on me when someone else was touching me.

"I admit that sometimes I just wanted to make you jealous or mad, but baby, I don't know what the fuck I'm doing here — I've never felt this way about anyone and I didn't know how to get you. You've been breaking my fuckin' heart."

So that was why he had slept around so much — not out of want but out of loneliness. I could understand that and I wouldn't hold it against him because I had hurt him too.

Rocked Under ~ Cora Hawkes

"We've hurt each other. When I walked in on you and that girl having sex on the sofa, I wanted to scream it hurt me so much. The fact that you were using cocaine just made it ten times bloody worse. It reminded me of a similar place in my past that I would rather have forgotten."

He looked away. "Babe, I started using that while I was away. At first it helped me, took me away from life. I missed my dad and I missed you, but I couldn't call you in the state I was in." He looked at me, his eyes full of regret. "I didn't want you to see any weakness in me and I didn't want you to be with me out of pity. I was angry with you because of all the times you pushed me away." He brushed a hand over my hair. "You don't know how many times I almost called you and wrote text messages that I never sent. After a while, it was like I needed it to get through the day. I'm so sorry that I hurt you, babe. I was in a bad place and too proud to ask you for help, even though I knew you would have given it. You're so good. I don't think you understand what a breath of fresh air you are to me."

He rolled on top of me and kissed me. "You're mine, Emma. I love you more than anything and I'm not letting you go. I'll never do that shit again and I haven't since that night. You scared the shit out of me, you know. I thought you were going to die in my arms..." He shut his eyes for a moment before opening them again. "I can never go through that again." He rained kisses all over my face before smiling down at me. His face was relaxed and content, and that looked good on him — he was more gorgeous now than he ever had been.

I stroked his hair. "I didn't want to push you away. I was afraid because of my parents, but that doesn't matter now because I know that I'm unhappy when you're not with me. The thought of you going away for months on tour is horrible. I want you to stay with me."

Scott's face lit up. "That's good because you're coming with me."

"Oh?"

"I'm not taking no for an answer, babe. If you don't come with me, then I'm not fuckin' going."

"You don't need to persuade me. You're asking someone who wants to be a tour manager when she grows up to go along with a real touring band? Like I would ever say no to that."

"And I don't want you to move either."

I sat up and he rolled to the side. "I've already given my notice to the agent. He knows that I'll be leaving."

"That agent works for me."

I frowned. What was he talking about?

"My dad owned this house and when he died everything got passed to me. This house is mine and I want — I'm *asking* — you to stay." His green eyes were hopeful and I couldn't say no to that.

"Okay, I'll stay, but Ash might be a bit annoyed — the new place had a jacuzzi and a great view."

He threw me a look that said *I don't give a fuck*, then he pulled me back and tucked me next to him.

I put my hand on his chest and snuggled — sleep was calling.

"I love you, Emma," he murmured as he drifted off.

"And I love you, Scott." I kissed his chest and sleep took me quicker than it had in a long time.

What lay ahead seemed bright. All my worries had vanished — he made me feel stronger than I had ever felt and my fears were finally being buried along with the hurtful memories. I was looking forward to the future again, — a future where I got to be with Scott every day, a future that had a tour in it. I couldn't wait.

Rocked Under ~ Cora Hawkes

To be continued…

Rocked #2
Coming 2013

Printed in Great Britain
by Amazon.co.uk, Ltd.,
Marston Gate.